Thomas Edward Brown

Fo'c's'le Yarns

including Betsy Lee, and other poems

Thomas Edward Brown

Fo'c's'le Yarns
including Betsy Lee, and other poems

ISBN/EAN: 9783337402402

Printed in Europe, USA, Canada, Australia, Japan

Cover: Foto ©Andreas Hilbeck / pixelio.de

More available books at **www.hansebooks.com**

FO'C'S'LE YARNS

INCLUDING

BETSY LEE, AND OTHER POEMS

London

MACMILLAN AND CO.

AND NEW YORK

1889

First Edition 1881.

New Edition 1889.

CONTENTS

To sing a song shall please my countrymen,
  To unlock the treasures of the Island heart :
With loving feet to trace each hill and glen,
  And find the ore that is not for the mart
Of commerce : this is all I ask.
No task,
    But joy, GOD wot !
    Wherewith " the stranger " intermeddles not-

Who, if perchance
  He lend his ear
As caught by mere romance
  Of nature, traversing
  On viewless wing
  All parallels of sect,
  And race, and dialect,
Then shall he be to me most dear.

Natheless, for mine own people do I sing,
  And use the old familiar speech,
  Happy if I shall reach
  Their inmost consciousness.
One thing
  They will confess—
I never did them wrong :
And so accept the singer and the song.

I

BETSY LEE

I said I would? Well, I hardly know,
But a yarn's a yarn; so here we go.
It's along of me and a Lawyer's Clerk,
You've seen mayhap that sort of spark !
As neat and as pert, and as sharp as a pin,
With a mossel of hair on the tip of his chin ;
With his face so fine, and his tongue so glib,
And a saucy cock in the set of his jib ;
With his rings and his studs and all the rest,
And half a chain cable paid out on his breast.
Now there's different divils ashore and at sea,
And a divil's a divil wherever he be ;
But if you want the rael ould mark,
The divil of divils is the Lawyer's Clerk.
Well—out it must come, though it be with a wrench,
And I must tell you about a wench
That I was a courtin of, yes me !
Aye, and her name it was Betsy Lee.

Now most of you lads has had a spell
Of courtin and that, and it's hard to tell
How ever a youngster comes to fancy
That of all the gels it's Jinny or Nancy,
Or Mary or Betsy that must be hisn.
I don't know how it is or it isn,
But some time or other it comes to us all,
Just like a clap of shoot[1] or a squall,
Or a snake or a viper, or some such dirt,
Creep—creep—creepin under your shirt,
And slidin and slippin right into your breast,
And makin you as you can't get rest :
And it works and it works till you feel your heart risin—
God knows what it is if it isn pisin.

You see—we're a roughish set of chaps,
That's brought up rough on our mammies' laps ;
And we grow and we run about shoutin and foolin
Till we gets to be lumps[2] and fit for the schoolin.
Then we gets to know the marks[3] and the signs,[3]
And we leaves the school, and we sticks to the lines,
Baitin and settin and haulin and that,
Till we know every fish from a whale to a sprat ;
And we gets big and strong, for it do make you stronger
To row a big boat, and to pull at a conger.
Then what with a cobblin up of the yawl,
And a patchin and mendin the nets for the trawl,

---

[1] Sudden fall of soot in the chimney.
[2] Good-sized lads.   [3] Of the fishing grounds.

And a risin early and a goin to bed late,
And a dramin of scollops as big as a plate,
And the hooks and the creels and the oars and the gut,
You'd say there's no room for a little slut.
But howsomdever it's not the case,
And a pretty face is a pretty face ;
And through the whole coil, as bright as a star,
A gel slips in, and there you are !

Well, that was just the way with me
And the gel I'm speakin of—Betsy Lee.
Ah, mates ! it's wonderful too—the years
You may live dead-on-end with your eyes and your ears
Right alongside of the lass that's goin
To be your sweetheart, and you never knowin !

That's the way.   For her father and mine
Was neighbours, and both in the fisherman line ;
And their cottages stood on the open beach,
With a nice bit of garden aback of them each.
You know the way them houses is fixed,
With the pigs and the hens and the childher mixed ;
And the mothers go round when the nights begin,
And whips up their own, and takes them in.
Her father was terrible fond of flowers,
And his garden was twice as handsome as ours—
A mortal keen eye he had for the varmin,
And his talk was always of plantin and farmin.
He had roses hangin above his door,

Uncommon fine roses they was to be sure,
And the joy of my heart was to pull them there,
And break them in pieces on Betsy's hair.
Not that Betsy was much of a size
At the time I mean, but she had big eyes,
So big and so blue, and so far asunder,
And she looked so sollum I used to wonder.
That was all—just baby play,
Knockin about the boats all day,
And sometimes a lot of us takin hands
And racin like mad things over the sands.
Ah ! it wouldn be bad for some of us
If we'd never gone furder, and never fared wuss ;[1]
If we'd never grown up, and never got big,
If we'd never took the brandy swig,
If we were skippin and scamp'rin and cap'rin still
On the sand that lies below the hill,
Crunchin its gray ribs with the beat
Of our little patterin naked feet ;
If we'd just kept childher upon the shore
For ever and ever and ever more.

Now the beauty of the thing when childher plays is
The terrible wonderful length the days is.
Up you jumps, and out in the sun,
And you fancy the day will never be done :
And you're chasin the bumbees hummin so cross
In the hot sweet air among the goss,[2]

---

[1] Worse.   [2] Gorse.

Or gath'rin blue-bells, or lookin for eggs,
Or peltin the ducks with their yalla legs,
Or a climbin, and nearly breakin your skulls,
Or a shoutin for divilment after the gulls,
Or a thinkin of nothin, but down at the tide,
Singin out for the happy you feel inside.
That's the way with the kids, you know,
And the years do come and the years do go,
And when you look back it's all like a puff,
Happy and over and short enough.

Well, I never took notions on Betsy Lee,
Nor no more did she, I suppose, on me,
Till one day diggin upon the sand—
Gibbins,[1] of course you'll understand,
A lad that was always a cheeky young sprout,
Began a pullin of Betsy about ;
And he worried the wench till her shoulders were bare
And he slipped the knot of her beautiful hair,
And down it come, as you may say,
Just like a shower of golden spray,
Blown this way and that by a gamesome breeze,
And a rip-rip-ripplin down to her knees.
I looked at Betsy—aw dear ! how she stood !
A quiv'rin all over, and her face like blood !
And her eyes, all wet with tears, like fire,
And her breast a swellin higher and higher ;
And she gripped her sickle with a twitchy feel,

[1] Sand-eels.

And her thumb started out like a coil of steel,
And a cloud seemed to pass from my eyes, and a glory
Like them you'll see painted sometimes in a story,
Breathed out from her skin; and I saw her no more
The child I had always thought her before,
But wrapped in the glory, and wrapped in the hair,
Every inch of a woman stood pantin there.
So I ups with my fist, as I was bound,
And one for his nob, and knocks him down,
But from that day, by land and sea,
I loved her! oh, I loved her! my Betsy Lee!

It's a terrible thing is love—did you say?
Well, Edward, my lad, I'll not say nay.
But you don't think of that when the young heart blows
Leaf by leaf, comin out like a rose,
And your sheets is slacked off, and your blood is a prancin,
And the world seems a floor for you to dance on.
Terrible—eh? yes, yes! you're right,
But all the same, it's God's own light.
Aw, there was somethin worth lovin in her—
As neat as a bird and as straight as a fir;
And I've heard them say, as she passed by,
It was like another sun slipped into the sky—
Kind to the old and kind to the young,
With a smile on her lip, and a laugh on her tongue,
With a heart to feel, and a head to choose,
And she stood just five feet four in her shoes.
Oh, I've seen her look—well, well, I'll stop it!

Oh, I've seen her turn—well, well, then! drop it!
Seen, seen! What, what! All under the sod
The darlin lies now—my God! my God!

All right, my lads! I shipped that sea;
I couldn help it! Let be! let be!
Aw them courtin times! Well it's no use tryin
To tell what they were, and time is flyin.
But you know how it is—the father pretendin
He never sees nothin, and the mother mendin,
Or a grippin the Bible, and spellin a tex,
And a eyein us now-and-then over her specs.
Aw they were a decent pair enough them two!
If it was only with them I'd had to do.
Bless me! the larned he was in the flowers!
And how he would talk for hours and hours
About diggin and dungin, and weedin and seedin,
And sometimes a bit of a spell at the readin;
And Betsy and me sittin back in the chimley,
And her a clickin her needles so nimbly,
And me lookin straight in ould Anthony's face,
And a stealin my arm round Betsy's wais'.
Aw the shy she was! But when Anthony said
" Now, childher! it's time to be goin to bed "—
Then Betsy would say, as we all of us riz,[1]
" I wonder what sort of a night it is;"
Or—" Never mind, father! I'll shut the door;"
And shut it she did, you may be sure;

[1] Rose.

Only the way she done it, d'ye see?
I was outside, but so was she!

Ah, then was the time! just a minute! a minute!
But bless me the sight of love we put in it!
Ah, the claspin arms! ah, the stoopin head!
Ah, the kisses in showers! ah, the things that we said!
Yes, yes! and the cryin when I went,
Aw the Innocent! the Innocent!

Now listen, my lads, and I'll give you the cut
Of what I calls a innocent fut.
For it's no use the whole world talkin to me,
If I'd never seen nothin of Betsy Lee
Except her foot, I was bound to know
That she was as pure as the driven snow.
For there's feet that houlds on like a cat on a roof,
And there's feet that thumps like a elephant's hoof;
There's feet that goes trundlin on like a barra,[1]
And some that's crooky, some as straight as an arra;
There's feet that's thick, and feet that's thin,
And some turnin out, and some turnin in;
And there's feet that can run, and feet that can walk,
Aye, feet that can laugh, and feet that can talk—
But an innocent foot—it's got the spring
That you feel when you tread on the mountain ling;
And it's tied to the heart, and not to the hip,
And it moves with the eye, and it moves with the lip.

[1] Barrow.

I suppose it's God that makes when He wills
Them beautiful things—with the lift of His hills,
And the waft of His winds, and His calms and His storms,
And His work and His rest ; and that's how He forms
A simple wench to be true and free,
And to move like a piece of poethry.

Well, a lass is a lass, and a lad is a lad ;
But now for the luck ould Anthony had.
For one ev'rin,[1] as I was makin the beach,
I heard such a hollabaloo and a screech
That I left the boat there as she was, and I ran
Straight up to the houses, and saw the whole clan
Of neighbours a crowdin at Anthony's door,
For most of the boats was landed before.
And some pressin in, and some pressin out ;
So I axed a woman what it was all about ;
And " Didn ye hear the news ?" says she ;
" It's a fortin [2] that's come to ould Anthony Lee."
Then she tould me about the Lawyer chap,
That was in with them there, and his horse and his trap,
And his papers " with seals as big as a skate "—
Bless me ! how them women loves to prate !
And " a good-lookin man he was," she said,
" As you might see ! and a gentleman bred ;
And he's talkin that nice, and that kind, and that free !
And it's a fortin he's got for ould Anthony Lee !"

---

[1] Evening. [2] Fortune.

So I said—"All right !" but I felt all wrong ;
And I turned away, and I walked along
To a part of the shore where the wreck of a mast
Stuck half of it out, and half of it fast.
And a knife inside of me seemed to cut
My heart from its moorins, and heaven shut
And locked, and barred, like the door of a dungeon,
And me in the trough of the sea a plungin,
With the only land that I knew behind me,
And a driftin where God himself couldn find me.
So I made for the mast, but before I got at it
I saw Betsy a standin as straight as a stattit,[1]
With her back to the mast, and her face to the water,
And the strain of her eyes gettin tauter [2] and tauter,
As if with the strength of her look she'd try
To draw a soul from the dull dead sky.
Then I went to her, but what could I say ?
For she never took her eyes away :
Only she put her hand on my cheek,
And I tried, and I tried hard enough to speak,
But I couldn—then all of a sudden she turned.
And the far-off look was gone, and she yearned
To my heart, and she said—" You doubted me ;"
And I said—" I didn then, Betsy Lee !"

So her and me sat down on the mast,
And we talked and talked, and the time went fast,
When I heard a step close by, and—behould ye !

---

[1] Statue.   [2] Tighter.

There was the Lawyer chap I tould ye
Had come with the papers (confound the pup !),
And says he—" I'm sorry to interrup',"
He says, "such a pleasant têtertête ;
But you'll pardon me ; it's gettin late,
And I couldn think of returnin to town
Without payin my respects, as I feel bound,
To the lovely heiress, and off'rin her ——,"
And cetterer, and cetterer—
You know how they rattles on.   So we rose,
And all the three of us homeward goes.
But blest if he didn buck up,[1] and says he,
With a smirk, " Will you take my arm, Miss Lee ?"
And Betsy didn know what to do,
So she catched a hould, and there them two
Goes linkin [2] along.   Aw, I thought I'd split
With laughin, and then I cussed a bit.
And when we come up to the houses—the rushin
There was to the doors, and Betsy blushin,
And him lookin grand, and me lookin queer,
And the women sayin—" What a beautiful pair !"
Now it mattered little to me that night
What stuff they talked, for I knew I was right
With Betsy ; but still, you see, of[3] a rule,
A fellow doesn like to look like a fool.
And the more I thought of the chap and his beauin,
The madder I got ; so when he was goin,
And I held the horse, and gave him the reins,

[1] Play the *buck*, act pretentiously.   [2] Arm-in-arm.   [3] As.

And—"There's a sixpence," says he, "for your pains—
A sixpence, my man!" I couldn hould in,
And once I began I did begin,
And I let him have it *hot*, as they say;
But he only laughed, and druv away.

Now heave ahead, my lads, with me!
For the weeks rolled on, and ould Anthony Lee
Did just what he always wanted to do,
For he took a farm they called the *Brew*,
In a hollow that lay at the foot of a hill,
Where the blessed ould craythur might have his fill
Of stockin and rearin and grassin and tillage,
And only about a mile from the village.
And a stream ran right through the orchard, and then
Went dancin and glancin down the glen,
And soaked through the shilly,[1] and out to the bay,
But never forgot, as it passed, to say,
With the ringin laugh of its silv'ry flow—
"She's thinkin of you, and she tould me so."
Laugh on, my hearties! you'll do no harm;
But I've stood when the wind blew straight from the
    farm,
And I've felt her spirit draw nigher and nigher,
Till it shivered into my veins like fire,
And every ripple and every rock
Seemed swep' with the hem of Betsy's frock.

[1] Fine gravel.

But—of coorse! of coorse—Ah little Sim!
Is he off? little lad! just fist us the glim![1]
Ah, beauty! beauty! no matter for him!
No matter for him!   Aw, isn he gud?[2]
With his nose like a shell, and his mouth like a bud!
There's sauce enough in that there lip
To aggravate ever a man in the ship.
Did ye hear him to-day agate of[3] his chaff?
Well! how he made the skipper laugh!
Just come here and look at him, mates!
Isn he like them things up the Straits?[4]
Them picthurs the Romans has got in their chapels?
Brave little chaps, with their cheeks like apples!
Holdin on to their mawthers' petticoats,
And lookin as pert and bould as goats!
Bless me! the body them craythurs has got!
Clean! without a speck or a spot!
And they calls the little boy Jesus, and her
With her head wrapped up in a handkecher
They calls the Vargin, and all them starts
And patterin-nostrin, and—bless their hearts!
What is he dreaming of now, little lad!
Brother and sister and mother and dad?
And lobsters a creepin about the creel,
And granny hummin her spinnin-wheel?
Or him in the parlour a lyin in bed,
And a twiggin the spiders over-head?

[1] Light.   [2] Good.
[3] At work with.   [4] Up the Mediterranean.

" Hushee-bow-babby upon the tree-top !
And when the wind blows, the cradle will rock—"
Ah Simmy my boy, I've done my best—
Somethin like that—but as for the rest——

" Go on ! go on !"   Is that your shout ?
Well, what is this I was thinkin about ?
I'm in for it now, and it's no use bilkin—
Oh, aye ! the milkin ! ould Anthony's milkin !
I never thought on for the whys or the hows,
But I was always terrible fond of cows.
Now aren't they innocent things—them bas'es ?[1]
And havn they got ould innocent faces ?
A strooghin[2] their legs that lazy way,
Or a standin as if they meant to pray—
They're that sollum and lovin and studdy[3] and wise,
And the butter meltin in their big eyes !
Eh ? what do you think about it, John ?
Is it the stuff they're feedin on—
The clover and meadow-grass and rushes,
And them goin pickin among the bushes,
And sniffin the dew when it's fresh and fine,
The sweetest brew of God's own wine !
And the smell of the harbs gets into their sowls,
· And works and works, and rowls and rowls,
Till it tightens their tits[4] and drabs[5] their muzzle—
Well, it's no use o' talkin—it's a regular puzzle :

[1] Beasts.   [2] Stroking, trailing.   [3] Steady.
    [4] Teats.   [5] Makes wet.

But you'll notice the very people that's got to atten'
To the like, is generally very aisy men.

Aw ould Anthony knew about them pat,
Alderney, Ayrshire, and all to that !
And breedin, and rearin, and profit and loss—
Aw, he was a clever ould chap, ould Anthony was.
More by token that's the for [1]
Him and me had our first war.
You see, I was sittin there one night
When who should come in but ould Tommy Tite ;
Tight he was by name and by nathur,
A dirty ould herpocrite [2] of a craythur,
With a mouth that shut with a snick and a snap—
Tight, for sure, [3] like the Divil's own trap ;
And his hair brushed up behind and before—
Straight [4] like the bristles that's on a boar.
Well, that man was thin ! I never saw thinner,
A lean, ould, hungry, mangy sinner !
And he'd sit and he'd talk ! well, the way he'd talk !
And he'd groan in his innards, but an eye like a hawk—
And cunning written all over his face—
And wasn it him that owned the place ?

Well, there they were talkin and talkin away
About carrots and turmits, and oats and hay—
And stock and lock and barrel, bless ye !
The big words they had was enough to distress ye !

---

[1] Reason.   [2] Hypocrite.   [3] I can assure you.   [4] Just.

With their pipes in each other's faces smookin,
And me lookin and longin, and longin and lookin—
Lookin for Betsy's little signs—
The way them pretty craythurs finds
To talk without talkin, is raely grand—
A tap of the foot, a twitch of the hand!
A heise [1] of the neck, a heave of the breast!
A stoop like a bird upon its nest!
A look at father, a look at mawther!
A one knee swingin over the other!
A lookin lower, and a lookin higher!
A long, long straight look into the fire!
A look of joy, and a look of pain!
But bless ye! you understand what I mean.
So on they talked till all the fun
In her darlin little face begun
To work—and I couldn hould it in,
And I laughed, and I laughed like anythin.
My goodness! the mad ould Anthony got,
With his eyes so wide, and his cheeks as hot
And as red as a coal; and the other fellow
Was turnin green and turnin yellow;
And the ould woman bucked up [2] as proud as you plaze,
But ould Anthony spoke, and says he, he says—
"It's most unfortnit—I hope you will—
I mean it's most disrespectable——
But I hopes, Misther Tite, as you'll excuse—"
And so he went on with his parley-voos—

[1] Hoist, lift.   [2] Drew herself up.

"Just a young man from the shore," says he,
"As drops in in the ev'rin for company !
A umble neighbour as don't know batther,[1]
You see, Misther Tite, I knew his father."
Well I choked that down, but I says to myself—
Pretendin to stare at the plates on the shelf—
"You've got me, ould man ! but I'll owe you one
For that, before the stakes is drawn."
But it's my belief that from that day
He never liked me anyway.

"But about the milkin ?" all right ! all right !
I'm nearly as bad as ould Tommy Tite !
Spinnin round and round and round,
And never a knowin where am I bound.
Well, mostly every ev'rin, you see,
I was up at the milkin, with Betsy Lee.
For when she was milkin, she was always singin ;
I don't know what was it—maybe the ringin
Of the milk comin tearin into the can,
With a swilsh and a swelsh and a tăntărān,
A makin what the Lawyer gent
Was callin a sort of *accumpliment.*[2]
But the look of a cow is enough to do it,
And her breath, and her neck, the way she'll slew[3] it—
As if she was sayin, the patient she stood[4]—
"Milk away ! it's doin me good."

[1] Better. [2] Accompaniment.
[3] Turn. [4] She stood so patiently.

And the sun goin down, and the moon comin up,
And maybe you takin a little sup,
And the steam of the hay, and your forehead pressin
Agin [1] her round side ! but, for all, it's a blessin
When they're nice and quiet, for there's some of them
    rough,
And kicky and pushy and bould enough.

Now Betsy would sing and I would hear,
And away I'd be like a hound or a deer,
Up the glen and through the sedges,
And, bless me, the way I took the hedges !
For I'd be wantin to get in time to the place
To see the last sunlight on Betsy's face.
And when I'd be gettin a-top of the brew [2]
Where ould Anthony's house was full in view,
Then I'd stop and listen till I'd got it right,
And answer it back with all my might.
And when I come down, she'd say—"I heard !
You're for all the world like a mockin-bird."
She had her fun ! aw, she had her fun !
And I'd say—"Well, Betsy, are you nearly done ?"
And I'd kiss her, and then she'd say—"What bother !"
And the cow lookin round like a kind ould mawther.
One cow they had—well of all the sense
That ever I saw, and the imperence !
God bless me ! the lek of yandhar ould mailie ! [3]
A brown cow she was—well raely ! raely !

---

[1] Against.   [2] Hill.   [3] Cow without horns.

She's made me laugh till I abslit shoutit—
Pretendin to know all about it.

Well, one ev'rin I'd been laughin like a fool,
And Betsy nearly fallin off the stool—
In the orchard—and the apple blossoms there
Was shreddin down on Betsy's hair,
And I was pickin them off, d'ye see?
And the cow was lookin and smilin at me,
When—creak went the gate, and who should appear
But Misther Richard Taylor, Esqueer!
That's the Lawyer chap—and says he,
" Plasantly engaged, Miss Lee !"
So Betsy was all of a twitter lek,
And she catched her handkecher round her neck,
And straightened her hair, and smoothed her brat,[1]
And says—"Good everin !" just like that.

Well, I hardly knew what to do or to say,
So I just sat down, and milked away.
But Betsy stood up to him like a man,
Goodness ! how that girl's tongue ran !
Like the tick of a watch, or the buzz of a reel,
And hoity-toity ! and quite genteel—
Rittle-rattle—the talk it came,
And as grand as grand, the two of them—
Aw, I might have been a thousand miles away—
Of coorse ! of coorse ! I know what you'll say—

[1] Apron.

But I couldn stand it—so I watched my chance,
And I turned the tit, and I gave it him once,
A right good skute betwix the eyes—
Aw, murder! murder! what a rise!
With the milk all streamin down his breast,
And his shirt and his pins and all the rest,
And a bran new waistcoat spoiled, and him splutt'rin,
And a wipin his face, and mutt'rin—mutt'rin—
And at last he says—"I shall go," says he,
"And kermoonicate this to Misther Lee."
"Aw, Tom!" says Betsy; "Aw, Betsy!" says I:
"Whatever!" says she, and she begun to cry.
"Well," I says, "it's no wonder o' me,
With your ransy-tansy-tissimitee."[1]

But we soon made it up, and it was gettin late,
And again I heard the garden gate.
"There!" says I, "he's goin: so now, little missis!"
And kisses, kisses, kisses, kisses!
"Take care!" says she. "Never fear!" I said;
Yes, a fool! an ould fool! but she loved me, Ned.
So I cleared the fence, and the stream, and the pebbles
Chimin all night with their little trebles,
And tenors, and bassers down at the fall,
Answerin back with a kindly call
(She used to tell me it sent her to sleep)
(Just at the dam it was middlin deep);

---

[1] Burden of a song sung by children dancing—"Here comes three
Dukes a ridin."

And I crossed the glen, and I took a short cut,
And all at once I heard a fut.
I guessed it was him, and I was right,
With his boots goin winkin [1] through the night.
" Good night !" says I.   " Good night !" says he.
" And what did you tell ould Anthony Lee ?"
Aw, then he begun, and he cussed and he swore,
The divil behind, and the divil before—
And all what he'd do—and he'd have the law—
And "if it hadn been—"   "Come, stop that jaw !
Have it out ! have it out, Misther Taylor !" says I ;
" Here we are under God's own sky.
Have it out like a man, if it's a man you are !
Have it out ! have it out, my lad ! if you dare ;
And don't stand there like a blue baboon
With your long teeth chatterin in the moon !"
" Not if I knows it !" says he, " Tom Baynes.
No ! no !" says he, " I've other means."
" Have ye ?" says I, and I grips him straight,
And sends him flyin over a gate.
And gives a look, and nothing stirred ;
But he kep' his word ! he kep' his word !

This was in spring, and the summer come,
And, behould ye ! my gentleman still was dumb,
For he maybe thought about that spree
The less said the better for he.
For he's one of them chaps that works in the dark,

[1] Creaking.

And creeps and crawls—is a Lawyer's clerk;
And digs and digs, and gives no sign,
Spreadin sods and flowers at the mouth of his mine;
And he'll lay his train, and he'll hould his match,
And he'll wait and he'll wait, and he'll watch and he'll watch,
Till the minute comes, and before you sneezes
You're up to heaven in a hundred pieces.
Aw, it's a bitter poison—that black art,
The lie that eats into your heart;
A thing gath'rin round you like a seine
Round the fish, and them never feelin the strain;
A squall comin tippytoe off the land,
And houldin its breath till it's close at hand,
And whisp'rin to the winds to keep still
Till all is ready—and then with a will,
With a rush and a roar they sweeps your deck,
And there you lies a shiv'rin wreck.

Well, winter come, and then the cows
Was goin a milkin in the house.
And if you want peace and quietness,
It's in a cow-house you'll get it the best.
For the place is so warm, and their breath is so sweet,
And the nice straw bedding about their feet,
And hardly any light at all,
But just a dip stuck on to the wall,
And them yocked[1] in the dark as quiet as ghos'es,

---

[1] Yock = Yoke, plank sliding in a groove, and confining the cow's neck.

And a feelin for each other's noses.
And, bless me ! sometimes you'd hardly be knowin
It was them, excep' for their chewin and blowin.
Aw, many a time I've felt quite queer
To see them standin so orderly there.
Is it the Lord that makes them so still ?
Aw, I like them craythurs terrible !
Aye, aye ! the sea for the leks of us !
It's God's own work (though treacherous !) ;
But for peace and rest and that—d'ye see ?
Among the cows is the place for me.

And Betsy speakin so soft and low,
Or speakin nothin at all, you know ;
Or singin hymns, no matter what,
" Gentle Jesus," and the like o' that.
And that's the way she was one night,
Pressed to my heart as tight as tight—
" Sing *Glory be !*" the darlin said,
" And then it'll be time to be goin to bed "—
When all of a sudden at the door
Come a clatt'rin of clogs, and there for sure
Stood Peggy, the sarvant, all out o' breath,
And, " You're wanted," says she, " Miss Elizabeth !"
So I got up, and I was goin too ;
" Aw, no !" says Peggy, "that'll never do !"
And she went—and she went—and my heart gave a
      shiver—
And I never saw her again ! no never ! never !

Well! well! well! well!—What ails the ship?
Hold on! hold on!   I've got a grip.
Who's at the helm?   Is it Juan Cronin?
With all this criss-crossin and herrin-bonin!
My patience! or is it Tommy Teare?
That's a tervil onasy [1] fellow to steer.
Have another pipe? Why, thank you, Eddart,[2]
You're a feelin lad, and I allis said it.
Yes, give me the can! I'll just take a swipe—
Aye! another pipe—another pipe—
And, Eddart my lad, was that a letter
You got from home?   Is your father better?
Is your mother hearty?   I knew her well,
A nice little sthuggha [3] of a gel!
And, Eddart, whenever you'll be goin to write,
Tell them I was axin (I've got a light)
How were they.   And, Eddart, mind you'll put in
If ould Tommy Tite's lookin after the tin,
And if the herrins was plenty this year,
And is the gaery drained, d'ye hear?
And have ould Higgison rose the rent?
Aw, Eddart and me is well acquent.

Well, well! I didn know what was up,
Nor whether to go, nor whether to stop.
So I waited a bit, and I took off my shoes,
And, thinks I, the ould people's gone to roos';
And maybe she's waitin all alone,
And wond'rin and wond'rin am I gone.

[1] Uneasy.   [2] Edward.   [3] Thick-set, but well proportioned.

And I looked and I looked, and I crossed the street
As quite [1] as a mouse in my stocking-feet,
And I crep' in among the honey-suckles
At the porch, and I gave a tap with my knuckles,
Just this way, when the door gave a flirt,
And there stood ould Anthony in his shirt—
Hard and keen, and his ould bald head
Like Sammil when he was riz from the dead—
In the Bible, you know, yes! just the sem,
Isaac and Peter and the like of them,
That's allis got conks[2] like turkey's eggs,
And the wind blowin free round their blessed old legs,
Enough to frecken you in the night,
He was so awful and big and white.
And says he, " I thought it was you that was knockin—
Oh it's very shockin! it's very shockin! "
" What's shockin?" I says.   " Oh," he says, "it's no use
Pretendin, young man! "   " Well, why the deuce,"
Says I, "can't you give the thing a name?"
" Oh raely!" says he, " for shame! for shame!"
And " it's could," he says, "and I think I'll go in—
Oh it's an awful sin! an awful sin!"
" Sin," says I, "well, whatever it is,
Who tould you this? who tould you this?"
" Misther Taylor," he says; " Misther Taylor!" says I,
" Oh indeed!"   Then he tould me the why,
And all about it, how Jenny Magee
Had come home, and laid a child to me—

<hr>

[1] Quiet.   [2] Heads.

And " Nice purseedins," he says, "indeed ! "
And—*who was I?*—and the beggarly breed
The lot of us was, and—*how dar I*, says he,
How dar I look up to Betsy Lee?
" Is he here ? " I says.　" No ! no ! "　" That's well !
Thank God ! thank God ! for by heaven and hell,
If I had caught him in the wood,
The sun would have risen upon his blood."
" Oh ! " says he, quite freckened lek,
" What shockin feelins ! " and—Could I expec' ?—
And—*did I raely mean ?*—and before I could say
This or that, he was in, and turned the key.

Aw, up to that I was proud enough,
Bould as a lion, and middlin rough ;
But left there alone, that sore distressed,
All the strength of the night came upon me and pressed
And forced me down till I fell on my knees,
And I heard the moan of the long dead seas
Far away rollin in on the shore,
And I called to ould Anthony through the door—
" Aw, listen to me ! aw, listen to me !
Aw, Misther Lee ! aw, Misther Lee !
He's bought that woman," I said, " he's bought her
To swear that lie ; and it's after your daughter
He is himself ! aw, listen to me !
Aw, Misther Lee ! aw, Misther Lee ! "
Not a word ! not a word !—" It's a lie," I cried,
" It's a lie, if on the spot I died

It is, sir, it is, it is a lie!"
Never a word or a sound of reply!
"Aw, Misther Lee!" I says, "can I see her?
Aw, Misthress Lee! are *you* up there?
Let me see Betsy! she'll belave me!
Let me see Betsy! Save me! save me!
She hears me now, and her heart is broke!"
I said, and I listened, but no one spoke.
"She's dyin! you're stoppin her mouth!" I said;
"You're holding her down upon the bed!
Aw, you'll answer for this at the day of doom!
You're smotherin her there in the little room!
Betsy! Betsy! my darlin love!
Betsy! Betsy! oh Father above!"

And then I fell right forrid, and lay
Quite stupid, how long I cannot say;
But the first thing I felt when I tried to stand
Was something soft a slickin my hand.
And what do you think it was but Sweep!
The ould black coly that minded the sheep!
"God bless ye!" says I, "I've a friend in you!"
And he was a middlin sulky craythur too.
So I dragged myself up, and picked a bit
Of the honey-suckle, and buried it
In my breast, and I wandered round and round,
But not a mossel of light could be found.
I was like a drunken man the way I staggered,
And across the street, and through the haggard,[1]

[1] Stackyard.

And into the fields, and I know nothin more
Till they found me in the mornin upon the shore.

Well he was a villyan anyway?
He was a villyan—did you say?
A villyan!—Will you cuss him, Bill?
Aye, cuss your fill, boy, cuss your fill!
A villyan—eh? but before I'm done
You'll know something more about him, my son.
Now, men, what was I to do? can ye tell?
Just leave it alone? aye—maybe as well!
But I never would strike my flag to a lie
Before I knew good reason why.
No, no! my lads! it's not in my blood—
I never did, and I never would.

Well, I thought and I thought till at last a plan
Come into my head, and—"That's the man!"
I says—"The Pazon!—I'll go to him,
And I'll know the worst of it, sink or swim."
So I claned myself, and I had a draw
Of the pipe, and I went, but middlin slaw,[1]
For my head was workin uncommon hard
All the way, and I didn regard
For nothing at all, and the boats comin round
The Stack, a beatin up for the ground,
And a Rantipike schooner caught in the tide,
And a nice little whole-sail breeze outside,

---

[1] Slow.

Not much matter to me, you'd 'spec [1]—
No! but you'll allis be noticin lek.

Now the grandest ould pazon, I'll be bail,
That ever was, was ould Pazon Gale.
Aw, of all the kind and the good and the true!
And the aisy and free, and—"How do you do?"
And how's your mother, Tom, and—the fishin?
Spakin that nice, and allis wishin
Good luck to the boats, and—"How's the take?"
And blessin us there for Jesus' sake.
And many a time he'd come out and try
A line, and the keen he was, and the spry!
And he'd sit in the stern, and he'd tuck his tails,
And well he knew how to handle the sails.
And sometimes, if we were smookin, he'd ax
For a pipe, and then we'd be turnin our backs,
Lettin on [2] never to see him, and lookin
This way and that way, and him a smookin
Twis' as strong and as black as tar,
And terrible sollum and regular.
Bless me! the sperrit that was in him too,
Houldin on till all was blue!
And only a little man, but staunch,
With a main big heart aback of his paunch!
Just a little round man—but you should ha' seen him
        agate
Of a good-sized conger or a skate:

---

[1] Expect.　　　　　　　[2] Pretending.

His arms as stiff, and his eye afire,
And every muscle of him like wire.

But avast this talk! What! what did you say?
Tell us more about the Pazon—eh?
Well, well! he was a pazon—yis!
But there's odds of pazons, that's the way it is.
For there's pazons now that's mortal[1] proud,
And some middlin humble, that's allowed.
And there's pazons partikler about their clothes,
And rings on their fingers, and bells on their toes:
And there's pazons that doesn know your names,
"Shut the gate, my man!" and all them games.
And there's pazons *too* free—I've heard one cuss
As hard and as hearty as one of us.
But Pazon Gale—now I'll give you his size,
He was a simple pazon, and lovin and wise.
That's what he was, and quiet uncommon,
And never said much to man nor woman;
Only the little he said was meat
For a hungry heart, and soft and sweet,
The way he said it: and often talkin
To hisself, and lookin down, and walkin.
Quiet he was, but you couldn doubt
The Pazon was knowin what was he about.
Aye, many a time I've seen his face
All slushed with tears, and him tellin of *grace*
And *mercy* and that, and his vice so low,
But trimblin—aw, we liked him though!

[1] Very.

And he wasn livin above the bay
Where I was livin, but a bit away,
Over the next, and betwix the two
The land ran out to a point, and a screw
Of the tide set in on the rocks, and there
He'd stand in the mornin, and listen to hear
The dip of our oars comin out, and the jealous
We were of the Derbyhaven fellows!
And the way we'd pull to try which would be fuss![1]
And "Pazon!" we'd say, "are you comin with us?"
And the Derbyhaven chaps would call—
And the way he'd smile and say nothing at all!
Well, that's the Pazon, you'll understand,
Aye, the very man, the very man.
Aw, if I once get agate of him—
But some night again, if I'll be in the trim,
I'll maybe be tellin you more, if so be
You'll be carin to listen, and all agree.

Well, the Pazon was walkin on the gravel—
My conscience! the slow that man did travel!
Backards and forrards, and stoppin and thinkin,
And a talkin away to hisself like winkin;
And a pickin a flower, or a kickin a stone,
There he was anyway all alone.
And I felt like a reglar blund'rin blockit,
And I stowed the quid in my waistcoat pocket,
And I said, "Here goes! I don't care a fardin,"

[1] First.

And I opened the gate, and into the garden.
And—" Pazon !" I says, " I've come to you."
" Is it true, Tom Baynes?" he says, "is it true?"
And he looked—" No it isn !" I said, quite pale ;
" So you needn look that way, Pazon Gale !
It isn true !"   So the ould man smiled,
And says he, " Well, don't be angry, child !"
Child he called me—d'ye see? d'ye see ?
Child !—and he takes my hand, and says he,
" I suppose you've got a yarn to spin :
Come in, Tom Baynes, come in, come in !"
So in we went, and him smilin like fun,
Into the parlour ; but the Misthress run
Quite shamed lek, a whiskin through the door,
And dropping her things upon the floor.
And the sarvant keeked[1] over the landin-top—
A dirty trouss,[2] with her head like a mop—
And she gurned[3] like a cat, but I didn care,
Though they're middlin spiteful, them craythurs are.

So I tould the Pazon all that I had,
And he says, " God bless ye ! God bless ye! my lad !"
Aw, it's himself that knew my very soul,
And me so young, and him so oul'.
And all the good talk ! and never fear—
And leave it to him, and he'd bring me clear—
And Anthony wanted spakin to—
And on with the hat—and away he'd go—

---

[1] Peeped.   [2] Slut.   [3] Grinned.

And *young Misther Taylor* (*a son of ould Dan !*)
Was a very *intelligent* young man.
" Aisy ! Pazon," says I, and he went ;
And all the road home—" *in-tel-li-gent* "—
I said, " what's that ? " some pretty name
For a —— deng it ! these pazons is just like crame,
They're talking that smooth—aw, it's well to be civil—
" A son of ould Dan's ! " and *Dan* was a divil.

That was a Monday ; a Thursday night
The Pazon come, and bless me the fright
The ould woman was in, and wipin the chair,
And nudgin and winkin—" Is Thomas there ? "
He says—" Can I see him ? " So up I got,
And out at the door, and I put a knot
On my heart, like one of you, when he takes
A turn and belays, and houlds on till it breaks.
And—" Well ? " I says--then he looked at me,
And " Have you your pipe, Thomas ? " says he ;
" Maybe you'd better light it," he said,
" It's terrible good to studdy [1] the head."
And he wouldn't take rest [2] till I had it lit ;
And he twisses, and twisses, and—" Wait a bit ! "
He says, and he feels, and " We're all alone,"
Says he, and behould ye ! a pipe of his own.
And " I'll smook too," he says : and he charges,
And puffs away like Boanarges.
I never knew the like was at him [3] afore :

[1] Steady.   [2] Be satisfied.   [3] That he had such a thing.

And so we walked along the shore.
And if he didn behove to spin a yarn
About the stars—and Aldebar'n,
And Orïon—and just to consedher [1]
The grand way God had put them together,
And wasn it a good world after all,
And—what was man—and the Bible—and Paul—
Till I got quite mad, and I says—"That'll do!
Were you at the Brew, Pazon? were you at the Brew?"
Aw, then it all come out, and the jaw
Ould Anthony had, and the coorts, and the law;
And—*Jane Magee and her mother both*—
He had gone there twice, but she stuck to her oath—
And—*what could he do?* "I'm going," says I—
"Keep up your heart now!" "I'll try, I'll try."
"Good-night, and mind you'll go straight to bed!
God bless ye, Tom!" "And you, sir!" I said.
"Come up in the mornin! Good-night! good-night!
Now mind you'll come!" "All right! all right!"

And it's into the house, and "Mawther," I says,
"I'm off." "What off!" says she, "if you plaze!
Off! what off!" says she, "you slink!" [2]
And she was sharplin a knife upon the sink, [3]
And she flung it down, and she looked that way—
Straight and stiff; and "What did you say?
Off! off where?" and the sting of a light
Snapped quick in her eye—"All right! all right!"

---

[1] Consider.　　　[2] Sneak.　　　[3] Sink-stone.

I says, and away to the chiss [1] I goes—
"Stand by !" I cried, "I want my clothes ;"
And I hauled them out—aw, she gave a leap,
And "Lave them alone !" she says, "you creep !" [2]
And she skutched [3] them up, and she whisked about
As lithe as an eel, and still lookin out
Over her shouldher, and eyein me,
Like a flint, or some dead thing—"Let be,
Mawther," I says, "let go ! you'd batther !"
Aw, then if she didn begin no matther !
And she threw the things upon the floor,
And she stamped them, and down on her knees, and she tore,
And ripped, and ragged, and scrunched away,
Aw, hands and teeth,—I'll be bound to say
Them shirts was eighteen pence the yard !
Rael good shirts ! aw, the woman was hard.
Hard she was, and lusty, and strong—
I've heard them say when she was young,
She could lift a hundred-weight and more,
And there wasn a man in the parish could throw her.
And as for shearin and pickin potatoes—
Aw, well, she bet all, and always as nate as
A pin, and takin a pride in it—
For there's some ould women, they're hardly fit,
They're that dirty and stupid, and messin and muddin,
I wudn live with the like—No ! I wudn !
But yandhar [4] woman—asleep or awake—

---

[1] Chest. [2] Creeping creature—very common term of contempt.
[3] Caught. [4] Yonder—that.

Was a clane ould craythur and no mistake.
But hard—aw hard! for the ould man died,
And she looked, and she looked, but she never cried—
And him laid out, as sweet as bran,
And everything white,—like a gentleman.
And brass nails—bless ye! and none of your 'sterrits,[1]
But proud in herself, and sarvin the sperrits.[2]
And " Misthress Baynes now! was he prepared?"
"God knows!" says she—aw, the woman was hard.
But if you could have prised the hatches
Of that strong sowl, you would have seen the catches
She made at her heart, choked up to the brim,
And you'd ha' knew she was as dead as him.
But mind me! from that very day
The juice of her life, as you may say,
Was clean dried out of her, and she got
As tough and as dry, and as hard as a knot.
Hard—but handy, and goin still,
Not troublin much for good or ill;
Like the moon and the stars God only touched
Once long ago, and away they scutched;[3]
And now He never minds them a bit,
But they keep goin on, for they're used of[4] it.

Goin on! Well she did go on that night,
And up from the floor, and her back to the light
Of the fire (it was burnin middlin low),
And the candle capsized, and she looked to grow

[1] Hysterics.   [2] Serving out the spirits.   [3] Ran.   [4] To.

That big in the dark, and never a breath,
But standin there like the shadda of death—
Never a breath—for maybe a minute,
Just like a cloud with the thunder in it
Dark and still, till its powder-bags
Burst—and the world is blown to rags.
Aw, she gave it them with a taste—she did,
"And was it that flippity-flappity flid
Of a Betsy Lee? and she knew well enough
What I'd come to at last with my milkin and stuff,
And sniffin about where I hadn no call,
And the lines hangin rottin upon the wall,
And the boat never moored, and grindin her bones
To sawdust upon the cobblin stones [1]—
And the people talkin—And who were the Lees?
Who were they now after all, if you please?
Who were they to cock their nose?
And Lee's ould wife with her strings and her bows,
And her streamers and trimmins, and pippin and poppin
Her stupid ould head like a hen with a toppin! [2]
And had they forgot when they lived next door?
A lazy lot, and as poor as poor—
And—*Misses Baynes! the beautiful tay*
You've got—and I raely think I'll stay—
And—*could you lend me a shillin till to-morrow?*
And borrow, borrow, borrow, borrow.
Aye, and starvin, and him doin nothin for hours
But pokin about with his harbs and his flowers—

---

[1] Large stones on the beach.   [2] Crest.

The lig-y-ma-treih !¹ the dirty ould bough !²
And now it was *Misther Lee !* my gough !
Misther and Misthress Lee in the gig—
Make way, *good people !*—aw, terrible big !
And would I demean myself to them ?
You silly-billy ! for shame ! for shame !"
And at it again—" And what she would rather—
And me the very spit³ of my father !
And what was the matter with Jinny Magee ?
Your wife ! your wife ! and why shouldn she be ?
She was good at the work, and worth a hundred
Of your Betsy things—and why should we be sundered ?
And Jinny and her would agree, never fear her !"
Aw, she was despard⁴ though to hear her.

"Hush ! mawther !" I says, "aw, mawther, hush !"
And she turned to the fire, and I saw her brush
The tears from her eyes, and I saw the workin
Of her back, and her body jerkin, jerkin :
And I went, and I never said nothin lek,
But I put my arm around her neck,
And I looked in her face, and the shape and the strent',⁵
And the very face itself had went
All into one, like a sudden thaw,
Slished and slushed, or the way you've saw
The water bubblin and swirlin around
The place where a strong man have gone down.

---

¹ Taking time, dilatory.   ² Poor (creature).
³ Exact likeness.   ⁴ Desperate.   ⁵ Strength.

And I took her and put her upon the bed
Like a little child, and her poor ould head
On my breast, and I hushed her, and stroked her cheek
Talkin little talk—the way they speak
To babies—I did ! and then I begun
To think of yandhar Absalun,
And David cryin " My son, my son ! "
And the moon come round, and the light shone in,
And crep' on her face, and I saw the thin
She was, and the wore, and her neck all dried
And shrivelled up like strips of hide :
And I thought of the time it was as warm
And as soft as Betsy's, and her husband's arm
Around it strong and lovin, and me
A cuddled up, and a suckin free,
And I cried like Peter in the Testament,
When Jesus looked at him, and out he went,
And cried like a fool, and the cock a crowin,
But what there was in his heart there's no knowin.
And I swore by the livin God above
I'd pay her back, and love for love,
And keep for keep, and the wages checked,[1]
And her with a note,[2] and all correct.
Then I kissed her, and she never stirred ;
And I took my clothes, and, without a word,
I snicked the door, and by break o' the day
I was standing alone on Douglas quay.

---

[1] Stopped at the owner's.   [2] Wage-note left at home by a seaman.

I shipped foreign of coorse, and a fine ship too,
China bound, the *Waterloo*—
Captain Davis—the time I joined her—
" Carry-on Davis? " aye, I thought you'd mind her,
A tight little ship, and a tight little skipper—
Hadn we a race with the Liverpool clipper,
The *Marco Polo*, that very trip?
And it's my opinion that if that ship—
But never mind! she done her duty,
And the *Marco Polo was* a beauty—
But still—close-hauled, d'ye see? Well! well!
There's odds of ships, and who can tell?
That was my ship anyway,
And I was aboard her two years to a day,
And back though for all, and her a dischargin,
And the hands paid off, so you'll aisy imargine
The keen I was for home, and the tracks
I made right away, and no one to ax,
Nor nothing—" And surely hadn I heard
From nobody? " Bless ye! not a word!

It was dark when I come upon the street,
And my heart hung heavy on my feet,
And—all turned in, but in the ould spot
A light was burnin still, and the hot
I felt, and the chokin, and over the midden,
And up to the pane—and her face half-hidden,
And her sure enough, and the ould arm-chair,
And as straight as a reed, and terrible spare!

And the needles twinklin cheerily,
And a brave big book spread out on her knee,
The Bible—thinks I—and I was raely plased,
For it's a great thing to get ould people aised
In their minds with the lek o' yandhar,[1] and tracks,
And hymns—it studdies them though, and slacks
Their sowls, and softens their tempers, and stops
Their coughin as good as any drops.
And if they don't understand what they're readin—
The poor ould things—it's a sort of feedin—
Chewin or suction—what's the odds?
One way's man's, and the other God's!

"But how about Betsy?" well, wait a bit!
How about her? aye, that was it—
And what a man knows, you see he knows,
So I lifts the latch, and in I goes.
"Mawther!" I says—aw then! the spring
She gave, and says she—"It's a scandalous thing,"
She says, "Comin back in their very closes!
And it's bad enough, but I'll have no ghos'es!
Be aff!"[2] says she, "be aff! be aff!"
Well, I raely couldn help but laugh.
"I'm Thomas Baynes, your son!" I said;
"I'm not a ghost." "And aren you dead?"
"No!" I says, and I took and gave her a kiss:
"Is that like a ghost?" "Well, I can't say it is."
"And—Betsy, mawther?" The look! the look!

---

[1] Things like that.   [2] Off.

"Betsy, mawther?"—the woman shook;
And she spread her arms, and I staggered to her,
And I fell upon my knees on the floor;
And she wrapped my head in her brat [1]—d'ye hear?
For to see a man cryin is middlin queer:
And then, my mates, then—then I knew
What a man that's backed by the divil can do.
For hadn this Taylor come one day,
And tould them I was drowned at sea?
And ould Anthony Lee, that might have knew better,
Never axed to see the letter
Nor nothin, but talked about "Providence;"
And the men at the shore they hadn the sense;
And the Pazon as simple as a child,
And that's the way the villain beguiled
The lot of them, for they didn know
What to do or where to go,
As if there wasn no owners nor agent,
Nor Lloyd's, where they might have heard immadient.

And Betsy, be sure, heard all before long,
They took care of that, and then ding-dong,
Night and day the ould people was at her—
And would she marry Taylor? and chitter-chatter!
And never a word from Betsy Lee
But "It cannot be! it cannot be!"
And thinner and thinner every day,
And paler and paler, I've heard them say;

[1] Apron.

And always doin the work and goin,
And early and late, and them never knowin,
For all they thought theirselves so wise,
That the gel was dyin under their eyes.
And—"Take advice, and marry him now!
A rael good husband anyhow."
And allis the one against the three—
And "It cannot be! it cannot be!"

One night he was there, and words ran high—
Ould Peggy was tellin—and "Let me die!"
She says—"let me die! let me die!" she said,
And they took her upstairs, and put her to bed,
And the Doctor come—I knew him well,
And he knew me—ould Doctor Bell—
A nice ould man, but hard on the drink,
And the fond of Betsy you wouldn think!
He used to say, but he'd never say more,
Her face was like one he'd seen afore.
Aw, that's the man that had supped his fill
Of troubles, mind! but cheerful still.
And a big strong man; and he'd often say
"Well, Thomas, my lad, and when's the day?"
And "would I be axin him up to the feed?"
The day indeed! the day indeed!
So he went up all alone to see her,
For Betsy wouldn have nobody there,
Excep' himself: and them that was standin
And houldin their breaths upon the landin

Could hear her talkin very quick,
And the Doctor's vice uncommon thick—
But what was said betwix them two
That time, there was none of them ever knew :
God knows, and *him ;* but the nither[1] will tell ;
Aw, he was safe to trust was Doctor Bell.
But when he come down—" Is she raely dyin ?"
Ould Anthony said ; but the Doctor was cryin.
And—" Doctor ! Doctor ! what can it be ?"
" It's only a broken heart," says he ;
And—*he'd come again another day*—
And he took his glass, and went away.

And when the winter time come round,
And the snow lyin deep upon the ground,
One mornin early the mother got up
To see how was she, and give her a sup
Of tea or the like—and—mates—hould on !
Betsy was gone ! aye, Betsy was gone !
" Gentle Jesus, meek and mild !
Look upon a little child !
Pity my simplicity !
Suffer me to come to thee !"
That's the words I've heard her sing
When she was just a little prattlin thing—
And I raely don't think in my heart that ever
She was different from that—no never !
Aw, He'd pity her simplicity !

[1] Neither of them.

A child to God ! a woman to me !
"Gentle Jesus !" the sound is sweet,
Like you'll hear the little lammies bleat !
Gentle Jesus ! well, well, well !
And once I thought—but who can tell !
Come ! give us a drop of drink ! the stuff
A man will put out when he's dry ! that's enough !
To hear me talkin religion——eh ?
You must have thought it strange ?— *You didn*—ye say ?
You didn !—no !—what ! you didn—*you !*
Well, that'll do, my lads ; that'll do, that'll do.

So of coorse the buryin—terrible grand,
And all in the papers you'll understand—
" Elizabeth, daughter of Anthony Lee
And Mary his wife—and twenty-three."
But bless me ! you've seen the lek afore—
And the Doctor waitin at the door,
And wantin somethin—and "Could I see her ?"
And "Yes ! aw yes !" and up the steer [1]—
And he looked, and he looked—I've heard them say—
Like a man that's lookin far away ;
And he kissed her cheek, and he shut the lid,
That's what they tould me the Doctor did.

But, however, you musn suppose, my men,
That all this was tould me there and then—
Aw, I thought I'd somethin to tell ye, mind !

[1] Stair.

That wasn much in the spoony line—
No! no! the words ould mawther said
Was—"Betsy is dead, Tom; Betsy is dead!
And it's Taylor has kilt her anyway,
For didn he tell you were lost at sea!"
Nothin more—and up I sprung
To my feet, like a craythur that had been stung,
And I couldn see nothin but fire and blood,
And I reeled like a bullock that's got the thud
Of the slaughterer's hammer betwixt his hurns,[1]
And claps of light and dark by turns,
Fire and blood! fire and blood!
And round and round, till the blindin scud
Got thinner and thinner, and then I seen
The ould woman had hitched herself between
My arms, and her arms around my neck,
And waitin, waitin, and wond'rin lek.
Aw, I flung her off—"He'll die! he'll die!
This night, this very night," says I:
" He'll die before I'm one day ouldher;"
And I stripped my arm right up to the shouldher—
"Look here!" I says, "hasn't God given
The strength?" I says, "and by Him in heaven,
And by her that's with him—hip and thigh!
He'll die this night, he'll die! he'll die!"
"No! no!" says she, "no, Thomas, no!"
For I was at the door intarmined[2] to go.
And she coaxed and coaxed, and "wouldn it be better

---

[1] Horns.   [2] Determined.

To speak to him fuss, or to write a letter—
Will you go to the Pazon?" says she; I laughed—
"Will you go to the Pazon?" "It's not his craft,"
I says; "the work I've got to do
Is no Pazon's work." "Will you go to the Brew?"
Aw, when she said that, I made a run—
But she held me, and—"Oh my son! my son!"
And crying and houldin on to me still—
"Will you go to the Pazon?" "Yes! I will,
If that'll give you any content."
Not another word, but away we went—
And her in the dark, a-keepin a grip
Of my jacket for fear I'd give her the slip,
And a-peggin away with her poor old bones,
And stumblin and knockin agin the stones—
And neither the good nor the bad was said,
And the one of us[1] hadn a thing on our head—
And the rain it rained, and the wind it blew—
Aw, the woman was hard, but the woman was true.

"Missis Baynes!" says the Pazon, "Missis Baynes!
    Missis Baynes!
Will you plase to tell me what this means?"
And white as a sheet, and he cuts a caper,
And he drops the specs, and he drops the paper,
And backs and gets under the lee of a chair—
I'm blest if the Pazon didn look queer!
I racly thought he was goin to fall—

[1] Neither of us.

And says Mawther—"He isn dead at all!
Don't be freckened!" and—holy Moses!
Wasn he paid to look after ghos'es?
Aw, then the joy he took of me!
"And the only one saved from the wreck!" says he;
"What wreck?" I said, "there wasn no wreck—
Just Taylor's lies!" and I cussed him lek.[1]
"For shame then! Thomas!" and up she stood.
"Let him cuss!" says the Pazon, "it'll do him good."
And the look he gave, and the sigh, and the sob!
And he saw in a minute the whole of the job.
And he tried to speak, but he wasn able,
And I laid my head upon the table—
Quite stupid lek, and then them two
Began to talk, and I hardly knew
What was it they said, but "the little drop!"
I heard, and "you'll 'scuse him," and "Woman, stop!
The lad is drunk with grief," he said,
And he come and put his hand on my head;
And the poor old fingers as dry as chips!
And the pity a tricklin off their tips—
And makin me all as peaceable—
Aw, the Pazon was kind and lovin still!
Full of wisdom and love, and blessin,
Aw, it's kind and lovin was the Pazon!

So at last, ye see, whatever they had,
I didn say nothin, good or bad;

---

[1] Apologetic use of this flexible word.

And they settled betwix them what would I do,
And neither to go to the town nor the Brew,
" But off to sea again, aye straight !
And, if I could, that very night."
So they roused me up, and " Me and your mawther "—
The Pazon says—" Aw, ye needn bother,"
Says I, "all right !" and then I'll be bail
I took it grand out of Pazon Gale—
"Now Pazon," I says, " you know your man—
And a son of ould Dan's too ! a son of ould Dan ! "
We were at the door just ready to go—
Aw, the Pazon couldn help smilin though—
A son of ould Dan's !—aye, just that way—
A son of ould Dan's !—eh ? Billy ! eh ?

Well, I kept my word, and off at once,
And shipped on a coaster, owned in Penzance ;
But it was foreign I wanted, so very soon
I joined the *Hector* bound for Rangoon.
Ah, mates ! it's well for flesh and blood
To stick to a lass that's sweet and good,
Leastways if she sticks to you, ye know ;
For then, my lads, blow high, blow low,
On the stormiest sea, in the darkest night,
Her love is a star that'll keep you right.
But there wasn no sun nor star for me—
Drinkin and tearin and every spree—
And if I couldn keep the divil under,
I don't think there's many of you will wonder.

Well, divil or no, the *Hector* come home :
We raced that trip with the *Flying Foam*,
And up the river the very same tide,
And the two of them berthed there side by side ;
A tight run that, and the whole of it stuck
In the paper—logs and all—good luck !
And the captain as proud, and me like a fool
Spreein away in Liverpool—
And lodgins of coorse, for I never could stand
Them Sailors' Homes, for a man is a man,
And a bell for dinner and a bell for tay,
And a bell to sing and a bell to pray,
And a bell for this and a bell for that,
And " Wipe your feet upon the mat ! "
And the rules hung up ; and fined if you're late,
And a chap like a bobby shuttin the gate—
It isn raisonable, it isn :
They calls it a Home, I calls it a Prison.
Let a man go wherever he chooses !
Ould mawther Higgins' the house that I uses—
Jem Higgins' widda—you'll be bound to know *her*—
Clane, but not partickiler.
There's Quiggin's too, next door but one,
Not Andrew, of coorse ! but Rumpy John—
She's a dacent woman enough is Nancy,
But Higginses allis took my fancy.
There's some comfort there, for you just goes in,
And down with the watch and down with the tin,
And sleepin and wakin, and eatin and drinkin—

And out and in, and never thinkin—
And carryin on till all is blue,
And your jacket is gone and your waistcoat too.
Then of coorse you must cut your stick,
For the woman must live, however thick
You may be with her : and I'm tould there's houses
Where the people 'll let ye drink your trousis ;
But Higginses ! never ! and it isn right !
Shirt and trousis ! honour bright !

But mostly afore it come to the spout
I'd ask if the money was all run out,
And she'd allis tell me whether or no,
And I'd lave my chiss, and away I'd go.
And so this time I took the street,
And I walked along till I chanced to meet
A shipmate, somewhere down in Wappin'—
And "What was I doin? and where was I stoppin?"
And "Blow it all ! here goes the last copper !"
And into a house to get a cropper.[1]

It was one of them dirty stinkin places,
Where the people is not a bit better than bases,[2]
And long-shore lubbers a shammin to fight,
And Jack in his glory, and Jack's delight—
With her elbers stickin outside of her shawl
Like the ribs of a wreck—and the divil and all !
And childher cussin and suckin the gin—

---

[1] Crupper, a small measure of spirits.   [2] Beasts.

God help them craythurs! the white and the thin!
But what took my eye was an ouldish woman
In and out, and goin and comin,
And heavy feet on the floor overhead,
And "She's long a dyin," there's some of them said.
"Dyin!" says I; "Yes, dying!" says they;
"Well, it's a rum place to choose to die in—eh?"
Aw, the ould woman was up, and she cussed very bad—
And—"Choosin! there's not much choosin, my lad!"
"And what's her name?" says I; says she,
"If ye want to know, it's Jinny Magee."
Aw, never believe me but I took the stair!
And "Where have you got her? where? where? where?"
"Turn to the right!" says she, "ye muff!"
And there was poor Jinny, sure enough!
There she was lyin on a wisp of straw—
And the dirt and the rags—you never saw—
And her eyes—aw them eyes! and her face—well! well!
And her that had been such a handsome gel!

"Tom Baynes! Tom Baynes! is it you? is it you?
Oh can it be? can it be? can it be true?"
Well I couldn speak, but just a nod—
"Oh it's God that's sent you—it's God, it's God!"
And she gasped and gasped—"Oh I wronged you, Thomas!
I wronged you, I did, but he made me promise—
And here I'm now, and I know I'll not live—
Oh Thomas, forgive me, oh Tom, forgive!
Oh reach me your hand, Tom, reach me your hand!"

And she stretched out hers, and—I think I'm a man,
But I shivered all over, and down by the bed,
And "Hush! hush! Jinny! hush! hush!" I said;
"*Forgive ye!*—Yes!" and I took and pressed
Her poor weak hand against my breast.
"Look, Tom," she said, "look there! look there!"
And a little bundle beside a chair—
And the little arms and the little legs—
And the round round eyes as big as eggs,
And full of wondher—and "That's the child!"
She says, and she smiled! the woman smiled!
So I took him up, and—"His name?" "It's Simmy:"
And the little frock and the little chimmy![1]
And starved to the bones—so "Listen to me!
Listen now! listen! Jinny Magee!
By Him that made me, Jinny ven![2]
This child is mine for ever, Amen!"
And "Simmy!" I says, "remember this!"
And I put him to her for her to kiss;
And then I kissed him; but the little chap
Of coorse he didn understand a rap.
And I turned to Jinny, and she tried to rise,
And I saw the death-light in her eyes—
Clasped hands! clenched teeth! and back with the head—
Aye, Jinny was dead, boys! Jinny was dead.

"Come here," I says, and I stamped on the floor,
And up the ould woman come to be sure.

---

[1] Chemise, shirt.   [2] Dear.

"See after her!" I says, "ould Sukee!"
And "All very well!" she says, "but lookee!
You gives yourself terrible airs, young man!
Come now! what are you goin to stand?"
But I took the child, and says I, "I'm goin:"
"Indeed!" she says, "and money owin!
And the people 'll be 'spectin a drop of drink,"
And cussin, *and who was she, did I think?*
And the buryin too, for the matter of that!
"Out of the way!" says I, "you cat!"
And down the stair, and out at the front,
And the loblollyboys[1] shoutin "Down with the
　　blunt!"[2]
And a squarin up, and a lookin big,
And "hould him! down with him! here's a rig!"
"Stand back, you Irish curs! stand back!"
Says I, for there wasn a man in the pack:
"Stand back, you cowards; or I'll soon let ye see!"
So off we went—little Simmy and me.

Is that him there asleep? did ye ax?
Aye, the very same, and them's the fac's.
And now, my lads, you'll hardly miss
To know what poor little Simmy is.
Bless me! it's almost like a dream,
But the very same! the very same!
Grew of coorse, and growin, understand ye!
But you can't keep them small agin nathur, can ye?

---

[1] "Loafers" about the docks.　　　　[2] Money.

Look at him, John ! the quiet he lies !
And the fringes combin over his eyes !
I know I'm a fool—but—feel that curl !
Aw, he's the only thing I have in all the world.

Well, on we marched, and the little thing
Wasn so heavy as a swaller's wing—
A poor little bag of bones, that's all,
He'd have bruk in two if I'd let him fall.
And I tried all the little words I knew,
And actin the way that women do.
But bless ye ! he wouldn take no rest,
But shovin his little head in my breast,
For though I had lived so long ashore,
I never had carried a child before.
And not a farlin at me ;[1] so the only plan
Was to make tracks straight off for Whitehaven,
And chance a lugger loadin there—
Aw, heaps of them yandhar—never fear !
And the first time ever I begged was then,
And the women is raely wuss till[2] the men—
" Be off !" says my lady, " be off ! you scamp !
I never give nothin to a tramp !"
So I made her a bow, for I learnt with my letters,
To " ordher myself to all my betters."
But when the sun got low in the sky,
Little Simmy began to cry.
" Hungry !" I says, and over a gate

---

[1] Not a farthing in my possession.   [2] Worse than.

And into a field, and "Wait then, wait!"
And I put him sitting upon the grass—
Dear o' me! the green it was—
And the daisies and buttercups that was in,
And him grabbin at them astonishin!
So I milked a cow, and I held my cap,
And I gave it to the little chap;
And he supped it hearty enough, the sweep!
And stretched hisself, and off to sleep—
And a deuced good supper and nothin to pay,
And "Over the hills and far away."

So by hook, or by crook, or however it was,
I got down to Whitehaven at last;
And a Ramsey lugger they call the *Map*—
Jemmy Corkhill—I knew the chap.
"Hullo!" says I—"Hullo!" says he;
"It's yourself that's been on the divil's spree,
And a baby at ye too—my word!"
"All right!" says I, and heaves him aboard—
And—*Bless his soul the fun! and a chile in!*[1]
So that's the way I got to the Islan'.
I landed at Ramsey and started off
The soonest I could, and past Ballaugh,
And Kirk Michael, and the Ballacraine—
I hadn been there I couldn tell ye the when.
And you may think how he wasn much of a load,
But I was checked[2] when I come on the mountain road;

---

[1] A child in the case. [2] Tired.

And I found a spot where the ling was high,
And terrible thick and soft and dry—
And a big rock standin Nor-east by East—
The way of the wind—aw, a beautiful place!

So I laid me down, and the child in my arms,
And the quick little breath, and the dogs at the farms,
And the curlews whistlin, passin by—
And the noise of the river below, and the sigh
Of the mountain breeze—I kept awake,
And a star come out like a swan on a lake,
White and lonely ; and a sort of amazement
Got hould on me, and the leads of a casement
Crissed-crossed on the sky like a window-frame,
And the long, long look! and the far it came!
Aw dear! I thought it was Jinny Magee
In heaven makin signs to me.
And sleep at last, and when I awoke,
The stars was gone, and the day was broke,
And the bees beginnin to think of the honey,
And who was there but little sonny—
Loosed from my arms, and catchin my hair,
And laughin ; and I laughed too, I'll swear.
And says I—"Come, Simmy, my little buffer !
You're small, but what is it sayin ?—*Suffer*
The little children to come to me—
So here goes! Simmy ;" and " Glory be,"
I said, and " Our Father," and two or three
Little hymns I remembered—" Let dogs delight,"

The first two verses middling right—
And "Little boy with cheerful eye,
Bright and blue as yandhar sky;"
And down, and takin the road to the Lhen,
And the clear the sun was shinin then,
And the little church that white; and below—
The stones—and—well—you know! you know!

But at last I come to the shore, and I ran,
For though it was early I saw a man
Diggin lug [1] on the beach, and I didn want
To meet the like, so I made a slant,
And back and in by the Claddagh lane,
And round by the gable—Ned knows what I mean;
And in at the door; and "Mawther!" I said,
"Mawther!" but she was still in bed.
"Mawther! look here! look here!" I cried;
And I tould her all how Jinny had died,
And this was the youngster, and what I intended,
And she heard me till my story was ended,
And just like a stone—aw, never a word!
And me gettin angry, till this little bird
Chirrups up with a crow and a leap—
And—"Mammy sceepy! Mammy as'eep"—
Just that baby way—aw, then the flood
Of the woman's-life come into her blood;
And she stretched her arms, and I gave him to her,
And she cried till she couldn cry no more.

---

[1] Sand-worms for bait.

And she took to him grand, though of coorse at fuss [1]
Her hand was out, ye see, to nuss.
But after dinner she had him as nice—
And a singin, bless ye, with her poor ould vice.

The sun was down when I left them awhile,
And up the Claddagh, and over the stile,
And into the ould churchyard, and tryin
To find the place where Betsy was lyin.
It was nearly dark, but I wasn alone,
For I seen a man bending over a stone—
And the look, and the heave of the breast—I could see
It *was* a man—in his agony.
And nearer! nearer! the head! the hair!
The stoop! it was Taylor! Taylor—*there!*
Aw, then it all come back again,
All the throuble and all the pain,
And the one thought in my head—*him there at her grave!*
And I stopped, and I said, " May Jesus save
His soul! for his life is in my hand—
Life for life! it's God's command,
Life for life!" and I measured my step—
"So long he shall live!" and I crep and crep—
Aw, the murderer's creep—"God give him grace!"
Thinks I—then to him, and looked in his face.
Aw, that face! he raised it—it wasn surprise,
It wasn fear that was in his eyes;
But the look of a man that's fairly done

[1] First.

With everythin that's under the sun.
Ah, mates! however it was with me,
He had loved her, he *loved* her—my Betsy Lee!
"Taylor!" I said; but he never spoke:
"You loved her," I said, "and your heart is broke."
And he looked—aw, the look—"Come, give us your hand!"
I says—"*Forgive you?* I can! I can!
For the love that was so terrible strong,
For the love that made you do the wrong."
And, with them words, I saw the star
I tould you of, but brighter far:
It wasn Jinny, but Betsy now!
"Misther Taylor," I says, "we cannot tell how,
But it was love—yes! yes! it was love! it was love!
And He's taken her to Hisself above;
And it's Him that'll see that nothin annoys her,
And——" "Watch below! turn up!" "Aye, aye, sir!"

CHRISTMAS ROSE

THE Pazon! the Pazon! just stop a bit!
Where to begin—Is that lamp lit?
I've got it, I've got it! It's like you'll mind
The big storm in hunder-thirty-nine—
You do? at least some does—then think of your sins!
For that's the time my story begins.

It was Christmas time, if I remember,
Or at any rate well in the month of December—
They were up at the School that night practisin
(And even then the wind was risin),
Ould Hughie the clerk, and Jem—Jemmy—Jem;
Aw well there was a pair of them—
And Dicky-Dick-beg agate[1] of the fiddle,
And the son and the daughter, and him in the middle—
Carvels[2]—of coorse—again the Ail Varey[3]—
You'll mind it, Ned! you and me and Mary,

---

[1] At work at.   [2] Carols.   [3] Eve of Mary, Christmas Eve.

And all the gels and the lads from the shore,
Carryin on outside of the door.
It was blowin hard when they went to bed,
And "There'll be jeel[1] to night!" the ould man said.
But childher sleep sound; and the first I knew
Was mawther shoutin for any two—
And I jumped, and I looked, and there was the wall,
But the divil a roof there was at us at all—
Divil a straw; but the bits of spars,
And the sand and the spray, and the scud and the stars:
And all the houses stript the same,
Hardly a rafter, hardly a beam—
And the tearin and callin one to another,
And "Jenny! where are ye?" and "Mawther! Mawther!"
And all the lot of them comin flyin
Out on the street—and the shoutin and cryin,
And this way, that way, and the pullin and haulin
And "Give us that rope!" "Make fast that tarpaulin!"
Bless my heart! the confusion though!
But the ould man took for the beach, you know—
Aw a right ould sea-dog! keen on the scent—
Sniffin and snuffin away he went,
And round the gable, and out on the strand,
And crouchin and slouchin a-back of his hand,
And a-layin his head to the wind like a bullet,
And a-edgin out to the side of the gullet—
Wasn I after him? knowin his ways,
And a hold of his arm, and we saw the blaze

[1] Damage.

Of a rocket go up, and "Studdy!"[1] he said,
"There's a ship ashore on Conisthar head."
And a gun come boomin through the roar
Of the waves, and "A ship! a ship ashore!"
The both of us shouted, and we ran like mad—
Aw it's the wonderful wind the ould man had!
And "Here! all hands!" he says, "just as ye are!
There's a ship ashore on Conisthar!"

Ashore, but not where we might have got at her,
You'll mind, but out in shoaly water—
The Scranes they calls it, and deep inside;
But the Scranes shoals bad, and a ten-knot tide
Rakes them, and at Spring ebbs you'll get
About a fathom—eh Ned? that's it?
Well that's where she was; *And could you see*
The people aboard? aye, aye! let be!
My lads, let's drop it! let's drop it, however!
Could a boat have lived? tut! bless ye! never!
Never! no life-boats, nor apperaturs,
Nor nothin them times! Lord help the craythurs!
Well look here now! drop it, do! It was light,
Broad day, when she parted amidships—*All right!*
Was the word, and *Steady! all hands look out!*
Then never a word till one gave a shout
And another, and hands was gript in a minute,
And I looked at the trough, and what was there in it
But a nigger swimmin strong and hard

---

[1] Steady.

On his back? and a bundle—I didn regard[1]
What, but somethin white, and the lift
Of the sea curled round him, and swep' it adrift;
And he turned on his face, and he made a bite
With his teeth, and he caught it, and held it as
    tight
As tight; and struck out, but rather slow,
Aw, a pluckier nigger I never saw;
Nor nobody else—and pluck is pluck;
But whether it was his heart was bruck[2]
With the strength of the sea, I cannot tell;
But when they got hould of him he fell
In their arms; and, sure enough, he was dead!
Poor fellow! But what d'ye think he had
Clenched in his teeth that they had to cut
The tapes with a knife, they were that tight shut—
What but a little child? a gel!
And livin too! aw well, well, well!
If you'd ha' heard the cheer, and the women cryin,
And runnin, and takin their turn and tryin
To warm it at their breasts, and rockin,
And doublin themselves over it—well it was shockin!
And *go and tell the Pazon!* such squealin;
But the Pazon was there already kneelin
By the black man's side: and he'd got a book,
And workin the rules; and he wouldn look
At the baby a bit, for he said, and he smiled,
"The women 'll be sure to look after the child."

---

[1] Notice.   [2] Broken.

But all the rules of the Royal Human [1]—
Tryin and tryin—they wouldn do, man!
Aw he worked them well, and they all of them worked,
And lifted and shook him, and rolled him, and jerked,
And rubbed him and all; and a fine man, look'ee!
Of his limbs, though his legs was a little crooky—
As big as me, or maybe bigger—
And the Pazon manœuvering over the nigger—
And some of the men fit enough to cry [2]
To think that a man like that should die,
And him in their hands! But they had to give in
At last, and the Pazon tied up his chin
With his own handkecher, and strooked
His arms by his side; and he looked and looked
And then he kissed him! aye, aye! he did!
He did though! and these is the words he said—
And all with the hats off, holdin their breath—
"Thou hast been faithful unto death—
I will give thee a crown of life"—
Them's the words, and turns to the wife;
"And now let's see the baby!" says he,
And took it and nussed it as nice as could be.
And of every sowl aboard that wreck
That's all that had a chance, I expec',
To reach the shore; for a ship that catches
On the Scranes is very soon turned into matches.
Some of the cargo was got to land—
Not much—no divers, you'll understand.

[1] Royal Humane Society.　　[2] Very nearly crying.

F

Convanient to yandhar place; but her name
Was found on a bit of plankin that came
In the trawl one day: but no manifess,[1]
Nor log, nor list of passengess,
Nor nothin—only the name, d'ye see?
The Hidalgar—so it's a Spaniard she'd be.

Well the little gel was took up to the church,
And next day the Pazon come down to search
For a nuss, and got an aunt of mine—
Just the woman! in the washin line—
And shuited capital—aw the best
Of chărācters—aye—and no sort of address,
No sign, nor marks, except on its shirt
An I, and a D, and a thing like a sort
Of a haythen god, or some of these charms—
I think they called it a *coat-of-arms;*
But, howsomedever, that's the why
They thought the child was terrible high.

And the nigger was buried as grand as you plaze,
In the Pazon's ground, just a bit of a raise
At the top of the churchyard; and a mortal sight
Of people, and sarvice, and everything right;
And *dust to dust,* and the clerk with the muck
On the point of the spade—and the nate he shuck[2]
And the sollum—a-makin believe that way
They were all agate of a Christian—eh?

<hr/>

[1] Ship's manifest.   [2] Shook

And a stone ! aye, a stone, and the very verse
The Pazon said over him at first—
I know the man that cut it, and he tould me
In the teens of pounds ! in the teens, behould ye !
And a stunnin job at Jemmy Bluitt—
Aw the man could do it ! the man could do it !

And the little gel did thrive for all—
Aw man-alive ! and straight, and tall,
And strong on her feet ; and every faythur [1]
Like a child twice her age—the little craythur !
Dark though, and keen, and soople [2] still,
And the Pazon loved her terrible.
I've seen him with her beside him a sittin
On the darkie's grave, and her a gettin
Daisies and that, and a pokin them straight
In his face, and him with the love and the light
And the strength and the strain of his soul's desire
All round the child like a glory of fire.
Aw it's truth I tell ye—but I've heard them say
The misthress wasn much that way.
She'd look middlin sharp now and then at the pair,
And bite her thread with a wrench, and stare ;
But quite [3]—aw quite ! just hemmin and hummin
A bit—she was hard to make out—that woman ;
At least I'm told so—I was middlin young
Them times, and the misthress was close o' the tongue,
A dry sort of woman, and no-ways free,

---

[1] Feature.   [2] Supple, lithe.   [3] Quiet.

But allis civil enough to me.
What did they call the child? eh, Dan?
Wasn I goin to tell you, man?
My patience! there's chaps—but I knows what I knows—
Well—they called her the Christmas Rose.
And was the water hove [1] *in her face*
On a name like that? Just so if you plaze—
Christmas Rose—d'ye hear? d'ye hear?
Christmas Rose. Now then what cheer?
Christmas Rose! you'll 'scuse me, mates.
But I like to chastise these runagates.

    Now the Pazon had childher, George and James,
Sons the both, and that's the names;
And that's the lot that ever they had;
And such times as they come, I've heard it said,
The wife and himself was middlin ould.
And the woman was dry—that's the way I'm tould—
I believe she was, and bony uncommon,
Aw it's dry and bony was the woman.
I've raelly thought many a time she was jus'
Like yandhar Sarah in Genesus,
The time she took Hagar, that was imperint [2] to her,
And jawed her, and put her to the door.
Only the misthress, whatever annoyed her,
Had a way to keep the divil inside her:
Like them burnin mountains seems done their burning,
But the fire is in them churnin and churnin

---

[1] Thrown in her face; was she baptized?   [2] Impudent.

The brimstone—ah dart[1] such women ! I say—
They'd break the heart of Methusaleh.
Now the time I'm tellin the boys, you know,
Was little things just beginnin to go—
George was the ouldest, a tidy bit ;
I don't know was James in perricuts yet—
Just little things with the little bare pelt
Of their legs and their arms, and never a belt,
But a runnin string, and a blue check brat,
And big round eyes, and all to that.[2]
I don't believe that ever the mother
Herself was used to take much bother
About them—middlin fond of the bed
She was ; and, as for the Pazon, he said
To my aunt when she spoke to him middlin free,
" Now 'Tilder," he says, " don't worry me
About the lek ;[3] for, I tell ye, 'Tilder—
I'll have my childher like other childher."
I don't know was it because he got
No pride in him ; or maybe he thought
It was good for childher to be together,
And out in the muck, and out in the weather ;
And sweatin and tearin and fightin away ;
And a gettin strong, as you may say :
And hard, and apt to take their part,
And hand with hand, and heart with heart ;
And free and bould in the talk, and givin
And takin, and laughin and lovin and livin

---

[1] Drat.   [2] So forth.   [3] That sort of thing.

With the rest : and rough, if you like, but ready,
With the stuff in them that when they'd get steady,
And 'd know their place, them's the boys, by jing,
That 'd have go in them for anything.
Like trees, that grows in the open air,
Eh, lads ? and chances it, rain or fair,
Blow high, blow low, they've got the grain
In their heart that'll polish and polish again.
Now did he do right, or did he do wrong ?—
Is it me ? chut ! capers ! get along !

Bless me ! the imps they got, and the pluck !
But that was long after the Pazon took
The strange child home ; for then, no doubt,
They were innocent baby things, runnin about,
And terrible fond it's lek they'd be
Of the little sister that come from the sea.
But when they grew to be lumps[1] the fond
They got of me, you'll understand,
And me of them, and the heads like wool—
That curly, and all of them beautiful !
And when they got big and took sense they begun
To take a pride in theirselves, and done
Theirselves that nice, and their clothes that fine
And soft and differin lek from mine,
That I loved to touch them : and when they were rowin
In the boat with me all stripped and showin
Their arms that white and strong, for all,

---

[1] Good-sized urchins.

And their neck like a tree and their back like a wall—
I'd miss my stroke for lookin—yes !
Aw, I couldn take no rest.

And mawther was allis scouldin of coorse,
She was the woman that could, and never got hoorse—
And who was I, and what was the good?
And place was place, and blood was blood.
But let them grow a bit and I'd see
They wouldn take up with the leks of me.
But the Pazon was terrible wise, you know,
And he saw at once which way the wind blow.
Aw, I have him now with the ould blue eyes—
The tender, the lovin, and the wise.
So with her it was allis "babby !" and "fool !"
And when was I goin to begin to cool?
But there wasn a thing goin under the sun
But the Pazon knew the way it was done :
For his heart was just four pieces joined,
A man and a woman and a child, and a kind
Of a sort of Holy Ghost or another—
So he knew what was at me [1] better than mawther ;
Just a fit that was on me lek
That would have its time and then it 'd break
Like a spell of weather, and I'd be wakin
Swivel [2] enough, and no good to be shakin
A poor craythur that's draemin, but all the same
If he's draemin, his drame is a happy drame.

[1] What ailed me.   [2] Quickly.

And I believe there was more till[1] that;
I believe the Pazon knew what he was at:
I believe he knew it was good for us,
For me and for them, for better for wuss,
That all we had in us should have fair play,
And all give account at the judgment day.
Aw the heat of young blood is a terrible thing,
And it swims in your head, and makes it sing
Queer songs enough—but doesn't it loose
Your soul like a bud that's sticky with juice,
Till it creaks, and it cracks, and it opens free
In the eye of the sun most gloriously?
Anyway—look at the other surt,
A steppin their tippytoes over the dirt!
Bless ye! keepin no company
But only with the top of the tree;
And no spunk in them, and no chance if they had it,
And—*marry a fortin, and be a credit!*

Aw well but the Pazon was kind, and he'd say—
"Come up man, Thomas!" or "Stay la,[2] stay!"
Aw as free as free! and the servant tould
To give me my dinner, bless your soul—
In the kitchen of coorse; and them comin creepin
Across from the parlour, the divils! and peepin;
And her with a clout a hittin them sudden,
And me lookin foolish and workin the puddin.
And he'd play with us too, would the Pazon, yes!

---

¹ Than.   ² Interjection.

Tops and marbles, and not amiss,
Not him—and laughin at all their jokes,
And knuckle down, and take his canokes [1]—
Duckstone—no! nor Hommer-the-let—
Well—no! I don't think it would hardly be fit
For a Pazon to run with his shirt all-amuck
Of sweat, and singin out "Double the Duck!"
And eyein and creepin just the same 's
An ould black cat; besides them games—
They doesn' do—of coorse they doesn'—
Without a little bit of cussin.
But out with the ferrets agate of the warren,
Or in the haggard [2] playin But-thorran,[3]
And them two boys with their imperince mockin,
And trippin the Pazon up most shockin;
And floorin him, and rollin him over,
And tryin to bury him in the clover,
Or straw, or the lek; and him a strugglin
Pretendin lek, and his ould throat gugglin
And splutterin out the stuff; and me
As shamed as ever I could be—
Aw the hat flyin here and the stick flyin there—
Well the shy and the shamed—aw never fear!
"A blessed ould fool!" you'll be thinkin? not him!
But a sort of a blessed ould Cherubim,
If you like: and who can tell the sorrows
He was working out of him with them sparrows?—

---

[1] In the game of marbles.   [2] Stackyard.
[3] Hide-and-seek round the stacks.

Lyin and kickin—and if he had thought
The limb I was, and the way I taught
Them boys to cuss, it isn't there
I'd have been, it's lek; aw dear! aw dear!
Childher is strange; for nearly the fuss [1]
I knew them I axed them could they cuss.
And they said "No;" and I wouldn take rest [2]
But they must learn—and the words—"Say this!"
I said, and "Say that!" and to it we went,
Bless my heart though the innocent!
And I don't know—but Him that's above,
Which they say His name is Love,
He'll be knowin all the same
Was I as innocent as them.
Aw I taught them though; and the ouldest was clever;
Well he could work it, for sure,[3] however;
But James was quiet over it still,
Noways hearty, though comfible.

But *the gel*—did you say? I know! I know!
The gel! the gel! just so! just so!
Gels! gels! gels! and sorrow and sin
They're in everythin, in everythin.
And *what was she lek?* yes! yes! I hear—
What was she lek? aye—never fear!
The little girl that was took from the wreck?
What was she lek eh? what was she lek?
Is it what was she lek? stop! stop a bit!—

[1] First.　　[2] Would not be satisfied.　　[3] Really.

The way she'd stand, the way she'd sit !
And George and her, and takin an oar,—
And up in the church—and down on the shore—
And the turn, and the spring, and the lookin behind
And the eye all full like a cup with wine—
And—what was I sayin? let's see ! let's see !—
I can't ! I can't ! the leks o' me
Draw a picthur of her ! come ! that's a rig !¹
But *was she little or was she big?*
Little or big? What's in my head ?
Little or big I think you said ?
And me that never looked at her
But almost trimblin, mind ye—there !
Lord bless your sowl ! you ignorant noddy !²
Wasn there fire come out of her body—
Aye all over her a blaze
That beat you back, like the Bible says
The sword of fire afore now at the door
Of the garden of Eden though to be sure—
And burnin and burnin
And turnin and turnin
Every art,³ that no base⁴ of a divil
With his cuts and his capers, no matter how swivel,
And dirt in his heart, and mowin and mockin,
Could enter the place where God was walkin !

Well they were wonderful them three—
To see them together was something to see.

¹ Joke.   ² Ignorant blockhead.   ³ Way.   ⁴ Beast.

Well they were scand'lous [1] though for all!
And the whole of the three o' them middlin tall;
And her in the middle, and them either side,
And the strength, and the step of them, and the pride!
George was the biggest a goodish lot,
And the curly yellow hair he got!
And the eyes as blue and as soft as a wench's,
But a splendid strappin lad of his inches.
And bould he looked, and keen, defyin
The world, like a lump of a bull [2] or a lion.
He was middlin red in the face was George;
And so was James, but not that large
In the shouldhers and back like the ouldest, but rather
Stoopin lek, and favourin [3] the father.
But pluck! aw bless ye! there wasn a patch [4]
Betwix them—I never saw their match—
Game to the heels—aw make your bet!
The true breed them! and never fret!

But if they were red then she was white—
The way I tould ye—with the sheets of light
Comin off her skin, like it's sayin about Moses—
With the fire on his face and all his closes.
But what's the use of me?   I shouldn
Be tryin the lek, and I said I wouldn,
But just one thing, and that's her hair—
Well it wasn right—no! no!   I'll swear

---

[1] Marvellous.   [2] A big bull.   [3] Resembling.
[4] The slightest difference.

It wasn—some charm or the lek no doubt
Was put on it—aye! Says you "Get out!"
Aisy all! Some witch or another
Must have spun that stuff; neither father nor mother
Done that, my lads! It was black as nubs,[1]
But streaks of red, like you'll see in the dubs
Where they're cutting the turf; or down in the river,
Where it's deeper and darker and redder than ever—
And all like a cloud around her scutched[2]—
Aw she must have been wutched![3] she must have been
     wutched!
The three of them—the three of them!
I see them now, and it's like a dream;
A dream it's like—and it's strange to a man,
But I'm allis seein things that's gone.

She was proud, 'deed[4] she was uncommon proud—
Aw that's what the Pazon himself allowed!
Aye many's the time I've seen the ould man
At the door, and houldin the hat in his hand;
And her on the step, and him that narvous,
And backin and fillin, and at-your-sarvice!
And bowin and bowin; and her on the step
With the sit of her head and the curl of her lip—
Sweet, but proud; and her foot like a queen's,
And her only just comin into her teens!
Aw I'll never forget the time—no never!
One day she was coming across the river,

---

[1] Coals.   [2] Caught.   [3] Bewitched.   [4] Indeed.

Not far from the shore, where the stones is high
And far betwix—and to see her fly
Like a bird all colours ! bless your hearts !
The way they gets them in foreign parts—
And a jumpin delicate lek, and lettin
On a stone like a feather ; and then she'd be gettin
Her perricuts round her, and balancing
Like a image set on a fine hair spring.
And I got aback of the bushes below,
The way she wouldn see me, you know ;
And my heart in my mouth—when—what was the spree
But her hair got caught in the branch of a tree—
Nuts, or trammon,[1] or—never mind !
But there she was, clane caught behind ;
And whatever she'd do ! and took that sudden—
It wudn let go ! it wudn ! it wudn !
So in I goes, nearly up to my waist—
No stones for me ! it was just a race !
And a plunge and a kick and a scramblin through—
And up to her before she knew,
It's lek with the noise of the water thund'rin
In her ears, and me with my hand a sund'rin
The hair—aw she turned ! and, believe it or not !
She made a leap, and she cleared the lot,
And she stood all shiverin ! and the flashes
Of her eyes was awful, reglar splashes
Of fire they was—and " It's not afraid "—
Says she—" but how dare ye ? how dare ye ? " she said—

---

[1] Elder.

"How dare ye?" Lord bless me! I didn stand
To think, I can tell ye, but away I ran,
And never stopped for gate or stile,
Till I'd done the bettermost part of a mile.
But that same night I couldn sleep,
And back to the place, and I made a sweep
Overhead on the chance, and I caught the hair
That was hangin still on the trammon there—
Aw the tingly it felt in the dark, and the quick
It run up aroun' my finger lek!
You'd ha' thought it was steel—the coil it had,
And the spring—but am I goin mad?
Eh boys? aw laugh! laugh hearty! I say;
For that's despard[1] nonsense anyway!

But the very next mornin I'll engage
Down come George in a terrible rage;
And him and James in their Sunday clothes,
And says they, "You've 'sulted Christmas Rose."
"'Sulted her?" "Yes! 'sulted her!" they says;
"And it's up to the church you must go and confess
On your bended knees this minute!" they said,
"And apologize!" that's the word they had.
Aw they wouldn take rest but up I should;
So I claned myself the quickest I could,
And away with them; and as stiff as may be,
Talking together, but not to me.
I didn like it a bit, mind you!

[1] Desperate.

And I didn hardly know what to do.
" But what must I say ? " says I, " when I'm there ; "
" Aw it's all put down in the paper here,"
Says James, and whips it out of his pocket—
" Listen to this ! " he says, " you blockit ! "
And sure enough they had it as grand
As any lawyer in the land—
Aw the terrible big words that was in,
And the *wicked* and *imperint* I'd been ;
And *inasmuch*, and *seein how far*,
And *the court*, and *the prisoner at the bar*—
Aye ! and they stopped in the highroad twice
For to make me ply it to say it nice.
And *wasn I ouldher?*   I don't say nay ;
But they come over me that way—
Ouldher of coorse ; but it's no use o' talkin,
The art that was at them boys [1] was shockin—
Aw they'd work it, bless ye ! and, whether or no,
They said the word, and you had to go.

Well behould ye ! there she was
Out in the garden, and a chair on the grass,
The Pazon's chair, with its arms like a gig,
Took out of the study o' purpose, and big
Enough to hold half the parish with aise—
And—cock her up with a stool, if you plaze,
Under her feet ! and if she hadn [2]
A scarf or the lek, with yallar and red in,

---

[1] Those boys had.   [2] She must needs have.

Twisted through her hair to give her
A look like a crown on her head, did you ever?
Aw a reglar queen; and behould ye! a fan
And tippin it this way and that in her hand;
And frownin and frownin—and "Let him draw near!"
Says she, and I tried, but it didn appear
I had it at all—but middlin handy
Down on my knees like a jack-o-dandy,
Or a play-actor, or the lek, and them
And me betwixt us, and—*Miss* and *Mem!*
Humblin—bumblin—and "no offence!"—
And up's with her chin, and "Take him hence!"
She says, and she says—"I forgive his rudeness;"
And "He has his pardon"—his pardon! My goodness!
I'm laughin now, but I didn laugh then;
And the boys to lift me, and all hearty again,
And shakin hands, and "*Never mind!*"
But it was necessary, and terrible kind;
And—*Just be careful lek! That was it!*
And—*the same friends as ever!* and coaxin a bit.

But she got up, and she took a sweep
Of the grass with her frock, and I felt like a creep—
And the swing of her waist, and the ribbons flyin—
Aw a creep! a creep! there's no denyin—
And the pick and the peck, and the in[1] with a taste—
And "'Scuse me, marm!" and "I ast[2] your grace!"
And the way and the look—"He have his pardon!"

---

[1] Into the house she goes.   [2] Ask.

If ever there was a fool in that garden,
It was me, aw it was—but, right or wrong,
She held me, she did though, uncommon strong—
Her vice of coorse—aye that's the thing—
Sweet! aw the sweet! astonishin!
If she'd cussed ye, it 'd ha' been the same—
Aw hard as steel and soft as crame;
Something betwix a hawk and a linnet—
Aw the music of her soul was in it.
Music! soul! you've heard tramhurns,[1]
And clarnets, and their twisses and turns,
And curlin and purlin, and pippin and poppin,
And booin and cooin, and stippin and stoppin—
Well they were all just fools, d'ye hear?
To that darlin voice—Ah Betsy, dear!
Yes, yes, yes, yes! the difference!
I know, I know! and taken hence—
That's it—we must—and—Come, come, come!
Shouldher arms and march to the drum!
Life is life, and the best foot fust!
'Scuse me, lads! I was thinkin just—
Thinkin—thinkin—Aw certainly,
Clear as a bell; but it's sharp it could be,
Sharp as a knife, and stingin, stingin—
But bless ye! the angels isn allis singin—
But a-hailin the divils; and "Enter not!"
They're shoutin, and givin as good as they got,
Lookin over the wall; for they leaves their hymns,

---

[1] Trombones.

And fights like Turks—them cherubims—
I've read in a book—but aisy ! I say !
She was the one could hould me anyway—
And shake me too—could Christmas Rose—
And, bless me, the way she had with her clothes !
The slackin and tautin, and liffin [1] and dippin,
And nippety-nappety trappin and trippin,
And a hitch to starboard and a hitch to port,
And a driggledy-draggledy all through the dirt ;
How are they doin it, Billy—eh ?
I don't know but they manage that way
That three or four foot of nothing—bless ye !
Is more to you till Europe or Asia.

But avast then ! anyway in she goes—
And me all right, and—clothes ! is it clothes ?
Aw blow the lot !   Aw I did it grand !
Aw I gave it them nice, you'll understand—
And away, and shook them off, and tearin
Blue murder and all, and cussin and swearin
The skin off your face, and makin tracks
And down the road—but then I slacks,
And into the hedge and cries like blazes—
And up come people, and I knew their faces—
And souljerin [2] on—as proud as you please,
And pretendin to look for blackberries—
And down to the shore, and up's with a creel
And into the boat with a kick of my heel

---

[1] Lifting.   [2] Soldiering, sauntering.

And off, and before you could preach or pray
I was crossin the tide and out to Mahay,[1]
And agate o' the lobsters, and haulin in,
And destroyin them congers like anythin—
Aye! aye!   I could do that—chit nish![2]
There's no mistake but I knew how to fish—
And up with the grapplin, and home, and the tide
Dead again me, and springs beside,
And the back at me mostly broke out of the hinges,
And pullin—aw pullin—pullin tremenjous!
And landed and moored, and a skip and a hop
And a into bed, and a slep like a top.

Well there's an end of everything under the sun,
And I must tell ye the way it was done—
And was it my fault it's not for me—
Maybe it wasn nobody—
And if it wasn for what the Bible is sayin
About Him that hears us when we're prayin,
And never a sparrow drops, for all,[3]
But He's handy close to see it fall,
I'd think some black ould witch was stuck
At the wheel of the world, and spinnin our luck,
And runnin the threads through her skinny fingers
Till our time was up, and then, by jingers,
It's whinkum-whankum, thrummity-thrum,
And she cuts you short with a snick o' her thumb.
But of coorse it isn, all the same.

---

[1] A famous fishing-ground.   [2] Come now!   [3] However.

It's Him—and blessed be His name !
They were tervil fond them three of the boat,
And they'd ha had her whenever she could float ;
But the Pazon was doin their schoolin at home
Hisself, you see, so they couldn come
Just as they pleased, but they had their taskses—
And grammar, and ciph'rin, and questions they askses—
Wonderful ! aw I could tell ye a dale
About yandhar [1]—but mind ye ! when Pazon Gale
Was about in the parish, or when they were done
With the taskses—aw it's away they'd run
Like hounds for the shore ; and her—yes, her—
The first of the three, and in, and a spur [2]
Rigged like a shot, and an oar I kept
O' purpose for her, and off we swept,
Her with the rullock—aw bless your souls !
As proud—but ours was square in the thowls, [3]
And pins, [4] you know—and she'd pull, she'd pull !
Aw man-alive ! it was beautiful !

One everin they come, and it's off to the Calf
Behould ye ! and long-lines stowed there aft
Ready baited, and her that had never been there
And—carry on ! and never care !
And a mist comin creepin up the Sound,
And wind to follow, you'll be bound—

[1] Yonder, that.   [2] Rowlock.
[3] Part of the oar which rests upon the gunwale.
[4] Pegs to keep the oar in its place.

But—*stuff-and-nonsense!* and a whiskin her hat
At the breeze, and "We'll do this and that!"
And George with the gun lookin out for a rabbit
On the cliffs above; but James rather crabbit
On the middle thwart, and houldin the sheet
In his hand, and just a turn on the cleat;
And eyein the offin—aw, sink or swim!
A sailor every inch of him.
And "Is it back?" I says; "No! no!" says she,
"The sea! the sea! the open sea!"
And a lot of rhymes; and George says, "Blow it!
Give her it, Tom! put her gunwale to it!"
Her gunwale to it! aye! aye! my heartie!
Her gunwale to it, says Buonaparte—
But it was *gunwale-to-it*, and no mistake;
For the wind come stronger, and I didn spake,
And I knew well enough what ought we to do—
But—give in before her! not me!   Would you?
No! no! and her that keen to be sure—
Aw she'd have danced if she'd had the floor—
But she danced with her eyes—dear heart! the light
That come into them! and the stretched and the tight—
Till they looked to be snappin fire in your face;
For the storm was in *her*—aw that's the place
That *was* the storm! aye, aye, man! aye!
All out o' the sea, and out o' the sky,
Catching it with her mouth like suck,
Drawing the strength of its heart till she shuck [1]

---

[1] Shook.

And shivered again—and when the big cloud
Come up with the lightnin, she gripped a shroud,
And she sprang to meet it like a bird to its nest,
Or a child to hang on its mammy's breast—
Or was it her sweetheart the cloud was lek,
And her a-leapin on to his neck,
And sighin and sobbin and slakin her drouth
With the thunder-poison from his mouth?
Sobbin—aye! but not with fear!
Aw bless my heart! I cannot bear
Them women aboard in a storm—can you?
Instead of the divil's own hollabaloo
And faintin, for them to go and rejice—
It isn nice! it isn nice!
Nor right nor raison nor nothing—eh?
For them to be carryin on that way.
Women is women, and it's in the blood,
And they should be freckened[1] a bit, they should.

Well the dark it got, and the lightnin strong,
Like it would slick up the sea with its red-hot tongue,
And a little dead dirt of daylight left
In the west, and we began to drift
On the rocks, for the boat couldn look at her course;
So it's down with the lug, and out with the oars—
Me with the one again them two,
And her in the stern with nothin to do
But enjoyin herself; and the head at her[2] bare,

---

[1] Frightened.   [2] Her head.

And the lightnin lookin all mixed with her hair,
Like flowers of fire! yes, yes! and a child!
But the wild she looked! the wild! the wild!
And the glad and the mad—was her father and mother
Out in the clouds? chut![1] bother! bother!
There's strange things happens in storms though yet—
Well it makes me funny to think of it!

So we pulled uncommon hard till we got
To the Thushla—bless me! that's the spot—
That's where ye gets the strenth of the tide—
Aw despard though! but slack inside,
And shelter from the sea, that's more ;
So that's what we were making for.
" Three strokes! my hearts! three strokes!" I said,
" Three strokes, and we'll be round the head."
Three strokes was given—aw the pluck of the lot!
Three strokes with a will—and in we shot—
Smooth water enough—but James had fell
Right aback from his taff,[2] with his head in the well—
" Dead as a herrin, for sure!" thinks I,
And has him up immediately—
And feels the heart, and goin still—
But as slow as slow—aw terrible!
So I took him aft, and I put him restin
With his head on her lap, and it was just distressin
The way she sat, and not a notion
To hould him, or nuss him, nor never a motion

---

[1] Tut! [2] Thwart.

To breathe on his cheek, or hould his hand,
The way with women, you'll understand—
But her knees that sharp all drew to a pint
Most comfortless! and every jint
That stiff! aw as sure as I'm a sinner
It was the divil of the storm that was in her!
Aye, aye! and mind my words, d'ye hear?
I don't believe it was her that was there—
Or if it was, I'll tell ye it,
Her soul was gone out of her for a bit—
Out and off! and up in the air,
With the clouds and the thunder—Lord knows where!
"Get along!" says you, and "Stuff!" what *stuff!*
Aw it might happen, mind ye! easy enough—
Well—lave it alone! but I saw—I saw—
And I gave a cuss, but middlin low
That she wouldn hear; and I says, "Miss Rose!"
I says, says I, "Lord only knows
If there's life in Masther James, and maybe
You'll nuss him a bit," I says, "like a baby.
He haven't got no sense," says I,
"To know what are you doin—aw try now! try!"
I spoke middlin free; "and heise[1] him," I says,
"Heise him, Miss Rose, agin your bress!
And warm him, and sing some ould tune to his ear!
Aw do, Miss Rose! aw do! that's a dear!"
I was trimblin when I said that word;
And afore it was out of my mouth—good Lord!

[1] Lift.

There come a flash that all the bay
And the boat and us was just like day—
Clap !—but betwix the darks behould yer !
George's face lookin over my shouldher
White as the dead ! and eyein them two—
White as the dead ! hurroo ! hurroo !
And I turned like a shot, and I saw her all
Like a tree when it doesn't know which way to fall,
And up with the arms and down again
All of a heap, and the boy gathered in,
With his head in her lap—I couldn tell how—
Aw the freckened I was that time ! and now
When I remember—but it's likely not—
But still now ? was it the sperrit—what ?
Come back to her like a bird off the wing,
Or did she see George—eh ? that's the thing !

Well we had a good two mile or more
To row agin [1] we got to the shore—
And not a word from the one of us
Till the boat was up to her moorins just—
But then ?—*how was he?* I axed, *and his head?*
Was it comin to?   " Aw he's better," she said ;
" He knows where he is."   " Thank God !" says I,
And gets him ashore, and middlin dry.
On a bit of the floorins ; and me agate of him
And George, the two didn feel the weight of him—
And up to the house, and in with us straight,

---

[1] Against, before.

And mawther there, and gettin a light,
And grumblin (I heard her; but lettin on [1] not)
And fixin her hair, and strooghin her brat,
And whippin a chair amazin swivel,[2]
And very nate and very civil—
Aw she could be that—and "Mother!" I said,
"Masther James must be put to bed
'Torectly,"[3] I says; "And get a sup
Of something hot, and I'll sit up "—
And this and that, and where and when;
For I was afraid there'd be a fight even then.
But there wasn though—no! I declare—
But "Aw the poor thing!" and "Dearee dear!"
And pityin, and lookin at Christmas Rose—
And—bless me! the way them women knows
What's up, in a general way—when you're sick—
And also about young gels and the lek—
It's terrible in the world,[4] it is;
For if two craythurs hev took a kiss
Anywhere by day or night,
Every ould woman 'll know it straight.[5]

So we got him to bed, and George run home
For to tell the Pazon, and down he come,
And pale enough; and nothing to me[6]
But "I see!" he says, "I see—I see!"
And down to the parlour—and lost no time,

---

[1] Pretending.   [2] Quickly.   [3] Directly.   [4] Intensive phrase.
    [5] Immediately.   [6] He said nothing to me.

You may aisy suppose; but turned like lime,
He did though, when he saw the lad,
For the faver was on him, and talkin like mad,
And never knowin the father a mossel [1]—
And down on his knees like the ould Apostle
With the chap in the Bible that nothin could hinder
But he must needs go and fall right out at the winder.
But the sollum—aw the beautiful hearin!
Prayin a little—but none of your tearin
And shoutin up to the rafters, like yandhar
Premmitives,[2] that calls like a gandhar
Before his gesslins[3]—and what d'ye think
The Rose went and did? aw the bonny blink
Of her eye that time—they're terrible though—
Them women—whether you like it or no—
She come behind, and she put her hand
On the ould man's head—Aw dear! the grand
It was to see her, and how he turned
And looked in her face! aw it's me that yearned
In my very heart—and " Papa!" says she,
" Papa!" aye just like that it would be;
But sweeter, bless ye! and like to cryin—
Aw she was a darlin—there's no denyin.

And didn the mother come? yes! she come—
And middlin snappish, and middlin glum
She looked; and her bonnet off, aw it was!
And titivated in our lookin-glass—

---

[1] Morsel, bit.   [2] Primitive Methodists.   [3] Goslings.

Well now! I was freckened, I don't know what at—
But our little parlour, and a lady like that!
And, it's no use o' talkin, she made me jump
With her hair like the handle of a pump
Stickin out, and no cap nor nothin, and as gray
As the divil—a sort of a wisp of hay—
And her never knowin I saw her there
Combin away in the big arm-chair.
But not till the mornin—not her, if you plaze!
What's your hurry? no lovin ways
With her—not a bit! and sittin as stiff
And rubbin her nose with her handkerchief;
And as grim; but mind ye! if you'd eyed her,
You'd seen that woman had something inside her—
Aye! but never mind! you'll hear!
"One at a time!" says Tommy Tear.

Well the days went on though, and James could sit
In the bed, but—a cripple! aw never fit
To earn his livin, nor nothin, but bent
All crooky—and crutches, and be content,
And hobble about! Aw dear I grutched [1]
A lad like him to look like wutched,
Or took at [2] the fairies or that, and him
A picthur to look at, every limb.
If he wasn that strong and that big like the brother,
I don't know where you'd ha' seen such another.

---

[1] Grudged.　　　　[2] Stricken by.

Aw, I tell you what! I loved the lad—
And to think of it now—it drives me mad.

Well just before he left our place,
And the doctors had settled about the case,
And cut, you know, I was sittin beside
The bed, us alone, and I cried and I cried;
And I said—"It was me! it was me! it was me!
Masther James!" I says; "of all the three
(Miss Rose don't count) it was me that done it—
It was me—yes it was—whosomever begun it—
I wish I was dead," I said, "I do!
Dead and in the grave with you—
Or dead by myself, no matter what!"
"Now Tom," says he, "what stuff have you got?
The three of us done it," he said, "I'll swear!"
And he out with a cuss—"what a fool you are!"
Aw the joy of my life! aw as free as free!
Just a little cuss, you see,
To keep me in heart! aw I thought I'd buss [1]—
"Thank God!" says I; "he can cuss! he can cuss!"
And then he swore me that I wouldn tell
What had he got [2]—but I knew as well—
I can't say how—but chut! I knew it,
I did, afore ever he put the words to it.
That night aboard the boat when he woked
From the fit, and felt the way he was yoked
In Christmas' arms, and her breath on his face—

[1] Burst.   [2] On his mind.

He didn know the time nor the place,
But only a sort of a dream, I expec';
And he kissed her knees, and he kissed her neck;
And all the words the poor fellow hed
Was—"Christmas! I love you—I love you!" he said.
Aw the poor lad! I loved him too—
Very good and gennal[1] and true.
He said that—he did—and "Oh" he said,
"She lifted my head! she lifted my head!
And whispered something in my ear;
But I was that weak I couldn hear,
Nor spake again; but her breath was warm
And sweet on my face; and the strain of her arm,
And all—and she loves me! she does!" says he—
"And look at me! and look at me!"
He says—and he looks at himself like this—
"And will she ever—?" "Yes! yes! yes!"
I says: "Aw Masther James, you knows
It's the rael thing is Christmas Rose:
And she'll be a good sisther to you no doubt:
And fixin ye nice, and help ye about,
She's handy enough is Miss Rose, and she'll try—"
Aw then the red come into his eye,
And he swore the big oath—"Aw," I says, " Masther James,
Cussin is cussin, and names is names—
If it's doin you good—aw go ahead!
But about Miss Christmas Rose," I said,
"Aw Masther James! be careful though!

---

[1] Kindly.

Be careful for all ! for how do you know
She loves ye ?" I said : " Because you lay
In her arms, and she nursed ye into the bay ?
Wouldn any gel have done the lek ?
And you that was dyin ! for goodness' sake,"
Says I, "be quiet, and let me wash ye !
The poor gel only didn want to cross ye.
And besides I know—" but I jammed my helm
Hard a lee there ; for I was goin to tell him
About George and the look in the boat—so he says
(And all the blood come into his face),
" What do you know ?" and he swore the big oath,
Uncommon big that I'd be loath
To say it again—aw 'deed I would—
But the boy was mad, and I done what I could—
And *it wasn nothin !* and bless me ! the names !
And "Aw Masther James ! Masther James! Masther James!"
And " You'll be kilt altogether," I said, "you will ;
You'll be kilt now, James, if you don't lie still."
Aw a hard fight for it betwixt us—hard !
And *I was everything ;* but I didn regard :
For the worse of it was the waker he got
The angrier he was, and the cross and the hot ;
And the flesh was wake, but the sperrit was strong,
And allis thinkin you were doing wrong.
And fits, aye fits ! and him I'd known
Such a hearty lad, and the strong and the grown !
Was it me ? was it me ? well the Lord He gave it,
And the Lord took away—so there let's lave it !

But he'd be havin me with him whenever he could—
Not long at a time; for every flood
I was out at the lines: but the very fust
I was up to see him, it's go we must
The two of us alone to the church,
And sittin there inside of the porch,
And the one thing, as you may suppose,
Nothing but Rose! and Rose! and Rose!
And the very first time they were alone together,
He tould me, he looked and looked to see whether
Or not—"and nothing," he said, "in her face
But pity just, and gentleness."
And "What'll I do?" he says; aw dear!
What would he do? and his eye that clear
And strong! and all that proud and keen,
And full of the life that should have been.
"Aw! drop it!" I says; "aw Masther James,
Drop it! drop it! it's only drames.
Isn she your sister?" I said, "since the day
God gave her to you from the sea?
Keep her what she is!" says I;
"And she'll be a blessin to you by-and-by."
"A blessin!" says he, "a blessin! a blessin!
Tom Baynes," he says, "you're a foolish pessin.
I'll spake," he says, "I will—and I'll know——"
Aisy, Billy!—you'd let them grow
A bit first, Billy? *Strange!* eh what?
Young craythurs carryin on like that—
Let them ate a bit more porridge fust,

II

Says you : aw Billy ! that's the wust
Of you, and it allis was, I'll swear—
You're coorse, man, coorse ! aw yes ye are !
Aw it's coorse it is.   And *Childher*, says you?
Young fools, you says ; go on now do !
Fools, you said ; and *they should be stript*,
I think you said, *at*[1] *their mammies, and whipt*—
And *you'd warm them*—would ye ? well listen to me !
I'm not a young fool, nor meanin to be ;
And I say them *young fools*—wasn them your words ?
Well—wait a minute, and I'll give you the Lord's—
Lovin much is much forgiven ;
And—*of such fools is the kingdom of heaven.*

Well he had it out the very next night,
Just at the dark, but fire light.
For the Pazon and the wife was away
At another Pazon's, and George in the bay
Agate of the lines—and rainin, for all,[2]
And blowin hard, but we were bound to haul—
And him on the sofa, and her a-clattrin
With the cups and saucers, and chittrin-chattrin—
Aw he tould me all ! and bless me ! he had it
Just like a picthur—you'd hardly credit,
Now would ye ? and him that mad, you know,
And distracted lek—aw he had it though,
He had it—and this and that and how
And where and when, and all the row,

---

¹ By.   ² However.

And the backard and forrard and here and there,
And the light on the wall and the light on the chair,
And the light on her all dancin lek,
And the tippin her head and the tippin her neck,
And the tippin behind and the tippin before :
And *Sarpints*, he said, *wasn nothin to her*,
Nor Royal Bengal Tigers—the way
She turned, a-shakin the fire like spray
Out of all her clothes, he beat me clane,
I didn know half of it what did he mane.
The quality, ye see, is reared to that—
Noticin lek, and which and what
Like some of them painter chaps that's mixin
A colour for everything, and fixin
The way it is ; and him and her,
And the very place, and the near and the far—
Bless ye ! the like of us wouldn be mindin
Was there light at all—let alone was it shinin
On her hips or her hocks, and *shaddhers fleein*—
Lord bless my soul ! what things to be seein
When your life is on the cast ! ho ! ho !
The quality's very curious though.

Well he was intarmint[1] for to spake,
And out with it all, to mar or to make.
So he just said her name—as low as low—
But the way he said it ! the way, you know !
Aw she come to her feet, and she looked at him straight—

---

[1] Determined.

The hard ! he said, the hard and the white,
And the keen, took sudden, ye see, that way,
And watchin what was he goin to say,
And houldin herself like a hound on the spring,
And a-tight'nin her heart for anything.
And *proud*, he said, she looked, and despisin
The lcks of him—now isn it supprisin ?
To think of that now ! *proud*—let it go !
But *despisin !* her ! no ! no ! no ! no !
And she looked, and he looked, and then it came
Out of his soul like the livin flame—
Love and hate and joy and sadness
All mixed together in a muck of madness.
And angels and divils, he said, was scourin
The soul of him, and the cusses come pourin
Out of him ; and talkin love
All the time, and " dear !" and " dove !"
And cusses again—" till at last," says he,
" I said—never mind ! she listened to me
Till then," he says, and never a breath
But the studdy look and the sthrong as death—
But then she shivered all over, and then
" James !" she said, and she said it again —
Three times she said it—" and the eyes lookin down,
And the voice—it might have been a sound
From Heaven," he said, " far off," he said,
" Like one that 'd be speakin from the dead,"
He said—" far off "—and " James !" says she,
" I am your sister," she says ; " there's three,"

She says, "of us, and we love one another;"
She says, "O brother! brother! brother!"
She says, and—"yes! I will! oh yes!"
And she come, for he made his mouth for a kiss,
Beggin lek, and she gave him one,
And he fell as dead as any stone.
That's all he remembered—but the sarvint was tellin
How she came to her, and her eyes all swellin
With the big of tears, and "quick! quick! quick!"
She says, "Masther James is very sick,"
She says to the sarvint—that's all she said,
And never a bonnet upon her head
Nor nothing—and "Take good care of him, Jane!"
And out in the rain—aye, out in the rain.
And "It's over," he said; "I know! I know!
It's time to go! it's time to go!"
"But," I said, "Masther James, she didn say
But what *might* be, for all—" "*a year and a day*"!
Says he, "Oh yes! *and she'll think of it yet!*
Tom Baynes," he says, "you're a idiit!"

Well! George and me was comin in
That night, and a terrible time we'd bin,
With the wind off-shore, and blowin strong,
But him the hearty it didn seem long:
And shovin her nigh to the rocks, to cheat
The squalls; and says he all at once—"Did you see't?"
He says; "See what?" says I, "A ghost?"
"Look out!" says he, "and let's come close!"

So it's close we pulled—and behould her lyin
On the breast of the rock—aw we thought she was dyin—
And her hands all clenched in the tangles[1] there,
And the water sip-soppin up to her hair—
And *What had happened?* and *Bless my heart!*
And wondherin; and "Come! let's start!"
Says he; and in with her into the boat,
And covered her up with an oilskin coat
That was at us there.   But mind ye! before
I could get him to steady down to his oar,
He stooped, and he kissed her; "She's spakin!" he said;
And list'nin, and houldin down his head
To hear—and sure enough she was—
"Take me home!" she said—aw an albathross
Or a gannet wasn nothing to him then,
The way he pulled, like twenty men—
One, two, three, with a sweep and a swing!
And a four for the queen and a five for the king!
And into a gully that was lyin back
Under the church itself; and a track
Windin up through the goss;[2] for I knew,
If we went to the shore, what a hullabaloo
There'd be, and the talk—aw dear! if they'd seen us.
So up—and her goin a-carryin between us;
Very weak and slack; but I saw
Masther George had to stow the jaw,
Let alone the kissin! aye!
He had though, I tell ye! "It's you bein by,"

[1] Long seaweeds.   [2] Gorse.

He whispers to me : but she straightened her head
That stiff on my shouldher—" Look out ! " I said :
And " Look out ! " it was ; for, right or wrong,
He had to look out, he had, before long.

The Pazon wasn at home when we got
To the house ; so I stood out on the plat ;
And George took her in—aw the gel could walk
That time ; and then he come out for a talk
And a smook sittin under the sycamore
That stretched from the garden to the door ;
A fine tree too, for the country, and tall ;
For they're runnin rather stunty and small
Over there is trees—and the wind would come
And shiver it all, and make it hum
Like a brave big top, and tappin the pane
Of the Pazon's study till he'd laugh again—
Aw he liked it well ! but—I don't know,
Trees is very curious though !
If there's ghoses[1] takin[2] anywhere
It's in trees it is.! Aw they've got their share
Has churchyards and that—but mind you me !
I've seen funny things in a sycamore tree !
Aye, aye ! my lads ! Aw lower down—
All right of coorse ! all right, I'll be bound—
You can grip them there, and feel the stuff
That's in them—aw all right enough !
But—up in the branches ! I say !—they're about ;
But never mind ! look out ! look out !

----

[1] Ghosts.   [2] Haunting.

Well we talked and talked, and it was him begun ;
And he gave a big sigh, and he says " It's done ! "
He says " It's done ! " and he hung his head ;
And " I couldn help it, Tom Baynes ! " he said.
And then he tould me the hard to bear
It was, and the trouble, and the care,
And tryin and tryin to do his part,
And stampin the heavy upon his heart,
Puttin out the fire that kep burnin still—
Aw, he said, *it was terrible.*
Where does it come from ? where ? where ? where ?
Is it in the ground ? is it in the air ?
Is it sucked with your milk ? is it mixed with your flesh ?
Does it float about everywhere like a mesh
So fine you can't see't ? is it blast ? is it blight ?
Is it fire ? is it fever ? is it wrong ? is it right ?
Where is it ? what is it ?   The Lord above—
He only knows the strenth of love :
He only knows, and He only can,
The root of love that's in a man.
Aw isn it true ? and Him as quite,[1]
Seein all in the clear sweet light
That's runnin through Him all day long,
And all the night—and the angels' song—
" Holy ! holy ! holy ! " they're sayin—
And us poor craythurs prayin ! prayin !
And Him so quite [1]—and " Gentle Jesus ! "—
And waitin—waitin—but ah ! He sees us !

[1] Quiet.

What was I sayin? aw yes! *the fire ;*
And what could he do? and he *wasn wire,*
Nor nails, he said : and how he'd kep'
Out of her road ; and the hold and the grip
There was at him reglar :[1] and allis out
After the lines, and knockin about
With the gun, and tryin to clear his head
And studdy hisself. "And James!" he said,
"James!" he said—"God help us then!
Poor James!" he said—(Amen! Amen!)
"I thought," he said, "I thought I was stronger—
But oh, Tom Baynes! I can't stand it no longer!
Yes! Yes!" he says, "he loves her true ;
And what am I to do? what am I to do?
And I've tried and tried to give him fair-play—
Haven't I, Tom? now haven't I—eh?"
"You have," I says; "but listen! listen!
Masther George!" I says : "Now it is or it isn;
But tell me for all what makes you suppose
That either o' ye is for the Christmas Rose?"
" *What makes me ?* " he says, and gives a cuss ;
"And who is for her, if it isn us?
James or me?" he says. "Hullo!
I see!" he says, "I see! ho! ho!"
He says, and he jams his face chock up
Again mine, and he says—"Have you got a sup?
By Jove!" he says, "it's you ye manes!
You're for the Christmas Rose, Tom Baynes!

[1] He always maintained.

You then, you!" and he turned and he laughed—
Aw the bitter! and fore and aft—
At least up and down—and about with a wheel,
And churnin the gravel under his heel.
"You!" he said—"Well!" he said, "the cheek
Of some people! and what for don't ye speak?"
He says, quite quick, and stands as straight
As a boult before me: and "Will ye fight?"
He says, "or what will ye do? come! out!
Out with it! will ye? you're freckened, I doubt."
"Masther George!" I said—quite studdy, you know—
"Masther George! it isn a minute ago
You were all in the dumps; and now it's fightin
You're after; and maybe you might or you mightn
Have the best of it: but there's one thing I thought
You couldn mistake, let alone the *ought*—
One thing, Masther George, and knowin what you knows—
Me! me, did ye say? for the Christmas Rose!
Is there a thought?—You'll strike me, will ye?
(He was goin), or a wish I wouldn tell ye?
Haven I tould you every word,
To the very keel of my heart—good Lord!
What can I do more? that's it! that's it!
Pitch into me! I don't care a spit!
Knock my head off! but never a blow
From me to you! aw no! no! no!
Not this time, Masther George, if you plaze!
Not exactly! George!" I says.
And I laughed—and be hanged! the two of us laughed—

Aw people in love is ticklesome craft :
For it's laughin and cryin and foolin and fightin,
And cussin and kissin and lovin and bitin
All in the one—crabs and crame ![1]
And the very birds is just the same—
Let alone monkeys and dirts like that—
Aw they've got their troubles, I'll tell ye what !

Well the laugh cleared the fog away nicely though
That was hidin us from one another, you know—
You know what I mean—all hot and huffed—
And we talked chance talk, and puffed and puffed
At the pipe.   And I remember the jump
He gave when he heard the jerk of the pump,
Thinkin the Pazon had come in
Unknownst at the back !   And bless me ! the din
There was at[2] that pump; and apt to run dry,
And bad for the soak,[3] and never say die !
But work away !—aw a reglar brute !
And a rusty boult that roored[4] like the hoot
Of a owl or a dunkey ; and suckin and sobbin,
And retchin and cretchin, and slibbin and slobbin—
It's lek you know how a hoss is goin
When his wind is broke, and ah-in and oh-in
That bad—they're ugly to hear in the night
Is them pumps, like a thing lek that wouldn be right
Someway !   And the ould people used to be sayin—

---

[1] Cream.   [2] With.
[3] Water poured into the pump when the *sucker* is dry.
[4] Roared.

But bless my heart! it was only Jane
The sarvint, gettin water of coorse,
But mind ye! she done it with a foorce![1]
The arm she had—But it's idikkilis![2]
I'll never come to an end like this—
Pumps! my goodness! Well we laughed, and a bat ·
Come wheelin about, and he gave me a pat
In the face with his nasty ould webby wings—
Aw the terrible I hate them things—
Away went the pipe, broke out o' my cheek—
The strenth of the divil! and the boostly[3] squeak!
Aw dart[4] the father of him! I say—
I never liked them critters anyway.

Aw then the laugh! But he come at me again,
And "Tom," he says, "I want you to 'splain.
You're in some sort of love with her, that's clear."
"Now I'll tell ye what!" says I, "look here!"
Aw I got hot—"I'm not goin to stand
This talk," I says, "from the lord of the land.
I've tould ye and tould ye, and what's the good?
The more the tellin the less understood.
But mind my words, Masther George!" I says, "anyway—
The Christmas Rose isn for the one o' ye!
No she isn—not a bit," I said:
She's far far far above your head.
"Poor James!" I says; "poor James! well! well!
Of coorse—but you to come over the gel

---

[1] Force.   [2] Ridiculous.   [3] Beastly.   [4] Drat.

With your dainty curls, and your bit of a stachya,[1]
And the strong and the handsome; and '*Have me! bless ye!*'
Thinks you; 'most sartin, and only too glad!'
And *whistle and I'll come to ye, my lad!*
Them's your thoughts; but where's your fax?
Where? aye where indeed! I may ax
The where, bedad, and the when and the why."
Aw it's then he made a leap and a cry
Like a tiger, and at me; but I gave a duck,
And the fist went over my shouldher, and struck
The tree like a hatchet—aw dear! the smash!
And his knuckles all jammy, and the blood splish-splash!
"You're not the man for me to be 'fraid of:
You're not made of the stuff that Christmas is made of!
No, George Gale," I said, "you're not."
Aw the leap again, and flew at my throat.
But then I gripped him, and—yeo! heave ho!
And a lift and a twist—and over you go:
And let him down the softest I could
And it's only raison you allis should,
And give a man a chance—yes! yes,
And pick him up agin isn amiss.
Well he was middlin giddy, ye see;
So I studdied him against the tree—
And he says—"What's this for?" "For!" I said—
"For! ye come at me that vicious, ye did!"
And he hung the head middlin sulky though.
"Come, Masther George!" I said; "take a blow

---

[1] Moustache.

Of the pipe," and I took and charged it for him,
And got it to draw; and—jann myghin orrym ![1]
If he didn smoke it sweet enough !
Hard to light though—ye know the stuff.

    Well then I talked very sirrious,[2]
Uncommon though ; and I gave a cuss
And I said—" It's hard for the leks o' me
To tell you how I love Betsy Lee,
And how I love the Christmas Rose :
But I love the two of them, God knows !
The two of them—but the why and the whether— "
" How happy could I be with ether !"[3]
Says he, half laughin—some dirty ould song
He had, you know—" Now get along !
Masther George !" I says; " and listen, man !
I've got it now—the very plan !
Look here ! you're lovin a nice young gel,
And she's lovin you—very well ! very well !
That's right ! that's good ! that's—aw that's sweet !
And to meet and to part, and to part and to meet
Is all your thoughts—*and when will it be?*
Aw when ? aw when ? says you, says she.
And it comes at last, and the bells is ringin,
And the Pazon waiting, and the ould shoes a-flingin—
And home in the ev'rin, and settlin down—
And as happy as happy, I'll be bound.
That's love ; and thank my God it's in ![4]
For without it we wouldn be worth a pin.

    [1] Mercy on us !   [2] Seriously.   [3] Either.   [4] It exists.

But, George," I said, "isn there no love
That's greater than that, that's risin above
The lek o' that—why can't there be
No love without wivin and all that spree?
Couldn ye love, and never make to her
No love nor nothing, nor never spake to her?
Couldn ye look to her like a star
Up in the heavens quite reggilar,
Shinin down on all the same,
And maybe not even knowin your name?
Couldn ye love her up that high?
And kiss her with your soul through all the sky?
A sweetheart! aw Betsy ma veg![1] ma veen![2]
Aye, aye! but a queen! a queen! a queen!
That's another thing, and I don't care who knows,
My queen, my queen is the Christmas Rose!"
"Your queen indeed!" he says; "hear! hear!
Your queen! aw dear! aw dear! aw dear!
You're gettin quite rermantick," he said;
"Who put that nonsense into your head?
Why raelly," he says, "you're almost poetical!"
"Avast!" says I; "I'll have no reddikil.[3]
She's my queen, I beg to state!"
My queen! now wasn that first-rate?
Queen—d'ye see? aw the fancies come quick
In my head them times, aye as thick—as thick
As the hairs outside; but now hurroo!
The hairs is gone and the fancies too.

[1] My little (one).   [2] My darling.   [3] Ridicule.

Aw he laughed and he chaffed and he carried on
But wasn I right? eh Billy? eh John?
It's like lovin God : for it's seemin to me,
When you're lovin the loveliest things you see,
It's lovin God that made the things—
That made them—eh? and the birds they sings,
They does, and it's God that gives the notes,
Stretchin the bags of their little throats :
And the sun is bright, and the sky is blue;
And a man is strong, and a horse is too,
And God's in all—But I'll tell ye the when
You can see His face, if you ever can—
It's when He lights sweet holy fire
In the eye of a woman ; and lifts her higher
Than all your thoughts, a woman true
But not for you man, not for you.
Who for?   No matter ! if you've got any sense,
Of coorse you'll know the difference :
You'll know when you're wanted and when you aint
And never make no sort of complaint,
But touch your hat—" My sarvice, Madam ! "
And her not knowin you from Adam.
Bless me ! d'ye think she's nothing to me
Because mayhap she doesn know me ?
Har ! har !   I picks her out, and says I,
" You're my queen ! keep up in the sky ! "
I says; " keep up ! shine on, my queen !
Who the divil am I? it's all serene !
It's all serene ! " says I, with a bow—

Where's your huggin and ruxin now?
You've seen them picthers the Romans has got—
Merdonners they calls them—women, what?
Women, aye! with the blood in their veins,
And life and love, and the way they strains
Their eyes to a height that's far above them?
Who can look on them, and not love them?
Avast all Popery, says I,
And idols and every sort of guy!
And Irish divils anyway—
Protestant boys 'll carry the day!
But whoever made the likes o' them—
Their feet was in Jerusalem;
Whoever thought that a woman could look
Like that—he knew the Holy Book;
He knew the mind of God; he knew
What a woman could be, and he drew and he drew
Till he got the touch: and I'm a fool
That was almost walloped out o' the school,
I was that stupid, but I'll tell ye! I've got
A soul in my inside, whether or not,
And I know the way the chap was feelin
When he made them picthers—he must ha' been kneelin
All the time, I think, and prayin
To God for to help him; and it's likely sayin
He was paintin the Queen—they calls her the Queen
Of Heaven, but of coorse she couldn ha' been—
But that's the sort—a woman lifted
To heaven, with a breast like snow that's sifted,

I

And a eye that's fixed on God hisself—
Now where's your wivin and thrivin and pelf?
And sweethearts, and widdies well stocked with the rhino?
Ah! that's the thing likest God that I know.

Well up come the Pazon at last—no doubt
This time, and helpin the Misthress out,
Very lovin; and a-givin a scrape
Of her skinny ould leg agin the step—
And "Oh Misther Gale!" and "How awkard ye are!"
And him a fussin and—"Well I declare!"
And "I beg your pardin!" Bless me! the perlite!
And Jinny dodgin about with a light;
And me with ould Smiler's nose in my hand,
The horse that was at them,[1] you'll understand,
And laughin like fun; and George goin nudgin
With his elber the way it was time to be trudgin—
So I takes the hint, and away like a shot,
And down the gully and into the boat,
And pullin her round to the moorins all right,
And home, and mother sittin up straight
In her chair, and a-sulkin, and suckin hard
At her ould black pipe, and never a word
But—"Here ye are! ye Lhiggey-my-traiee![2]
Go off to bed!" "I'm goin," says I.

Well poor James died—he did though—yes
That was the first and the last kiss—
He'd never see her again—no! no!

---

[1] They had.   [2] Unpunctual.

Till the day he died—"Let me go! let me go!"
He'd say. It'd be some time about harvest—
I was shearin that year for ould Juan Jarvis—
But I was up at the buryin; and, what's more,
That's the first white shirt that ever I wore.
Save us! the row the ould mawther made
About yandhar shirt, and the terr'ble 'fraid
It wouldn be ready—aw quite delighted!
And *me invited! me invited!*
She wouldn ha' cared if it wasn for that—
And a black clout pinnin round my hat—
And the ould man's Sunday clothes took out
Of the chiss—and *mind what was I about!*
And none of my cryin and booin! she said;
I had other things to think of, I had—
"Buck up," says she, "and look like a man!"
And how to walk and how to stand—
Aw dear! I was tired—"And don't let me see
A speck on that coat, ye fenodyree![1]
When ye come back"—she says; "but in case
You must cry, hold the handkecher to your face!
That's dacent enough—but drabbin still
On your clothes—it isn respectable"—
She said—"let alone the cloth goin a-spilin."[2]
God bless my soul! the woman was rilin.

So I felt like a fool at the buryin,

---

[1] Properly the "lubber fiend" of Milton; here *awkward fellow.*
[2] Getting spoiled.

For I couldn be sorry nor anythin
In them boostly[1] clothes, but takin care
And mindin my eye like a prig[2] at a fair.
She'd got a thing warped around my neck
Would ha' choked ould Harry himself I expec'.
Well, well ! they're terr'ble—But even them clothes
Couldn hinder me lookin for the Christmas Rose.
And I saw her, I saw her sittin all alone
In a window—just like a block of stone—
Sittin, and lookin straight at the moul'[3]
That was heaped round the grave—upon my soul !
The way she sat—aw a queen on her throne !
But a block of stone—a block of stone !
" Her heart was stone," says you—Well ! well !
I suppose then, Billy, you knew the gel ?
You didn ! no ! I knew you didn !
Well then, ould gandhar ! stick to your midden !
Stick to what you're used of, Billy !
Christmas Rose, or Christmas Lily—
They're not much in *your* line, Illiam,[4] eh ?
Hard-hearted—well now I've heard them say
She *was* hard-hearted : but if they'd said
Strong-hearted not *hard*, why then they'd had
Some raison—Look here now ! is it the same—
Hard and *strong?* and a craythur that came
Like foam from the sea—But it isn *strong*
Nor it isn *hard:* you're wrong ! you're wrong !
It's far off it is, and different,

---

[1] Beastly.   [2] Pick-pocket.   [3] Mould.   [4] William.

A kind of a surt of a splenthar [1] sent
From another world—like moonstones just—
They haven't got the same subjecs [2] as us.
There's oncs comes into the world like that,
Even among their own people—what?
Haven't ye seen them? lonely things—
They haven't got crowns and they haven't got
    wings—
They're not angcls azackly [3] nor divils ether, [4]
And us and them will grow up together:
But their roots isn twisted someway with ours;
And the flowers that's at them [5] is other flowers;
And they're waitin, I'm thinkin, to be transplanted
To the place where the lek o' them is wanted:
And our love isn their love, and they cannot take it;
Nor our thirst their thirst, so we cannot slake it:
There's no food in us for them to feed on,
There's nothing in us that they got need on, [6]—
So there they are, with kith and kin,
Sittin in the middle, and wondherin.
And *love* and *heart*—why how should it be?
There's no heart made in them yet, d'ye see?
Just wild-fire flashin here and there,
Or if it's at them anywhere,
It's like a bud that sucks the air
Through its baby lips, but open? no!
Till the westlin winds begin to blow,

---

[1] Splinter.   [2] Substance.   [3] Exactly.
[4] Either.   [5] Which they have.   [6] Have need of.

And drew at[1] the sun with a strong sweet strain
It opens and never shuts again.

But, say what you like, and say what you will,
The Christmas Rose was a puzzle still.
It wasn no baby buds in her,
But a big woman's heart, that wouldn stir
To other hearts, but took its motion
From the winds and the clouds and the waves of the ocean.
It was bred in the storm ;
It was fed in the storm—
She'd run to meet it, she'd see it comin,
She'd smell it, I believe ; she'd hear it thrummin
A hunderd miles off—out she'd be !
But secretly ! aw secretly !
Crouchin and crouchin behind a wall—
I've seen her, but she didn know at all—
And lookin behind—Ah hah ! my Queen !
Was she seen? she was thinkin, *was she seen? was she seen?*
And flittin like a bird, or a gel
That's stealin away to the lad she loves well—
Ould eyes, she thinks, *aren't allis dim—*
" Hush ! hush ! that's him ! that's him ! that's him ! "
And then to the rocks, and a-loosin her hair
To the wind, aye, aye, and her neck all bare ;
And her mouth all open, and a-gaspin to't,
And the shivers of joy running down her throat—
What had she ? what was at her,[2] my men ?

---

[1] Drawn by.   [2] The matter with her.

Was it her heart that was makin then?
But think of her father! think of her mother!
That's it! so one thing with another,
And love for love, and tit for tat,
What would ye do with a gel like that?

There was another thing I seen that day—
A Pazon come from over the bay
For our Pazon lek, *to do the duty*—
That's their talk—well he was a beauty!
Well the purtiest little bit of a man
That ever I saw—and the little hand
And the little foot, and the little squeak
Of his little vice; and the little cheek
So rosy and round; and the legs—my gough!
And the little hem! and the little cough!
Well he was a nice little divil though,
He was now; and his mouth like a little red O—
My senses! that little chap beat all—
A pippity-poppity—talk of a doll!
Why I'd just have liked to took and stowed him
In my trousis pocket, and had him and showed him
To the childher—only a penny a peep—
Well he was the natest little sweep!
You might have put the little dandy
In your mouth, and sucked him for sugar-candy.
And he up's to the Pazon, and bless us! the sollum!
And the head goin like what-d'ye-call-em!
And "A great affliction"—and—tiggle—taggle—

And *the Lord was great*—and—wiggle—waggle ;
And the Pazon never lookin at him,
But out to the round of the blue sea-rim
(It was clear that day) ; but what he saw—
Never mind ! the little chap had the jaw.
Well, you see, I couldn cry, triced [1] up
In the ould woman's rig, so I didn stop,
But out on the gaery [2]—and what did I do
But off with the coat and the waistcoat too—
Aw laugh ! I did ; and I hung the pair
On a lump of [3] a thorn that was growin there ;
And then I set to for a hearty bout,
And I had it out, I had it out.
But I was that disthressed and done, I tell ye,
That harvest, I couldn go to the mheillea [4]—
Aw it's a fac ! and Betsy there !
Aw poor James ! aw Betsy dear !

Now, you see, after the buryin,
George couldn help it but he must begin
To talk very comfortin lek and nice
To Christmas Rose, and once or twice
He put his arm round her, and called her name,
Just comfortin lek, and wantin the same—
Aw wantin it bad, for he loved his brother—
And there they'd be, and the father and mother,
Terrible quiet, just sighin and lookin—

[1] Fastened.	[2] Piece of waste land.
[3] Good-sized.	[4] Harvest-home.

The Pazon, I mane, and sometimes he'd be smookin,
But the pipe 'd allis be goin out,
And him never knowin, and used to be stout,
And gettin thin, they were tellin me;
And the wife with the Bible on her knee,
Reading away, but very quick
And sharp with the temper, and givin a click
With her needles, and lookin up though still—
George tould me it was dreadful uncomfible—
Terrible quiet—and the everins[1] long,
And—what to do? and, right or wrong,
He couldn help it, but layin his head
On Christmas' shouldher, and "dodgin," he said,
Aye! "dodgin," he said, poor fellow! for fear
The ould people would see; aw dear! aw dear!
The way the Christmas 'd shake, and the shiftin
Onaisy[2] lek, and the "Don't!" and liftin
The big black eyes, and axin lek
He wouldn do that; and curling the neck—
And dhrivin him mad; and *why?* and *how?*
And "Mightn she now? aw mightn she now?"
And everything that miser'ble—
And all the house like a broken mill—
And wasn it her duty?—aye!
Her duty, he said, *at least to try*
Could she love him, and not be that contrary?
Aw a fine brave lad, but simple very!
"And have ye spoke plain to her?" I said;

---

¹ Evenings.   ² Uneasy.

"Yes! aw yes!" and 'deed he hed—
Plain enough—for the day before
He met her walkin upon the shore,
And he axed her *what was it*, and *what did she mane?*
That was middlin plain, eh? middlin plain!
Well she was a darlin, for when them two
Was alone together—aw it's true! it's true!—
She met him as lovin, and she spoke
The way she ought—aw it's fit to choke
I am [1] when I'm tellin ye—yes—straight
And plain to me as the gospel light—
To *me*—God knows how is it to me,
For George couldn twig it—ma chree [2]—ma chree!
The strange—and him that eddicated!
Aw a power of schoolin! And he should ha' waited—
But still—what good! aw the true and the keen!
My queen! my queen! my queen! my queen!
I know it! I know it! but him—well! well!—
She said—"My darlin" (didn he tell
Every word to me?)—"my darlin," she said,—
"My darlin brother!" (aw *the white and the red*—
He was tellin me!)—"my darlin brother!"
(Aw he clasped her then!) "no other! no other,"
She said, "can ever be to me
What you are," she said (d'ye see? d'ye see?
Brother—eh?) "But oh!" she said,
And she cried very bad, and she stooped her head
Agin [3] his breast, and he kissed her and kissed her—

---

[1] I'm nearly choking.   [2] My heart!   [3] Against.

(Aye, aye! I know!) and "Darlin sister!"
And that—but then—"George! George!" she says;
And the tears! the tears! and she lifts her face;
"George! George! no more! no more than this"—
And she gives him a long long lovin kiss;
And with that kiss—"George! George! here! here!
I give you all—oh dearest dear!
Oh brother mine—oh look and see!
It cannot be! it cannot be!
This—this! Forgive me, George, forgive!
I don't know how I come to live—
I should have died that time!" Ah Rose!
And the strange! the strange! and the green grass grows—
"I'm so different—(she said it! she said it!)
And so unhappy—(aw let it! let it!)
Would God that I had never been!"
She said—My queen! my queen! my queen!
"It's strange," says George. "Well, yes!" says I,
"Uncommon strange!" but I tould a lie;
For it wasn strange—the gel was right;
But a blind man never will see the light.

And George, ye see, got desperate,
And carin for nothin, and stayin out late;
And down at the public-house that was there,
In the village, and heavy upon the beer,
Aw drinkin hard, I tell ye, hard!
For a lad like him, and didn regard
For nobody—but "Come! let's go

And have a pint !" and whether or no,
And in on the door—and the dirty ould trouss,[1]
One Callow's wife, that was keepin the house,
Smilin and winkin, and plenty to say,
And drawin and drawin, and scorin away—
Bad work ! bad work !   And cards, and tossin,
And glasses round, and winnin and lossin—
And me that was ouldher backin the lad,
Aw very bad ! aw very bad !
But what could I do ? what could you expec' ?
You see I was shockin fond of him lek—
And proud uncommon—aye that was it—
Proud—bless ye ! proud ! for there we'd sit,
Him, d'ye see ? in the elber chair,
Hardly noticin was I there ;
And me on the settle ; and him in his glory,
Singin a song, or tellin a story :
And all the chaps delighted, you know ;
And " Isn he good ?" and " I tould ye so !"
And—" Listen ! listen !"—and me nearly cryin
A-thinkin of all ; and tryin and tryin
Not to let on ;[2] and proud though still—
And as much as to say—" Very well ! very well !"
But lookin the way I'd say to the others—
" Him and me is just like brothers !"
And " Capital !" and " Go it ! go it !"
Aw I shouldn ha' done it, and I know it.

---

[1] Slut.   [2] Betray what I thought.

What did ye say?—*if a chap's in the trim*
To have a spree, that's a matter for him!
And *why not have a spree when you can?*
No! you shouldn with a gentleman—
No! no! my lads! it's a different case—
Honour bright! I know my place.
But still the proud! and blow the fellows!
Who were they? and middlin jealous.
For some o' them chaps would make too free,
And then I'd be hintin if it wasn for me
He'd see the lot at Jerusalem
Afore he'd make sport for the likes o' them.
And "Isn he first-rate, Tom?" and "Hip!
Hip! hooraa!" and me bitin the lip
As contimptible as contimptible,
And lookin to say "Of coorse! but still
What's that, bless ye! to the fun
When him and me is together alone?"

Well drink is drink, and funny is funny,
And jink is jink, and money is money—
And a long score owin—that's the raison
He went partners with me for the mackarel saison.
Aw he was a partner—for I'll be dished
If a better fisherman ever fished—
Crafty uncommon, and never contented
With our ould dodges; but took and invented
New streamers, new poundrhels,[1] new guts, new plyin,

---

[1] Weights.

New everything, and tryin and tryin,
And changin often and calkerlatin,
And terrible tasty about the baitin.
Aw if there was a fish in the sea
He'd have it out though anyway—
Studyin lek.   And that time o' the year
The nights is short, so we didn care,
And maybe not in bed for a week,
But sittin in Callow's till the day would keek,[1]
And out the very first skute [2] of light,
For that's the time the divils 'll bite—
Sittin—and maybe three or four
Of the other chaps upon the floor;
And all the fun and all the spree
Peaceful enough, and leavin to me
Mostly to watch—aw they knew who they had—
Very wakeful and clear, they said !
And the clock goin tickin, and ould mawther Callow
A-snartin and snortin in the parlour—
Disthressin bad—'deed many a night
I've gone and pinched her to be quite.[3]
And George 'd mostly be down with the head
On the table, and his arms outspread
For a piller lek ; and the curly hair
Sthrooghin [4] among the rings of beer
And tobacco-dust and the lek ; and I'd take
And rise it up, and give it a shake,
And feel it a bit, for I loved him though,

---

[1] Peep.   [2] Squirt.   [3] Quiet.   [4] Trailing.

And reddyin[1] it, just with my fingers, you know;
And tuck it nice, and give it a ply
Aback of his ears, and so—Oie Vie![2]

But the first sign of day, we'd be down to the boat,
And him rather heavy and stupid to 't,
And blundherin lek, and stumblin about;
But as soon as ever we'd get out
A mile or that, he'd say—"Here goes!"
And half-a-minute, and off with the clothes,
And over the side, and in like a shot,
And me lookin sharp, and markin the spot,
And measurin lek—and, I'll be swore,
Maybe a cable's length or more—
And up with a jerk, and shakin the water
Out of his hair, and callin me ater[3]—
And "Come in! Tom Baynes! come in! come in!"
And the teeth that white, and the round o' the chin,
And his cheeks all red with the risin day
Like another sun comin out o' the sea—
And the green water swirlin around the ring
Of his shouldhers, and fit for anything.
And—"Try it, Tom! come! try, man, try!"
"Go ahead! go ahead! go ahead!" says I;
"I'm busy!"   But, bless ye! heel or toe—
I never cared much for the water—no!
In the heat of the day it might do, ye see;
But they're very strange is the quality.

---

[1] Combing.   [2] Good-night.   [3] After.

Well that's the style, and goin and goin—
And it's lek you'll ax was the Pazon knowin
About Callow's?—well—I cannot say—
Lek enough—but he had a way
Houldin on, you know, and hopin still,
And patient, patient terrible—
And livin in a sort of drame, I suppose,
And happy enough in the Christmas Rose—
And thinkin no evil, and trustin a dale—
Aw the best of fathers was Pazon Gale.

But he got to know it at last for all;
For who should go and give him a call
But ould mawther herself—and *was he aware?*
And this and that, and *the cards and the beer!*
And *well enough for him to spree*
That could easy afford it, but how about me!
And *she'd better be takin a bag at once,*
And about the country, and them that had sons
Should look after their hours—and no disrespec'!
And curtseyin and curtseyin, and trimblin lek.
And the Pazon, I'm tould, got terrible red,
And "I'll spake to him, Mrs. Baynes!" he said:
But he didn say much—aw the man was aisy!
Lazy though, mawther said, or *crazy!*
Aw she wouldn spare! but bless her chatter'n!
Good people isn all the 'zac[1] same pattern;
For some is very strong and bould,

---

[1] Exactly.

And some very tender, not willin to scould.
But whatever he said, poor George ! he felt it,
Aw aisy froze and aisy meltit !
And I'll be bound to say he didn come
To the Bull for a week, and very glum
And silent lek ; and the fellows lookin,
And never a word, and smookin, smookin.

But soon as bad as ever though,
And gettin in at the window, you know—
Aw I see the spot, and the very ould trammon [1]—
Faith ! I'm not goin to deny it, I amn [2]
Heisin [3] him up there in the tree—
I couldn help but back him, don't ye see ?
And *The Rose ? The Rose ? it's lek she knew ?*
Well—I think she did ; but what could she do ?
Was she to go and take him straight [4]
Because he was gettin drunk every night ?
And I'm not goin to say one thing or another ;
I know she loved him like a brother :
And there's many a sister that's got to let be,
And wait and see—and wait and see !
But that wasn the way of coorse to come at her,
Though maybe it wasn so very much matter ;
For the gel was moulded, ye see, and sent
Into the world to be different.
But still for all, if you want to catch
Young love asleep, you must lift the latch

---

[1] Elder tree.   [2] Am not.   [3] Lifting.   [4] Immediately.

K

Middlin aisy, I tell ye, for sure,[1]
And not go kickin at the door :
And if you want to take a bird, my son,
Alive for its beauty, no call for a gun ;
And snowdrops isn op'nin with puttin
A candle to them, nor neither shuttin ;
And the brightest brass is the better for ilin,
And never no egg wasn hatched with bilin.
Different—yes, different !
And never meant ! no, never meant !

But she couldn help noticin, whether or not,
It's differenter the two of them got ;
And furder [2] and furder, and sick and sore,
And lovin the Pazon more and more,
Aw a bird of the storm, if you like, but glad
Of a bit of rest, and all that she had
He done it, for, if the storm was in her,
The calm was in him—so there they were.
And she'd sit at his feet with her arms on his knees,
And look up like a thing that was lookin for peace,
And axin lek—and all the big troubles
A-strainin in her eyes like bubbles
Of fire and wonder ; and *who was she?*
And when and why? and the kind he'd be,
With his blessed ould face all full of love
And comfort for her to be drinkin of.
And she did drink too ; and off she'd go

---

[1] Indeed.   [2] Further.

To sleep the way with the babbies, you know.
Aw he was a reglar ould nussin mother
Was the Pazon, and 'deed she hadn no other.
For the Misthress wasn no use, but hard
And dry uncommon, and didn regard
For young craythurs, nor couldn fit
Her soul to theirs, aw not a bit !

And the two of them allis together though,
And larnin Spanish ; and George stuck to,
And larnin with them, and larnin grand ;
Aw quick at the schoolin, you'll understand.
I've got the book he was larnin from yet
In the chiss at me[1] here—I'll show ye it
Some night—of course it's lingo to me,
But George 'd be puttin it out quite free
In the English talk ; and of all the stuff !
Aw terrible nonsense, sure enough !
Fightin and women, and I don't know what—
And the name they had to it was Don Quixotte—
A sort of a Punch-and-Judy, or the way
The Whiteboys[2] is actin a[3] Christmas day—
Imprint craythurs ! and Rosinante,
A skinny ould hoss that he had ; and a banty
Fat little beggar called Sancho that got
For a governor—aye ! Don Quixotte !
And his shield and all the ould iron he wore—
Well the quality's—but I said that afore.

[1] My chest.   [2] Mummers.   [3] On.

And the picthers racly is funny amazin—
Bless me ! the barber and the bason !
And him agate o' the windmills—aye !
But I'll be showin ye bye and bye.

Well the time went on, and George had to go
To Oxford College, the way you know,
He'd larn for a Pazon—the for[1] they're sent—
And the spree the night before he went—
At the Bull ! and all the fellows there—
And him with a speech and "Hear ! hear ! hear !"
And shoutin and tearin ; and kissin ould Berry :[2]
But in the mornin thoughtful very
At the Coach : and "Tom ! do you know where I'm goin ?"
He says—and old Cannel waein and woin—
"I'm goin to the divil !" and he turned his head ;
Aw that's the very words he said !
And to the divil it was, for sure—
And sprecin, and bills, and the Pazon poor—
Not rich at any rate, no, no ! not he !
Just a little bit of proppity
On the Northside, a place they called the Height,
And mortgaged heavy to Tommy Tite.
The Misthress, it's true, was gettin the name
Of a fortin somewhere ; but how it came,
Or where it was, I cannot say ;
But the women is allis big that way.
And when he was home again—aw the work !

---

[1] Reason why.   [2] Betty.

And *what would become?* and that ould Turk
Of a Pazon's wife began to smell
A rat, and at him, and made him tell
About Christmas—and *he'd tried and tried,*
And he couldn help it, if he died:
And heaven help him! and what was the use?
And he'd either get her or he'd go to the deuce!
And at first she called him a fool; and she said
She raelly believed he was wrong in the head.

But she soon found that would never do;
And then she came over to the Brew
To see ould Anthony's wife; and says she—
"Oh Missis Lee! oh Missis Lee!"
And *would she advise her?* and—"Oh Missis Gale!
Sit down!" and—"You're lookin very pale!"
And *whatever?* And at it the two of them went,
And *a little sup of peppermint—*
"It's good for the narves"—and "Lawk-a-day!"
And "you gave me a start"! And "you don't mean to say!
Miss Christmas! mum—aw dear! aw dear!"
And out with it all—and "Did you ever hear!"
And *A terrible secret! and not to be tould*
On no account to a livin soul.
D'ye see how foolish the woman was?
And it's often the way with people that's close
And keepin back, and showin nothin—
They'll go to the very pesson they oughtn,
And demane theirselves to some ould churl

That's bound to blab it to all the world.
Aw dear! aw dear! they take a delight—
She tould it to Betsy that very night.
And what d'ye think the Pazon's wife
Had got to tell? God bless my life!
It wasn only George and Rose,
But the Pazon! Well you'll hardly suppose—
But the Pazon, I tell ye! gettin too fond
Of Christmas! and *the carryin on*—
And—*never sundered*[1]—aw as jealous
As the divil himself—and who blew the bellows
But Anthony's wife? And "O Missis Gale!"
And "Yes! Missis Gale!" and "No! Missis Gale!"
And *'deed and 'deed!*[2] *and scoffers would mock ;*
And *what a example to the flock!*
"And the family! the family
You come of! Missis Gale," says she—
"Some of the very first that's goin!
And to think! and to think! but there's never knowin!"
That was a nice sort of talk, I'll swear,
For a wife, and a Pazon's wife, to hear—
Aw takin it in as sweet as puddin—
And "Yes! my lady;" and *No! she wouldn!*
And the fortin she'd brought him, and her a match
For the best in the counthry, and glad of the catch!
"Aye indeed! You'll 'scuse me, mam!
But it's only spakin the truth I am!"—
And to think a woman that locked away

---

[1] Separate.   [2] Indeed and indeed.

Her soul in a safe, and hid the key,
Would give an ould craythur like Misthress Lee
The chance to take such a liberty?
But jealous! jealous! or mad? which is it?
Aw it's the divil's own claw in any one's gizzit![1]
And pride and dacency will go
When that ould cock begins to crow.
And Misthress Lee—d'ye think for a minute
The ould humbug believed there was anythin in it?
Not her! that's just the talk I heard
From ould Peggy long after—aw every word.
Of coorse! of coorse! But the very next day—
To Betsy—it was another say—
Poor Missis Gale now! dear! aw dear!
What was at her![2] and—terrible queer!
And—*the notions and the stuff she'd got!*
And *she ought to be ashamed, she ought!*
D'ye hear? of coorse! But true it ess[3]—
Rael good women is very skess![4]

And the two of them made it up, I suppose,
To have it out with the Christmas Rose.
And old Anthony's wife was tellin how,
And what she said, and all the row.
And they got her in the parlour together,
And George not at home, nor the Pazon either:
And then she turned up the whole o' the midden,
And Lee's wife backed her, but she said she didn,
But I know she did, but never mind!

[1] Gizzard.   [2] The matter with her.   [3] Is.   [4] Scarce.

And first about George—*the good and the kind*
And the studdy he was used to be—
"Now wasn he? wasn he? Missis Lee!"
And "Yes;" and *What had come over him then!*
And allis down at that wretched den.
Meanin the Bull—and *what was he doin*
At Oxford College? nothin but ruin!
And "Christmas!" she says, "what are we to do?
And—it's all—it's all—on account of you!"
And Christmas looked—but she sat quite still—
And looked; and her look was terrible—
Misthress Lee was sayin—and with that look
The Misthress got quite 'cited and shook
And trembled all over, and went on quicker,
All flurried lek, like a woman in liquor—
And cryin and cryin! and *what had she done?*
And—"Oh my son! my son! my son!"

But when she cried in that distress,
The Christmas flew like a bird to her breast,
And clung and clung; and "Mother dear!
Oh let me! let me! let me be here!
Mother! mother! oh be my mother!"
And Missis Gale gave a kind of a shuddher—
"Oh I long for your love! oh if—oh if—"
But Missis Gale got very stiff—
"If I could always be like this!
Your child! your own! oh one, *one* kiss!—"
And the mawther gave her a little pat

Betwix the shoulders, just like that !—
Coaxin though—"O mother ! mother !"
Says Christmas, "George is a darling brother—
But more than that—" and she kind o' moan't [1]—
"O mother ! mother ! oh don't ! oh don't !"
And—"Some other time," she says, "I'll try,"
Says the Christmas Rose, "to tell you why.
But now !" she says, and she cuddled to her—
"I never was like this before !
Love me, mother !"—Aw the Misthress's face
Was a thing to see—and "Listen !" she says—
"Will you have George ? oh I'm goin mad !
O Christmas ! have him ! for the love of God !"

Then Christmas lifted her face, and sent
All the love and the wonderment
And the pain and the longin and the sighs
Straight into that ould woman's eyes.
And—"Be merciful !" she said, and bent
Her head again ; but the woman meant
No mercy—no ! "Stand off !" she cried,
And all the rage and all the pride
And all the jealousy come tearin
In one blast through her soul, like the way you're hearin
A storm in the woods on a winter's day,
When the trees has no sap, and cranches away.
"Stand off ! you viper !" she said ; and *oh*
If she'd only known this long ago,

[1] Moaned.

" I'd have smothered her, I'd have smothered her
In her cradle!" she said—Missis Lee didn stir,
But snivelin lek—"I would!" she said:
" *Mother!* and *Mercy!*" and she spread
Her arms all wild—" Oh, I know your art;
And you've robbed me of my husband's heart!"
And then she went on, and ravin and ravin,
That Misthress Lee thought it was time to be lavin.
But—" No! Missis Lee!" and "The wretch! and the
          schamer!"[1]
And—" Look on her, Missis Lee! and shame her!"
And *what of Rose?* aye! what of Rose?
All the blood that was in her froze,
And she stood like an image made of stone,
A dreadful thing to look upon,
Ould Lee's wife said; and neither fear,
Nor anger, nor anything was there;
But just the beautiful and the strong—
And she cowed that ould woman with the bitter
          tongue
Till she hadn another word to say,
But down in a chair and snivelled away,
And the two of them lek houldin in,
And sniffin and snuffin and slobberin—
And never a word all the time from Rose,
But keepin her eye on them; and she goes,
And out on the door, and—" The fiend! the fiend!"
Says the Misthress then—my queen—my queen!

[1] Schemer.

And was the Pazon's wife raelly jealous!

Yes! and a woman should allis tell us

If so be we're not lovin enough—

In our ways, I mean; for we're apt to be rough,

Bein men, you know, and not thinkin about it—

But the women, you see, can't do without it.

They like to be loved, and the love to be showed

Middlin plain—aye that's the road!

And there's odds[1] of women and odds of men;

And this Misthress Gale she wouldn pretend

She cared, and dying all her life

Because she wasn a happy wife—

And the Pazon not knowin, the aisy he was,

The fire that was undher all that frost.

For she never made no sort of complaint,

And goin,[2] and seemin well content:

So that's the way she got mad, ye see;

At least—well a sort of mad it 'd be—

And plenty of love to have for the asin[3]—

Aw the poor Pazon! aw the poor Pazon!

I never knew was he tould or what,

But it's lek she'd be at him after that—

I don't know, and I don't want to know—

Poor ould man! But, whether or no,

He'd enough to put up with, I'll be bail,

Aw plenty! plenty! had Pazon Gale.

And George to Oxford again, and wuss

[1] Different kinds.
[2] Going about her ordinary pursuits.　　　[3] Asking.

Than ever, and kickin a terrible dust,
And makin the money fly like blazes,
As if the chap was as rich as Crayzus.
But not for long—for one fine mornin,
Without ever the smallest taste of warnin,
What did he do but ax a lot
Of chaps to his breakfast (a way they've got—
The quality—chut!¹ what a fool I am!);
And there was the eggs, and there was the ham,
Aw a terrible spread—but George, behould yer!
Was off long ago, with a gun on his shouldher
And a dog in a chain.   The chap that was tellin
Was at College with George; and his eyes was swellin
With tears when he tould—and a nice sort of lad,
And tould the Pazon all he had,
Bein come a-purpose, you know, and tryin
To tell it the best he could, and eyein
The Rose—yes! yes! for George had tould
The sore he was, and the sick in his sowl
About her; and her eye met yandhar young man's,
And then she hid her face in her hands:
And then the ould woman began with her talk,
And the Pazon gets up to go out for a walk;
And says he to the lad—"Will you come with me?"
And over the fields and out to the sea,
The young man said: but he didn tell
Much about that, and maybe as well.
But they walked till it was gettin night,

¹ Tut !

And the Pazon, he said, was very quite;
And at last he sat down, like for him to be goin,
And he says—" I'd wish to be alone !"
But kind—and the young man bowed and went—
Aw a very civil surt of a gent—
Not so free; but stayin at the Bull,
And sittin there, and the kitchen full,
And lookin—you know the way they'll stare,
And no pipe at him, but just a cigar—
And all of them knowin of coorse what for he
Was come, and very silent and sorry.
Aw the quality doesn think, d'ye see,
Such fellows has feelins—but let that be !

Well the next we heard of this poor chap,
He was seen somewhere a-drivin a trap
To a station, and never a dog or a gun,
And carryin on though with jokes and fun;
And then a-spreein away at a fair
Somewhere about in Lancasheer—
And took up with a hurdy-gurdy gel —
And trampin the country—aw well, well, well !
And grindin the urgan;[1] and her on the green
A-poundin away with the tambourine—
Aw mad though, and goin ahead like a fool;
And down at last to Liverpool;
And aboard a brig that was just a-startin
For Austrilia—the *Orpheus*, Captain Martin—

[1] Organ.

I knew the man—and up to the diggins,
And married there to a gel called Higgins,
I'm tould a dacent woman enough ;
And him stickin to her, but fond of the stuff—
And all to that ;[1] and twins, bedad !
The very first year ! aw bless the lad !
And losin the wife, and losin heart,
And losin all ; and makin a start,
And beggin about among the farms,
With them two childher in his arms.
That's the last I heard—aw every bit !
And I'm sore whenever I think of it.

Wait then ! wait ! and I'll try to tell
About the gel—about the gel—
About *her*—yes ! yes ! I know ! I know—
You'll not take rest [2]—just so ! just so !
Still—half-a-minute—and then—and then
(I'm feelin very strange, my men !)—
Half-a-minute (very queer)—
Half-a-minute—(aw dear ! aw dear !)
Half-a—half-a——Well, here goes !
This is what happened to the Christmas Rose.
It was harvest-time, and terrible warm,
And me a-shearin on the Lheargy farm ;
And rather late givin over though,
And home, and a good piece of road to go,
And takin the shortest cut I could,

---

[1] So forth.   [2] Be satisfied.

And crossin a stream and a bit of a wood,
And out on the headlands over the bay,
And I saw a cloud very far away,
But comin, comin, bound to come,
And the deep low growl of the thunder-drum ;
And steady, steady, sollum, slow,
As if it knew where it had to go ;
Comin, comin, like it would be
Comin a purpose for somebody—
(Was it *them* that had the power
Gave to them in that dreadful hour ?)
And low, rather low ; then higher, higher,
Till it kissed the cairn with a kiss of fire—
Once—like the twinklin of an eye—
Once—and the long back-suck and the sigh
Of the silence—and terrible far away
Flash flashed to flash behind the sea ;
And back and back till you couldn see fuddher,[1]
Like passin something to one another.
And—was it a sheep, or was it a flag
That white spot on the Belfry crag
I couldn tell, and wondhering,
And up through the goss, and up through the ling
As quick—it was her ! it was her ! Yes ! yes !
Dead though, dead, and gript in her fist
A bunch of blue bells that was growin there,
And sea-pinks twisted through her hair :
And never a spot and never a speck

---

[1] Further.

But just a black mark under the neck ;
And her breast all open—my God ! that breast !
The beautifullest and the loveliest !
But I covered it up—aw I did, and I ran
Down to the Pazon's like a crazy man,
And I shouted . . . well ! well ! that'll do ! that'll do !
They took her—aye, them two ! them two !
They took her, it's lek to be with them
In the Heavenly Jerusalem,
Or wherever it is.   And you'll aisy belave
Her grave is next to the darkey's grave—
And the Pazon is often sittin theer,
Partikler in the Spring of the year—
And to this day there's no man knows
Who or what was the Christmas Rose.

III

CAPTAIN TOM & CAPTAIN HUGH

You're wantin to hear about them two,
Captain Tom and Captain Hugh,
Very well! Very well!
But it isn much of a story to tell;
But—however—it's lek you know who you've got—
Middlin willin whether or not.

Now these two Captains they were all allowin
Was the best that was sailin out of Castletown;
And the two of them went to school together,
And never no relations either—
But up the Claddagh[1] agate o' buck-kyones,[2]
And ticklin troutses under the stones,
Or down at the Race, or out at the Mull,
Or over plaguin Lukish's bull,

[1] Marsh.   [2] A kind of fish.

Or any fun that was goin, ye see,
Where the one was, the other would be ;
And stickin mortal close, and backin
One another up, whatever was actin [1]—
Backin one another still,
And reared though very respectable,
Lek accordin to their station ;
And goin a-teachin navigation,
At [2] Masthar Cowin that was general known
For the grandest masther that was goin,
A one-armed man—aw, I'll be bound
You had to look slippy [3] if you went to Cowin ;
That's the man that could trim a scholar ;
Only wink, and the hook in your collar,
And wouldn listen to no excuse,
And workin the kiddhag [4] like the deuce.

So these two lads got on though, aye !
Got on, I tell ye, and passin by
Ouldher men, and very much lek'd, [5]
And studdier till [6] you'd expect.
So from one thing to another they came
To be skippers of smacks, the two of them—
Masther Corteen's—you'll have heard of him—
No ?   Well, racly ! but that's the way,
And every dog must have his day.

| [1] Going on. | [2] By. | [3] Sharp. |
| [4] Left hand. | [5] Liked. | [6] Steadier than. |

So when they got married, they wouldn be beat,
But it was two sisthers they were schamin to get,
And got them, by the name of Sayle,
And a nice bit of money to their tail;
And right enough, and not felt on the farm—
Aw a little money 'll do no harm,
Not it, but only just to take care   .
You'll have it on the land, d'ye hear?
Aye, that's your sort—aw very nice,
And the bigger the loaf, the bigger the slice;
But still there's some 'll take the huff,
And grab will never have enough:
But what with the lean, and what with the fat,
Maybe a hundherd pound or that;
And a little inthress [1] in the will,
Aye—bless ye! very comfible.
Good wives they were, let alone the tin,
And chrizzenin [2] for chrizzenin,
And as handsome a breed as ever you'd see,
And very nice and orderly.

For the sisthers was livin next door to each other,
And civil to all, but cautious rather;
And wouldn have their childher tearin
Out on the sthreet, and cussin, and swearin,
And raggin their clothes.   And Ned Ballachrink,
The uncle, that was mostly in dhrink,
Wasn never suffered to come nigh them,

[1] Interest.   [2] Christening.

As if his very look would desthroy them.

And still they might have been his own,

He was that fond of them ; and you'll never be knowin

What the lek is feelin ; but either woman—

No matter—let her see the uncle comin

And it was up the stair with the childher straight,

And longin shockin, but not a sight

To be seen of the one of them : and maybe he'd catch

A sound like little birds under the thatch,

Or the way they stirs themselves in bushes

Of a moonlight night—you'll hear these thrushes—

And the Ballachrink, he'd look and he'd listen,

And them knowin parfec[1] what was he missin,

But he darn say a word, or if he did,

It was—*some chickens they'd got on the laff,*[2] they said ;

And no lie for all, just a way to spake—

Aw, exlen[3] women, and no mistake.

Now it wasn often the husbands would chance

To be at home together, maybe once

On the summer, ye know ; and you'd see the whole crew

    o' them

Out in the garden that was doin for the two o' them.

They were looking fuss-rate was yandhar chaps,

And the women wearin their Sunday caps,

And all the little things as nate, ye know—

'Deed it was worth your while to go

Of an everin there, and look over the wall,

---

[1] Perfectly.   [2] Loft.   [3] Excellent.

And as nice and as happy though, for all ;[1]
And every one with his little bason
Under the trammon,[2] aw, putty amazin ![3]

And even the poor Ballachrink 'd be gettin
Admission them times, and the way he'd be sittin
And eyein the childher, and axin to taste,
Half tight, you know, but the love in his face—
The sowl—and well it's a pity too
Of the lek, and puzzlin what to do—
A good-nathured craythur, and would allis be hevvin [4]
His pockets stuffed with knobs to be gevvin [5]
To the youngsters ; and watchin, you know, and 'd try
To pop them in their porridge on the sly.
But big at the talk, aw very big :
And disputin there about the rig
Of a vessel, and reefin, and lee shores,
And this and that, and to work their course—
Aw, it's him that 'd larn them—and " Look ! " he'd say,
" D'ye see the thing ? "—and—" Here's the bay ; "
And—*such a wind*, and how he'd contrive her—
" Up peak, my lads, down jib, and jive [6] her ! "
Chut ! of all the foolishness !
And Captain Tom with the chin on the bress,[7]
And smookin studdy all the while,
And maybe just a little smile.

But that's the when [8] you'd see, mind you !

---

[1] However.   [2] Elder tree.   [3] Amazingly pretty.   [4] Having.
[5] Giving.   [6] Jibe.   [7] Breast.   [8] Time.

The difference of Captain Hugh,
That 'd turn very sharp, and walk a bit,
And rux[1] the shouldhers, and blow the spit,
Lek contemptible lek, and growl
Like a savage dog, and couldn hould[2]
To hear such stuff—aw, that was the man—
Impatient mostly, you'll understand—
Hot, very hot, in general—
That was Captain Hugh, for all.

So the years went by, and the childher grew,
And the ouldest boy of Captain Hugh
Fell in love with the ouldest gel
Of Captain Tom—aw terrible !
" Love again ? " now steady ! steady !
Fell in love though did this laddie.
And the nither of them knew a bit
How they ever come to think of it—
Bein reared like a sisther with a brother,
And used, you know, of one another.

Well this Hughie though was a reg'lar bould chap—
They were callin him Hughie after the ould chap—
Hughie, not Hugh, for a differ[3] lek—
Aw, a plucky lad and no mistake ;
A splendid hand aboord of a boat—
Aw, he'd stick to anything that 'd float—
Would Hughie—aye—and none of your sauce

---

[1] Shrug.   [2] Bear.   [3] Distinction.

Nor brag ; and the proud the father was
To see him when he was only a little mossel
With his two reefs tied, and his jib and fo'sail—
Stole [1] of coorse ; and the sea tha'd [2] be there !
And the owner shoutin on the pier—
And my lad with the taffystick [3] in his fist,
And strainin his back against the list [4]—
Aw, into the rail ! into the rail !
And as sollum as if he was carryin the mail—
And all the sheets trained aft to his hand—
And to see him lie to was raelly grand,
Waitin his chance to come over the bar,
And the father would call, and the owner would swear ;
And the little rascal would keck [5] like a gull
Under his boom, and wait for a lull,
And humoured the boat, and pacified her,
Feelin everything like a spider,
Till he saw the nick,[6] and afore you'd be knowin,
His helm was up, his jib was drawin,
And a lift and a leap and a jerk and a joult,
And he sent her in like a thunderboult.

Then of coorse he'd have to make the best of it,
Jawin and lickin and all the rest of it,
And done him no harm, the little midge,
And the Captain sthooin [7] him over the bridge—

---

[1] Stolen.   [2] That would.   [3] Tiller, lit. stick of toffy.
[4] Leaning over of the boat.   [5] Peep.
[6] Of time.   [7] Driving.

But aisy to see, whatever he done,
It's proud enough he was of the son.

He was rather silent lek was the Captain,
And not the sort of a man to be rapt in
A son or a gun—but he said one day
To the ould High-Bailiff down on the quay
That Hughie 'd take a boat through the Sound
With any man in Castletown.
So the High-Bailiff gave a little laugh,
And "What!" he says, "through the Sound of the Calf!
I doubt it, Captain!" he says, "I doubt it:"
And the people was tellin they had words about it.
But that may be—but still, dear heart!
There's no doubt at all the lad was smart.
I've seen him myself coming under our quarter,
And the skiff at [1] him there nearly full of water;
And he'd lay alongside for a bit to bail her,
And then he'd cast off, and take and sail her,
And just a little latteen with a hook at [2] it,
And he'd make the harbour when we couldn look at it.

Smart he was, but silent very,
Like the father, you know, and never merry
Nor frisky lek, but thoughtful still—
For the skipper could talk when he had the will;
Aw, it's himself that had the bitter tongue,
Partikler when he was a little sprung,

[1] With.   [2] To.

And terrible standin on his right;
But as for the boy he was allis quite.[1]
And if the father loved the lad,
He wasn showin it much, bedad—
Short and sharp and hard to plaze—
Aw, he wasn a lovin man in his ways
At all—no! no!   But the lad was lovin;
Even when he was a little thing he'd be shovin
Hisself betwixt the father's legs,
The way a little puppy begs;
And the Captain's hand on the little mop[2]
Just absent-lek, and wouldn stop
Whatever he was doin, or maybe
Doin nothin at all; and the little baby
Rubbin and rubbin and feelin him,
And the Captain sittin very grim—
And never a kiss for the little sowl,
Nor nothin, the craythur! so I'm tould.
But there's pessons like that though, isn there, John?
Starin out at the horizon!
Some people's allis up the mast
Cockin their eye to a spyin-glass.
It's well to look a little nearer,
And—bits of infants—what's more dearer?

But the son was lovin the father greatly—
Aw took up in him complately;
And grew to be the very prent[3]

---

[1] Quiet.   [2] Of hair.   [3] Print.

Of the skipper—he did—lek took and bent
To the shape of him—and the face and the walk,
And the turn and the look, and the nose like a hawk,
And the chin like an egg, and the throat like a bell—
Grew lek, grew; and of coorse you will;
Not thinkin, you know, but lookin—aye !
Lookin, lookin, and takin joy—
There's childher that doesn, and childher that does—
A surt of comedher,[1] I wouldn thrus';[2]
But still a father you know—that way—
And the fond and all, but it's hard to say—
There's men that's charmin other men,
And hardly knowin the lek is in[3]—
Hard men too, and gove[4] to be close—
Some power that's at them, I·suppose,
Like rubbed with somethin—what's its name?
Loadstun—aye; and women the same.
Hapes—that you wouldn be givin two screws for,
And gettin more love till they've got any use for,
And others aequal goin without,
And still a dale of it about.

Now this lad was a very gentle sort,
And hadn none of the fiery spir't
That was in the father—it's faithful he was,
Faithful, and houldin terrible fast
To them he liked, and perseverin

---

[1] Fascination.   [2] I would not trust, I rather think.
[3] That they exist.   [4] Given.

Uncommon—look at the either steerin,
And you'd know the odds;[1] for Hughie was all
For humourin, but the skipper would haul
On a wind no matter how it was blow'n,
Just like a dog would be peelin a bone,
Greedy, you know, like a hungry dog,
Greedy, suckin his luff like grog.
That's the way, and Hughie would look
On the sea like a man would read in a book,
Spellin big spells, and gettin them right,
But the Captain would stand like sniffin a fight
Far off—he would—like challengin,
Suspicious lek, like sayin—"Now then!
You're at it! are ye?   Who'll strike first?
Come on, ould stockin! do your worst!"
Like the sea and himself was swore in their teeth
To fight it out to the bitter death—
Half in anger, half in scorn,
Defyin it, as if he was born
A purpose to triumph and have the rule of it,
Or draw its cork,[2] and make a fool of it.

Chut! there's no luck with yandhar kind,
But never mind! never mind!
Lookin so proud—but the lek will get lave![3]
Rather like lookin for a grave—
Seemin to me—but—very well!

---

[1] Difference.   [2] Get the better of it.
[3] Such people will get leave = may do what they like . . . yet, etc.

And—maybe a notion—but time will tell.
And just the same ashore as afloat,
Allis restless, and facin to 't,
Like doubtin if he turned his back
The sea 'd be takin advantage lek.

   Do you see the men?—well—does or doesn,
Annie they were callin the cousin—
A shockin nice gel, but slandhar though,
Slandhar, and very scoople, you know;
And the hair she had, aw bless my sowl,
Cables and cables, and 'd take and rowl
And rowl them there, and stick a pin,
And the nice and the smooth astonishin.
She was a terr'ble modest gel was that,
And clane uncommon, and the little brat,[1]
And the little strings, and altogether—
Not azackly handsome either—
No, she wasn; but to see her smile—
Aw deed![2] I'd have walked a hunderd mile—
I would—the sudden it come to be sure,
The sudden and the sweet and pure,
And spreadin out like some lovely rose,
And fadin away like the sunset goes,
When you'd think it wasn willin to die,
And it's fit to make a body cry.

   So they fell in love like birds in the spring,

[1] Apron.   [2] Indeed.

And the mothers began to see the thing—
And lookin and signin, and hummin and hemmin,
And terrible plased—the way with women.
Aw, then the colloguin [1] that was done,
And her with the daughter, and her with the son,
And took a opportunity,
And had it out as nice as could be—
Hughie's mother that was spakin—
And—*whatever capers* [2] *were they takin !*
And—" Why don't you laugh, and why don't you talk ?
And why don't you hev a little walk ?"
And—" Come, man ! give your cousin a kiss !"
And—" Bless my heart ! what foolishness !"
Aw, if Hughie didn make for the door
Like a shot, and Annie on the floor ;
But made her tell, and aised her shockin
The way her heart was goin a-knockin—
Aw, yis !—and people should be kind
To the lek, and get them to clear their mind.
So she tould them though, and then they went
And looked for Hughie, and found him lent [3]
Against the trammon ; [4] and " Why, man, why ?"
And — " Nonsense, Hughie !" and " Try, man,
         try !"
And got him in, you'll understand,
And put them sittin hand in hand,
Aw beautiful, and left them there,
And the dark, you know, he could hardly see her.

---

[1] Consulting.   [2] Absurd ideas.   [3] Leaned.   [4] Elder tree.

Then the two women took a sthroull
Along the shore, and the nither[1] ould;
But still it's lek there 'd be a little sigh,
And I wouldn trust but a little cry,
Lek happy, you know, but middlin plain
Their time would never come again.
And I was tould there was some that seen them
    too,
And they were sayin that Annie's mother threw
Her arms very lovin around the sister,
And hung to her a dale, and kissed her—
And so they went together linkin,[2]
And very peaceful lek, and thinkin.
And tears is tears, no matter the from;[3]
But he was a fuss-rate husband was Captain Tom.

Fuss-rate he was—and gennaler[4]
There couldn be, nor heartier.
Aw, happy was the people that bred him,
And happy was the woman that had him.
But 'deed the happiest of the lot
Was the man himself the way he got
To make other people happy; his face
Was reglar bustin with happiness—
My sakes! the laugh! you never heard!
It was allis snugglin in his beard
Somewhere, you know, bein curly very;

---

[1] Neither of them.   [2] Arm-in-arm.
[3] Source.   [4] Kindlier.

But when he gave way, a blast in a quarry
Was just a fool to it—Nebuchadnessar !
Rattlin the very plates on the dresser.
And the same man was terrible wise,
And givin people good advice—
About business lek—there's some will remember—
But of coorse—dear heart ! the judge of timber,
And gardens and that—aw, every craft !
But he'd have his laugh, he'd have his laugh !

But the first these women had to do
Was to tell their story to Captain Hugh—
Mad—did ye say? God bless ye ! *mad !*
No, not him—the mad or the glad,
Nor the yes or the no, nor the good or the bad,
Nor the nothin arrim ;[1] just a spit,
And a puff o' the pipe to see was he lit,
And his head on his chin and his eye on the say ;
So the women had to go away.
" Well ! " says Annie's mother, " he's tould ! "
" Yes ! " says the sisther, but cryin, the sowl !
And it's allis the same—aw, very nice,
And raisonable to rejoice
When two young things is comin together—
But there's sure to be a bit of bother
About it someway—aw, by George !
There's lumps in every body's porr'dge ;
Like ould Jemmy the Red that drove to the packet,

[1] At him, on his part.

One hoss would go forrit,[1] and the other backit [2]--
" Dear me ! " the people said ;
" There's nothin puffeck,"[3] says Jemmy the Red.

   Now Captain Tom was in Ireland over ;
But the very minute they saw the *Rover*
(The smack he was skipper of) makin the Mull,
Aw, then the women took heart to the full—
'Deed if they were smellin Captain Tom in the offin
The whole of Castletown would be laughin
Mostly—the liked,[4] you'll understand—
Aw, a terrible man, a terrible man !
So somebody tould him, and he slapped the thigh,
And come ashore in a blaze of joy—
In a blaze—and " Where is she ? where is she, then ?
The little rascal ! " and—*how*, and *when ?*
And—*bless his sowl !* and—*to think the deep !*
And " Come here ! come here ! you little sweep ! "
And—" Hughie ! Hughie ! Tyre and Sidon ! "
And—" Annie ! Annie ! " but Annie was hidin.
But caught at [5] the mother somewhere in the yard,
" Ha ! ha ! " he says, " ha ! ha ! my bird !
What ! " he says, " you don't know me, maybe ! "
And took her off her feet like a baby ;
And clapsed her to his besom [6] there,
And kissed her eyes, and kissed her hair,
And kissed and kissed her everywhere—

---

[1] Forwards.   [2] Backwards.   [3] Perfect.
[4] Because he was so much liked.   [5] By.   [6] Bosom.

Shockin for kissin! noted for it
Was Captain Tom.   There's people horrit
That way with their slimin and slobberin,
But Captain Tom was differin—
But still—Well, in come Hughie, though,
And he dropt the gel, and he gave a crow
Out of him like a cock, very clear—
Like a cock that way—very pleasant to hear,
Hearty—eh? and gript him straight,[1]
And stood him off against the light;
And—"the sakes!"[2] and—"'Deed on[3] Hughie, for all![4]
Capital! Capital!"
And his face like the sun.   And—"Hould up!" says he,
"Hould up for all! I want to see—
(And Hughie lookin rather simple)
The polished corners of the temple—
What's this ould David is sayin in the Psalm?
Bless my heart! the stupid I am!
The corners, it's sayin, *the polished corners,*
And—*splendid sheep,* it's sayin, and the *garners*
Full of store.—I like you, my lad!
I like you! you'll do! you'll do!" he said.
And—"Where's your father?" he said to him then;
"Dear me! he isn half a man!"
And a passil of women outside gave a shout—
"You've got it!" they said; and he turned about—
"Hulloah!" says he, and a sort of a roar;

---

[1] Immediately.   [2] For all the sakes! an interjection.
        [3] Only to think of.   [4] After all.

"You're right!" says the women at the door.
"He's against the match!" says the women, "he is!"
"Come now! I tell ye! be off out of this!"
Says Captain Tom's wife—*Well, dear heart!*
And—*it was only the truth they were tellin.*   "Start!"
Says Captain Tom's wife; so the women cut,
And tossin the head, and—*A saucy slut!*
And, "Says is says, and thinks is thinks!"
And—*They were allis high, them Ballachrinks!*

And the talk was soon all over the town
That the one Captain knocked the other down,
And—*a desperate fight!* but of coorse they hadn,
And—*the evil eye that was on the weddin*
At[1] Captain Hugh, and—*Careless! chat!*[2]
No use o' talkin—he was a black man that!
But—*Captain Tom!* and—"Did ye see him there?"
And—*that was the man! aw dear! aw dear!*
Aw splendid!—the hearty and the kind!
Somethin like a father! aw, no fault to find,
But only them women!—a pair of slinks,
They hadn no patience with them Ballachrinks!

And it's lek there 'd be words; but—bless their stuff!
Captain Hugh was willin enough!
It wasn that.   There's pessins that bright,
The whole of their body is full of light;
Lek it's sayin in the Bible—"Take care!" it's sayin,
"If the light that is in thee turn dark again

---

[1] On the part of.   [2] Tut.

(Lek some devil's runnet [1] thick'nin it),
Bless me !" it's sayin, "the dark you'll get !"

But it wasn that.   And still no doubt
There's people that turns theirselves inside out,
And others that turns theirselves outside in—
Was that the sort? you'll be wonderin.
No! I don't think it—or was he haunted
At [2] some dirt of a sperrit? or was it wanted
Elsewhere he was? or a crick in his heart
That he had to look another airt? [3]
Or——well, ye see, what you're knowin, you're knowin ;
But I'll tell ye what, I'll lave it alone.

Well—this Masther Corteen I was tellin you of
Wouldn take no rest, [4] but it's a schooner he must have—
Aw, smacks wouldn do for him at all—
Schooners ! schooners ! that's the call.
Foolish—you're sayin?   Uplifted just—
Aw, uplifted scandalous !
For what is a schooner, if you come to that?
A slink of a thing with a side like a latt, [5]
And bearins—eh? and stowage? my gough !
A bilge like a plane, and a hould like a trough—
That's your schooners—idikkilis ! [6]
Give me the little gel that'll kiss
Ould Bags [7] in his teeth, and spin on her heel

---

[1] Rennet.   [2] By.   [3] Way.   [4] Be satisfied.
[5] Lath.   [6] Ridiculous.   [7] The wind.

Like a top, like your sweetheart dancin a reel
In the harvest moon—aw, a smack for ever!
Chut! you can twis' her tail like a heifer!
But—of course!—and them Douglas chaps 'd be talkin
And quiverin [1] there—aw, big though, shockin [2]—
Collister's ones, and Skillicorn,
And Moores, that was sailin a vessel for'n, [3]
And the lck of that—aw, brigs and barks!
And galliotts, and Noah's arks!
Aw, you couldn touch the Douglas fellows—
No! and feelin middlin jealous—
And "I'll have a schooner, up or down!"
And—*all for the honour of the town.*
And built at Boyds', and no mistake,
And goin a-launchin up the Lake,
Or the Claddagh—is it? aye! and the scholars
Let out of the school, and terrible colours;
And a cannon there, and would have a try,
And fired, and bust the bellman's eye—
Juan Jem—a squinty man he was,
And bust in bits—and—*not much of a loss
At all*—I've heard the women say;
But useful is useful any day.
And a beautiful launch, you may depend,
And off the ways as smooth as a swan;
And Jacks, and Blue Peters, and stars-and-stripes,
And the name they gave her was the *Clyps* [4]—

---

[1] Bragging.   [2] Very.
[3] To foreign parts.   [4] *Cyclops.*

Or the *Clops*, or the *Clups*—what is it—eh?
Well, it's the *Clyps* they were callin her anyway.

So then the talk was how would he man her,
And who'd be goin for a captain on her;
Aw, terrible talk—but of coorse they knew
It was either Captain Tom or Captain Hugh.
And a pazil[1] of fellows down at the Crow
Was shoutin for Captain Hugh to go;
But the company over at the Crown,
That was general countin[2] the best in town,
Ould Mollachreest, and Corkish the baker,
Was all for Captain Tom to take her.
So you see the people was mortal divided,
And a bit of a row, and reglar enjoyed it;
And—*Wait then! wait!*—and *All serene!*
He wasn no fool, wasn ould Corteen—
No! And who was the head man, d'ye think?
Who of coorse but the Ballachrink?
Down at the Crow there every night,
And glasses round, and as tight as tight;
And—*Healths apiece!* and—*What'll ye take?*
Bless me, the mischief them dunkies 'll make!

He got a notion that time, you see,
A notion arrim[3] how would it be
If he could just sundher the captains a lill[4]

---

[1] Parcel.   [2] Accounted.
[3] At him, in his head.   [4] Little.

That they wouldn be lek that agreeable
Lek they were used to be, on the one hand lek,
That the poor chap hadn the smallest speck
Of a chance, you see, to get his foot in
The either house ; for he didn care a button
About the sisthers, but just he was cravin
For the childher—aye ! aw, reglar ravin !
But how would it be now, how would it be !
" They'll have to give me more libbity !"
He says ; and then he begun to think,
And he seen there wasn the smallest chink
Betwix Tom and the wife ; and—" The smoother the wall
The harder to climb," says Ned, for all [1]—
Aw, Ned was sharp enough in his way—
He could tell was there shuggar in his tay,
Could Ned ; he knew where to hammer a tack in,
So it's Captain Hugh that he was backin.

Backin uncommon ; and terrible truck [2]
Betwix them too, like an aigle took [3]
To be friends with a pay-cock—that was about it—
And he puffed and he blowed, and he roored and he shoutit,
And he quivered the fist ; and " What !" he said,
" Captain Tom to walk over the head
Of Captain Hugh ; What sense !" he was sayin ;
And—*God bless his sowl ! and wasn it plain ?*
Captain Tom ! of coorse ! of coorse !
But—Captain Hugh, they were on diff'rin floors

---

[1] However.   [2] Communication, intimacy.   [3] Who had taken.

Altogether—Was it blind they were?
Did they know who they had?   Was there any com-
    pare?
And—" The two of them," he says, "is relations
Of mine," he says; "but, look here! my patience!"
And snaps the fingers, and taps the stick,
And gives a nod, and around as quick,
And faces up against one of the men
Behind him there; and at it again—
And over the Craves,[1] and all down New Street,
And up Kirk Arbory and Kirk Malew Street,
And the Green, and Cowles, and the Flukin' pool,
Everywhere you'd hear this fool—
But special at the Crow—Aw, there
He was all in his glory, and took the chair,
And wondherful, consider'n the gin—
You'd have thought it was the High-Bailiff himself that was
    in—
Proposed and seconded—and—*Them*
That's in favour—you know—aw, bless ye! it came
As natheral—amazin though
The way the lek can work the jaw—.
And he stuck to Captain Hugh like a leech,
And grips the arm, and over the beach,
And past the quay, and down the pier,
Showin him off lek walkin there,
And the nose on the cock, like snuffin a smell,
Lek—*Clear the road!* lek something to sell.

[1] A street in Castletown.

But howsomedever—Peter or Paul,
Captain Tom was the captain for all—
Aye, he was—of a Saturday night
The orders were out, and a reglar fight
At the Countin-house door—and—"Who then? who?
Is it Captain Tom? Is it Captain Hugh?"
And—"Hip hoorah!" and over the town,
And away to the Crow, and away to the Crown—
And the Ballachrink though, sittin as grand,
And the pipe in his mouth, and the glass in his hand—
Aw, a terrible big man at the Crow,
A sort of a gentleman, you know—
The way with these farmers—and his Sunday hat,
And a frill on his shirt, and all to that.[1]
And—"Well!" he says, "There's no mistake
Who's goin for Captain; it's all correct,"
He says, "it's settled," he says, "my hearties;"
And—*Of coorse!* and—*The influential parties
That was at Corteen, and not once nor twice;
But the man knew where to go for advice;
Aye! aye! and got it; and what for wouldn he?
A brother-in-law! and what for shouldn he?
But wait! but still—aw, dear! to think!
"I'll lave it to you then, Ballachrink."
In the parlour—aye!* "But mind ye! my men,
You'll never be mentionin this again!"
Aw, all in his glory—and the chaps goin nudgin
And winkin there, the way you'd be judgin

[1] So forth.

He'd see they were laughin ; and did and didn ;
Lek you'll see a cock upon a midden,
Scratchin—lek he was sayin to the hens—
"Look out!" he says, "my gough ! there's grains !
There's grains !" he says ; and the dirt goin flyin ;
And he'll scratch and scratch, and the hens 'll be eyein
One another, and smilin lek,
And may be bitendin [1] to give a little peck,
For manners, you know, lek knowin his way,
But just the same lek meanin to say—
For all he thinks hisself that clever—
"The ould chap's gettin wuss till ever !"

Well, there he was, so in comes a lad,
And—"It's Captain Tom that's got her," he said—
Aw, the poor Ballachrink !   "You sniffikin falla !" [2]
(You could ha heard him up at Ballasalla)
"You blockit !" he says ; "how dar ye !" he says ;
"Ger urro that !" [3] and quivers the fist—
Aw, the chap made tracks—And—"I must, I must !"
Says the Ballachrink, "or else I'll bust."
And he laughed and he laughed—and "Keep her so !"
And—"Certainly ! but knowin, you know !"
And the laugh—But it wasn long before
The whole mob-beg [4] was outside of the door,
And no mistake, and "Hip Hooraa !
It's Captain Tom—where's ould Dadaa ?" [5]

[1] Pretending.   [2] Insignificant fellow.   [3] Get out of that.
[4] Little mob ; mob of boys.   [5] Dad.

Meanin the Ballachrink—the fond
He was of the childher; and—" *Where was he gone ?* "
And—" Hurroose ! " Aw, bless ye ! no respeck
At [1] these lumps of boys, aw, that's a fack !

But the Ballachrink begun to look queer,
And he gave a start, and he gave a stare ;
And Corteen's head clerk come in through the row,
And no mistake about it now—
And the Ballachrink gave a leap and a cry,
Aw, dear ! but he made the pint-joughs [2] fly,
And his hair all on end, and his mouth all frothin—
" Hugh ! " he said ; but Hugh said nothin—
" I'll go myself," he says, " this minute ;
I'll know what raison is there in it ;
What right, what dacency, what sense !
Clear the road ! I'll go at once ! "
" Aw, stay where you are ! " says the clerk ; " when a bone
Is picked, it's better to lave it alone ; "
He says, says the clerk—Aw, then the fury—
You never—Herod, King of Jewry,
With all his tantrims, couldn touch him !
" *Ruch !* [3] is he ? the dirty ould fool ! I'll *ruch* him ! "
And out in the lobby, but he didn get no furdher—
" Here's ould Dadaa comin ! murdher ! murdher ! "
The people began ; and he strooghed [4] his clothes
And studdied hisself agin the post,

---

[1] On the part of.   [2] Ale mugs.
[3] Rich.   [4] Stroked, straightened.

And gave them a speech—aw, didn he though?
And this and that—and—*He'd have them to know ;*
And—*who was he ?* and—*a black disgrace,*
And a shame and a scandal to the place ;
And—" Justice ! " he says ; and—" We'll have it bynby ! " [1]
And—Captain Tom ! he wouldn deny—
But him to be captain of a schooner !
Did they think he ever worked a lunar
In his life, or heard of the lck ? not him !
And Captain Hugh that knew the trim
Of every craft that ever floated
And could work his distance ; and noted, noted !
Noted ! he said, *for the navigation—*
" God bless me ! let every man keep to his station ! "
" Hooraa ! " says the people, " that's the stick !
Give it to them ? give it to them, Dick ! "
And a hiss in his ear—" That'll do ! that'll do ! "
And turns—and there was Captain Hugh—
Like the thunder itself—and—" Draw these men
Some liquor ! " he said to the woman ; and then—
" Come ! " he says, and just like a stone—
The poor Ballachrink ! and liquor goin !
But it wasn no use—like a stone ! like a flint !
" Stand back the lot ! " and away they went.

And—" The childher ! aw, the childher though !
Aw, Hugh, good soul ! " and—*whither* [2] *or no,*
And—*it wasn his fault—now was it ? was it ?*

[1] By and by.   [2] Whether.

" Aw, the childher ! aw, the little closet !
Aw, Hugh ! " and—" You promised ! yes ! you did !
Aw, let me see the craythurs in bed ! "
And cryin—bless ye ! Wasn Billy Fauldher
Sheltrin behind a yawl there ?
And didn he hear ? and fit to split—
But I'd be thinkin it was rather a bit
Sorrowful lek—but all depandin [1]—
And he wouldn go on ; and he kept him standin
Agin the boat—and—" Do la ! [2] do ! "
" You're far too drunk to-night," says Hugh.
" No ! no ! " he says ; " just look at me then !
The sober I am is astonishin ! "
And coaxed and coaxed, and—*the careful he'd be !*
Till at last the Captain said he'd see.
" In bed ! in bed ! aw, honour bright ! "
Says the Ballachrink ; " All right ! all right,"
Says Captain Hugh ; " And you'll get them to say
Their little prayers though anyway—
Yes ! yes ! aw, Hughie ! the little prayers !
Aw, whose is God listnin to, if it isn theirs ?
Bless father and mother (the little birds !)
And Uncle Edward ! isn them the words ?
Eh ? Hughie, eh ? aw, the lovely things !
Like angels, lek tuckin their little wings
Under their shirts, and the hands it's lekly [3]
Goin claspin [4] there ! aw, let's start directly !

---

[1] Depending (on circumstances).　　[2] Interjection.
[3] Likely.　　　　[4] Clasping.

Come, Hughie!"   "The dhrunk ye are to be sure!"
Says Hugh; and so they come to the door.
And they axed for a light, and it's up they'd go;
But the mistress didn half like it, ye know,
Deed she didn—and *What sort of a state*
Was that to be comin, and couldn they wait
Till the mornin—and the childher fast—
And it was reglar out of all order it was—
Yes! And she did objeck, she did,
And they'd better take and be off to bed
Theirselves.   And—" As for that sot," says she;
" Aye, woman?   Is it erluding to me
You are?" says the Ballachrink, "now is it?
Because, if a gentleman pays a visit
To his brother-in-law," he says, "he's expectin
Quite a differin way of actin—
Now look here!" he says, "I'll tell you what!
It's just the dirty temper you've got—
That's it! the dirty temper—aye!
Aw, ye needn begin to cry—
You're the talk o' the town," he says, "with your tongue!
Capers!"[1] he says; "and you're not so young
But you might have some sense," he says, "with it too!"
" Hould your jaw!" says Captain Hugh—
"'The light!" he says; "I mean to have it!
The light! the light!" and the woman gave it;
And the brat[2] to her face, and followed them there,
And sobbin lek, and up the stair—

---

[1] Nonsense.   [2] Apron.

And freckened[1] of fire, and stood outside
The door—the soul! and cried, and cried.

So these two divils in to the childher—
And a little boy, and a little gel there—
Aw, beautiful! as white as snow—
The very best of calico!
Bless ye! there wasn no houldin[2] them chaps!
And the little frills around their caps
And all—aw, they'd have it! aw, 'deed they would!
They'd have it, and they'd have it good.
And three bedrooms there, and all with ceilins!
Money! bless ye! like priddha[3] peelins!
Aw, square was square, and round was round,
And Castletown was Castletown
Them times—aw, it's there the money was made—
Hapes! man; hapes! my word! the trade!

So the Ballachrink made a run and a dart,
And the little things wakened with a start—
And the big man there! and his face as red!
And the hair goin flyin about his head!
And slobberin, you know—but seein the father—
Aw, he was for atin them altogether,
Clane devourin—"Aw, dear! the soft!
The lovely!" he says—"Hands off! hands off!"
Says Captain Hugh—"Aw, just a touch!
Aw, one little foot! aw, it isn much!"

---

[1] Afraid. [2] They couldn't be held, or restrained. [3] Potato.

"No! no!" says Hugh; "Keep against that wall!"
The women, ye see, was tellin all—
Knowin! God bless ye! Peggy Shimmin!
What *ar'n* they knowin? catch the women!

So the Ballachrink got quite,[1] they were sayin,
Humble lek, and didn complain,
Nor nothin—but "The little prayer," he says,
"And the little hymn, and the little vess[2]—
Blessed Jesus! strong to save!"
Aye! but he promised he'd behave.
So then these little things was riss,[3]
And put on their knees agin the chiss;[4]
And "Our Father" they said though, very nice,
But rather trimblin with their little vice;
And then they rose the hymn—aw, dear!
Like little robin-redbreasts there—
Aw, the Ballachrink was done complate,
And he cried and cried most desperate,
Puttin them out, you'll understand;
And then these little mossels began,
And cried treminjus; and the mother couldn
    hould
Any longer, and she come in, poor soul!
And there was Ned, and the tears goin splatch,
Like the rain is drippin off the thatch:
But Hugh was turned away, and he stood,
And his face was fixed on the risin flood;

---

[1] Quiet.   [2] Verse.   [3] Raised.   [4] Chest.

And a scran [1] of a moon hung dead in the south,
And never a word from either man's mouth,
But—"Jean myghin orrin, peccee hric"[2]—
The Ballachrink was groanin—aye !
Lek you'd be know'n, if you could understand him,
For the Lord to have mercy lek upon him—
Just so—And "It's not much *myghin* [3] you'll get,"
Says the sisther, and hushed the childher a bit—
"*Myghin* indeed !"   But then she thought
He was her brother, and the ould spot,
And the times, you see, when they were young ;
And she checked the anger on her tongue,
And she went and put her hand on his shouldher,
And she saw the man the way he looked ouldher
And broken lek, and "Look up !" she said,
"Look up man, Edward ! be comforted !
And come down stairs with me, man, come !
And warm, and then you'll be goin home !"
"Aw, no !" he says, "I like this place—
There's a dale of pace,[4] a dale of pace
Here," he says ; but she coaxed him though,
And coaxed, and got him persuaded to go,
And sat a bit, but didn spake ;
And then the woman got him to take
A basin of milk to steady him,
And took and led him across the strame,

---

[1] Scrap (properly of a cheese).
[2] Lord have mercy upon us, miserable sinners.—*Litany*.
[3] Mercy.   [4] Peace.

And into the town and very quite,
And got the hoss, and home with him straight.

So you'll be thinkin? not a bit of it !
Bad blood ! bad blood ! and they couldn get quit of it.
For whatever you might do or say,
You know what was Hugh, so that's the way.
Bad blood ! I tell you.   And you'll aisy suppose
Whenever the *Clyps* was showin her nose—
Why, bless ye ! the very first trip that was arrer [1]
Captain Hugh was waitin for her
Aback o' Langlish ;[2] and the two of them,
The smack and the schooner in ballast trim ;
Aw, he gave her a dustin—and raison he would,[3]
Just a dead beat at them all the road—
Aw, she could have given the schooner 'crase,[4]
Mortal slippy in her stays
Was yandhar smack—the *Mona's Pride*
They were callin her, and built at Boyd
The same as the *Clyps*, but a dale more spring,
With the worked,[5] you know, and everything
Like shuttles runnin ; but new or ould,
A smack with a schooner ! bless my sowl !

So it was allis racin after that,
Racin, racin, for he wouldn be beat :
Blow high, blow low ; come fire, come thunder,

---

[1] At her, she had.   [2] Langness.   [3] Good reason he should.
[4] Increase, start.   [5] On account of having been worked so much.

Everything she could shiver under—
Sky-rakers, moon-scrapers—
And talk about them in the papers.
And he'd be hidin there with his topsail low'rt [1]
In Dreshwick somewhere, or under the Fort;
And Captain Tom 'd be lyin to,
To see would he go ahead, you know;
But the fo'sil 'd be over like a shot,
And he'd wait; and it's wuss and wuss he got,
Stickin to Captain Tom like a leech,
And they never come to no manner of speech
About it at all—Captain Tom would have lekt, [2]
But Hugh—well, now, you could hardly expect.

Then the Ballachrink got a notion, you see,
It was his duty to look after the family
When Hugh was away—aw, terrible big!
And he'd come and he'd sit outside in the gig,
And call to the sisther; and—for her *to look smart*—
And—this and that—and—" Bless my heart !"
And—" Look here !" and—*did she understand?*
And—*mind she wasn extravagan !*
And—" hould this hoss !" and *he'd have a look;*
And—*was she puttin everythin in a book ?*
And in with him there; and piffin and puffin,
And op'nin the cupboard, and sniffin and snuffin;
And—" Very well !" he'd say, " but you see
Of coorse your husband is lookin to me !"

----

[1] Lowered.   [2] Liked.

And up the stair, and eyein about him.
It's a wonder to me she didn clout him;
But no! she didn, but held the hoss—
A patient craythur if ever there was.

One day he come, and spades and picks,
And the man-servant with him, and—*They were goin to fix
The garden*, he said; and—what did they do
But took and divided the garden in two
With a lump of[1] a hedge? so the women said—
"Whatever!" "I'll tell ye *whatever*," says Ned:
"The *whatever*—it's a sundherin,"
He said, "a separationin!
Come now! that's the whatever!" says he.
Says the women—"Where's your 'torrity?"[2]
"'Torrity!" says Ned, "aw, dear!
Is it 'torrity?" he says, "look here!
Whose writin is that—eh? Chapter and vess!
I think you'd better go in," he says.
And sure enough he had the letter
From Captain Hugh: so says he, "You'd better
Go in," says the Ballachrink, "and mind
Your business," he says; and the women cryin,
But went; and the hedge was finished grand—
Separationin! bless the man!

So that's what Captain Hugh wanted,
And a fuss-rate job, and quicksets planted

---

[1] Good-sized.   [2] Authority.

By the time he come home—and the Ballachrink
To show him all; and—"See that sink!"
He says, "and the barrel there agen¹ it!
See the splendid brass tap that's in it
This side!" he says, "to share the water!
Aw, dear!" he says, "look at yandhar daughter
Of Captain Tom's," he says, "she's smilin!
Imprince!" he says; but Hugh was silen'.
But the Ballachrink was cock of the walk,
And swellin the breast, and workin the talk—
And wheelin the pipe, and pintin to this,
And pintin to that—and—"It isn amiss!"
And—"Take that handle! turn that tap!
Sherwood's best! I wouldn give a rap
For your rubbidge," he says; "just feel that movemen'!"
He says, "chut! a terrible improvemen'
Altogether, you know! aw, dear!"
And in to get a drop of beer.

And sure enough it was Annie they seen,
That was standin there with Bella Corteen,
A grand-daughter of the owner's—aye!
Aw, a reglar lady! but noways high—
Very gennal,² aw, reglar frens!³
She's married to a pazon since—
Yes—and indeed it's smilin she was
Was Annie; and she had a cause;
For she loved her uncle—the sort of a man

---

¹ Against.   ² Kindly.   ³ Friends.

That women 'd love, and not understand
What for were they lovin—the deep, I suppose,
And the dark, and the strong—but, goodness knows!
An uncle anyway—and the poor little woman!
Smilin—eh? and Hughie comin!
And 'deed he was entrin on the door
That very minute, and happy thallure;[1]
And out in the garden; and gave a run,
And over the hedge like the shot of a gun,
Hardly mindin the lek was in[2]—
But the Ballachrink was noticin,
Watchin there, cocked up in the windher;
And he turns, and "Hulloah!" and "Did ye see yandher?"
He says to Hugh—"You'll jump it, will ye?
Jumpin! jumpin, is it, my gillya?[3]
But for all the jumpin, if I was you,
I'd teach him——" "Drop it! drop it!" says Hugh;
And he turned, and he looked at a picture though
Of the wife afore they were married, you know.
And he looked very long, and then he went
And kissed her there; and then he leant
The head of him against the chimbley;
And then the wife come, very thrimbly,
Very lovin and gentle lek;
And she put her arm around his neck;
And you could see by the way his shouldhers was hove
The terrible the strong man strove—
And never a word! never a word!

[1] Enough.   [2] Noticing its existence.   [3] Lad.

But the woman was prayin to the Lord
In her heart, poor soul! fit enough to break—
Aw, bless them! bless them! bless the lek!
And the Ballachrink could only stare,
And got up, and took and left them there.

    And the hedge—aw, well it was left to stand;
But what d'ye think these sweethearts planned?
Hughie that schamed it—They took and sowed
A passil of plants that as soon as they growed
'd creep over the hedge, and mix the flowers—
And Hughie was settin convolvolars,
And Annie was setting these—what's their name?
Painted ladies! aye, the same—
Like butterflies mostly—lovely things,
With their little curly catchy strings!
"So you see," says Hughie, "whatever there 'll be,
These flowers 'll be standin for you and me;
And they 'all be twisted together," he says,
"And beathin in one another's face.
And when I'm far away, little gel!
There they 'll be whisprin and snugglin still,
Coortin there till the mornin light—
Aw, the hard it is to say good-night!
Aw, Annie——" But bless me! what am I at?
Well—of coorse their talk would be somethin like
    that—
Just fancyin lek—aw, I wouldn say knowin;
But I'll be bail there was kisses goin.

So when these flowers begun to grow,
They said you never seen the show!
Astonishin the strenth! like clover!
And the hedge goin cov'rin[1] over and over!
And little Annie 'd come and listen,
And settin two of them a-kissin—
And a notion at her[2] she heard them ringin,
Like a sort of a cling-a-ling-a-lingin,
Like a weddin, you know—and she'd take and kiss them
Herself, the little bogh![3] and she'd bless them;
And she'd coo upon them like a little dove,
And all in a wonderment of love—
Longin, you know—the little honey!
Aw, dear, the sweet they are and the funny
With their little ways—aw, they're very nice,
Aw, yes they are.   But she heard a vice,
And who was there but poor ould Ned—
And—" This place is goin to ruin," he said;
" It's altogether goin to ruin—
What's these painted-ladies[4] doin?
I see!" he says—" from the other side:
I'll larn ye," he says, " I'll tame your pride!
I'll make you know your place, ye trash!"
And out with the knife, and he gave a slash—
And—" Uncle! uncle!"—poor little Annie!
" Aw, don't then! don't then!" " *Don't!* your grannie!"
Says the Ballachrink—" I've a very great mind"—

---

[1] Getting covered.   [2] In her mind.
[3] Poor (little thing).   [4] Sweet peas.

"Aw, uncle, be kind! aw, uncle, be kind!
Lave them, uncle! lave them; will ye?"—
"Very like a trespass, I can tell ye"—
Says the Ballachrink—"indeed it is!"
But, however, he'd consider the case;
But didn do nothin—just puffin and blowin—
And so the flowers was left alone.

It was maybe a twelvemonth after that
Captain Hugh come in with a flat
That he took in tow—I forget her name—
And everybody praisin him.
But the people said he was terrible queer,
Heavier and silenter
Till[1] ever, they said; and takin no joy
Of anythin; and the light in his eye
Like a turf, like smouldhrin in a pit;
And there's plenty said he wasn fit
To be in charge of a vessel at all;
But howsomedever they hadn no call,
And it wasn no business of theirs—but still
Somebody ought to be 'sponsible.

So the very next tide he was settin sail
For Liverpool; and Billy Quayle,
That was used to work for him, took to his bed;
He didn like his looks, he said—
Just 'scusin; and, behould ye, though,

---

[1] Than.

The Ballachrink took a notion to go—
Knowin about a vessel? not a cent!
But took a notion, and off he went.
And the son, young Hughie, was servin mate,
Just the three: and, of coorse, the consate
Of the Ballachrink—and criticisin
Terr'ble, you know, and the big advisin,
And all to that—but you know the man,
Cacklin there like an ould hen
All the way—and a beautiful scamper
Before the wind; and the best o' temper
Comin up the river; and the way he was drast,[1]
And the style altogether—there was people ast[2]
"Who's your passenger!" 'deed they done[3]
And the 'spectable—astonishin!
That's what they were sayin comin up the river—
Aw, a credit to any vessel whatever!
Just lek a Pazon—aw, the coat as black,
And his hands in the tails behind his back
As tight—and the sate of his trousis showin
The tasty, every step he was goin—
For the thieves you know, bein warned that
     way—
Aw, bless ye, whatever ye may say,
The biggest man on the Prince's pier
And Maddharell's and everywhere—
Aw, the Ballachrink was the man that could—
Aw! bless ye! it was in the blood!

[1] Dressed.   [2] Asked.   [3] Did.

I was over there myself that time,
Just a running job with a cargo of lime
For Jefferson's; and the *Clyps* was moored
Alongside of us; so I jumps aboard,
And axed them were they wantin a man,
And glad enough of an extra hand,
So ships like a shot, and out of the basin
That tide—and the schooner, the trim for racin
She was in! but never a notion arr[1] us
That Captain Hugh was waitin for us
Just outside the Bell bwee;[2]
But, however, there he was, you see;
And every stitch, and more prepar'd,
And riggin out a stunsil yard
Like a fishin-rod goin slingin across;
But, bless me, the deep in the water she was!
"She'll never carry that canvas," says I :
Didn I see her high and dry
In the harbour only a week afore,
And noticin the strained and the wore
She was in the bottom—and natheral—
Nothin done to the boat at all
For years—*and whatever was he at!*
Draggin, draggin her like that!

So he got the wind of us, you know;
"Let's give him a hate!"[3] says Billy Crow,
That was at the helm—"let's give him pepper!"

[1] At us, in our minds.   [2] Buoy.   [3] Heat, race.

"Aisy! aisy!" says the skipper;
"Aisy," says Captain Tom, "my lad!
Just keep an eye on him," he said.
Then says Billy—"He started sooner"—
"Silence! silence aboard this schooner!"
Says Captain Tom; and a look at the clouds,
And twists his arm in the weather shrouds;
And keeps his glass on the *Mona's Pride*—
"Silence!" terrible dignified!
Aw, he could be that, for all
The hearty he was in general.

So on we went, but keepin a view of them,
And maybe a mile betwix the two of them.
How was the wind?   A leadin wind,
And very little of it to begin—
Hardly a list to it,[1] bless your sowl—
But about mid-channel a long dead rowl
Come up from the South; and far away
A white mist creepin over the say,
Creepin, creepin, the dirty thief,
Creepin—"All hands stand by to reef!"
Says Captain Tom; and reef we did—
"Get out your storm-jib! quick!" he said—
All right! and then by gough it come
With a rip and a roar, and a hiss and a hum—
Bizzz—and the schooner lept her lenth,
And if there 'd been another brenth[2]

---

[1] Hardly enough to make her lie over.   [2] Breadth.

Of canvas out, it isn here
I'd ha' been to tell ye, never fear!
Rip-rip-rip—you know the scranch[1] of it,
And into the hatches, every inch of it!
But come to her bearins beautiful,
And shakes herself, and away like a gull.

And what was the *Mona's Pride* about?
Anythin off her? not a clout!
Every stitch—and the green-seas flyin
Over her cross-trees, and never a sign
To shorten sail; but—*on you go!*
Slash her through it! keep her so!
And us that was sailin as light as light,
And humourin, and only right;
And Captain Hugh with his broadside to 't,
Reglar buryin the boat.
"Well, that's no sailin!" says Dicky Homm,
That was mate o' the *Clyps*; but Captain Tom
Kep his eye upon her strick,[2]
For the free she was sailed she was bearin quick
Upon us, you know, as if she meant
To overhaul us, and make a slant
Across our bows; and every man
On the schooner with a coil in his hand,
For any minute they were knowin
The smack might foundher like a stone.

And Hughie was tellin us, you know,

[1] Onomatopoetic.   [2] Strictly.

That the Captain tould him to go below.
"Father! father!" says the son,
"Take somethin off her, or we'll be done!
For God's sake, father!"—and he made a spring
To the weather halyards—"Touch a thing,"
Says Captain Hugh, "and I'll strike you dead!
You coward! say your prayers," he said.
"Look here! look here!" says the Ballachrink;
"If you'll go on like that, she's bound to sink!
You're mad!" he said, and out's with his knife—
"Villyan! villyan!! for your life,"
Says the Captain—"Villyan!" and struck him full,
And down on the combins [1] like a bull—
And a lurch and a rowl, and a shake and a shiver,
And the Ballachrink was gone for ever.
"Father! father! you've murdered him!"
And he looked, but the Captain's eye was dim,
Like wakin from sleep, and he gave a yawn,
And—"Hulloah!" he says, "hulloah! that's one!"
Then Hughie drew a long long breath,
And gripped him there for life or death—
The despard [2] grip; and the tiller dropt,
And the smack flew up, and the fo'sail flopt,
And took aback immadient,
And all sheets fast, and down she went.

"Stand by!" says Captain Tom, "stand by!
Listen if you'll hear a cry!

---

[1] Covering of the hatch.   [2] Desperate.

Look out!" he says; and it wasn long
Afore we saw Hughie swimmin strong,
And heaves him a line, and hauls him in
Like a shot, and—"Where's your father, then?"
Says the Captain, but Hughie couldn spake;
And the whole of us strainin our eyes on the wake.
But Billy Crow that seen him fuss,[1]
Driftin right under our stern he was,
Driftin lyin on his back—
"About! about on the other tack!"
Says Captain Tom, and heaves a rope—
But he didn look at it—"More scope! more scope!"[2]
Says the chaps, "Hould on! my gough! you'll lose him!
Noose him! Captain, noose him! noose him!"
And the noose went flyin over his head—
"Studdy! studdy!" the Captain said.
But he turned on his face, and he slipped his neck—
"For God's sake, Hugh! for Esther's sake!"
"Father, father!" says Hughie, "try!"
Then the two clenched fists went up to the sky—
"Never!" he says; and a big sea tore
Right over him with a race and a roar
Like a thousand guns, and just a minute
We saw the black head wrigglin in it—
And round and round—aw, it's thrue! it's thrue!
And that was the last of Captain Hugh.

Aw, it's an ugly job to be comin

1 First.   2 Line.

Home with news like that to a woman—
And the way she'll look, and the way she'll sob—
Aw, bless my heart ! it's an ugly job—
And the childher wondrin, and no help in for it,
And questions axin—aw, it's horrit !
And poor Annie, you know, and the fond she was
Of Uncle Hugh ; but lost is lost,
And that's a fact, and, do what you will,
The world must go on, and its good and its ill—
So married the chap, and what 'd prevent her ?
Married him that very winter—
Aye—and a nice little lump of jink—
Wasn she heiress to the Ballachrink ?
Aw, a beautiful proppity,
And no mistake, and so you see—
But of coorse—and love it was ! aw, yes !
But still whatever was hers was his—
Aw, married—and the very weddin day
Yandhar hedge was took away—
And the place where it stood they put a row
Of lilies, crocusars, you know,
Polyanthers—and every thing
That's comin up early in the spring—
Makin a garden very bright—
And so I think I'll say good-night.

IV

TOMMY BIG-EYES

I NEVER knew a man in my life
That had such a darling little wife
As a chap they were callin Tommy Gellin;
So how he got her is worth the tellin.

Now Tommy was as shy as a bird:
"Yes" or "No" was the only word
You'd get from Tommy.   So every monkey
Thought poor Tommy was a donkey.
But—bless your sowl!—lave Tommy alone!
He'd got a stunnin head of his own;
And his copies just like copper-plate,
And he'd set to work and cover a slate
Before the rest had done a sum:
But you'd really have thought the fellow was dumb—
He was that silent and bashful, you know;
Not a fool—not him—but lookin so.
Ugly he was, most desperate,

For all the world like a suckin skate.
But the eyes! the eyes! Why—blow the fella!
He could spread them out like a rumberella—
You'd have wondered where on earth he got them
Deep dubs of blue light with the black at the bottom—
Basins of light.   But it was very seldom
You could see them like that, for he always held them
Straight on his book or whatever he had,
As if he was ashamed, poor lad!
And really they were a most awful size;
And so we were callin him "Tommy Big-eyes."

The way that chap was knocked about
Was just a scandal.   You hit him a clout
Whenever you saw him—that was the style:
Hit him once, and you'd get him to smile:
Hit him twice, and he'd drop the head;
Hommer away till you'd think he was dead.
And he'd stand like a drum, as if his skin
Was a sheep's, and made for hommerin.
Then his hair was so thick it was nice to grab it,
And pull it back like skinnin a rabbit,
Till he'd have to look up, as you may suppose;
And then you could welt him under the nose.
I do believe the cruellest fien's
In the world is a parcel of boys in their teens,
One of them stirrin up the other.
But still, for all,[1] the divil's mother

---

[1] After all.

Should have looked a little more to the way
The chap was rigged ; for it isn't fair play
To dress a lad that's goin to school
As if he was born to be a fool.
Fancy a frill around his neck !
What in the world could the woman expec' ?
And his trousers buttonin outside
Of his jacket, like these fellows that ride
At the races.   Surely, it might occur——
Well, she'd a deal to answer for.

And that's the for this Tommy had
Such girlish ways—oh, very bad !
Just give him a needle and a bit
Of calico, and there he'd sit
In a corner, as happy as a prince,
And the gels goin on with their imperince,
And—"Are you wantin a sweetheart, Tommy ?
Poor thing ! as innocent as a lammie !
They said, if you'd give him a doll he'd frock it,
But he owned to a pin-cushion in his pocket.
" *Where did he come from ?* " did ye say ?
Somewhere over Lough Molla' way ;
And a road runnin in on the opposite side,
A long sort of road that went to Kirk Bride,
And joinin together, and leadin down,
And over the bridge, and into the town ;
And about a mile, I think it will be,
On the Kirk Bride road there's a path you'll see

Betwix the brews [1] that the sheep have wore,
And a cart-track leadin to the shore ;
And a pleasant little place they're callin—
What's this it is now ?—aye, " The Vollin "—
And a little house, and a garden to't,
And a little croft, and a mackarel boat,
And some trees they've planted, but they haven't thriven,
And that's were Nelly Quine was livin.

So you see these two would be meetin there
Every mornin, rain or fair.
For, mind ye, if this Tommy was late—
And he tried to be—little Nelly would wait.
Wait she would, and pretend a nest,
In the briars, you know ; or had to rest ;
Or a pin or somethin she was losin ;
Or sittin down to put her shoes on.
Then Tommy would come, and he'd give a peep
Round the corner, and then he'd creep
Close in to the hedge, and wouldn allow
He saw her a bit, and on like a plough.
And there they'd go—you'd have split to seen them—
One on each side, and the road between them—
And little Nelly lookin, lookin ;
And this poor bashful divil hookin
The best he could.   And every turn
In the road, no matter the bend, he'd burn
With the shame ; and he'd crib himself into a O,

___
[1] Hills.

Like feelin her bearin on him, you know.
And sometimes Nelly 'd give a race,
And get before him, and look in his face,
And he'd stop as dead—and she'd give a little snigger
Of a laugh in her nose, like the click of a trigger,
And lookin under to see could she prize
His big head up with a lift of her eyes—
Botherin this chap. But when they'd be near
The school, she wasn willin they'd see her
Comin with Tommy; and she'd tuck up her clothes,
And she'd shake her hair, and away she goes;
And the little feet twinkling—ha! ha! my men!
He'd look rather sharp, would Tommy, then.

And Dick, and Nick, and all the rest of them—
Miss Nelly could plague him with the best of them—
Indeed she could; and boo and hiss,
And put out her mouth like wantin a kiss,
And dance round him, and ask him to carry her—
" Do, Tommy! " and—*when was he goin to marry her?*
" When, Tommy! when la?"[1] just bewild'rin—
That's when she was with the other children.
" *Fiends* " I called them, did I? Well,
I shouldn then. It's hard to tell;
And it's likely God has got a plan
To put a spirit in a man
That's more than you can stow away
In the heart of a child. But he'll see the day

[1] Interjection.

When he'll not have a bit too much for the work
He's got to do. And the little Turk
Is good for nothin but shoutin and fightin
And carryin on ; and God delightin
To make him strong and bold and free,
And thinkin the man he's goin to be—
More beef than butter, more lean than lard ;
Hard, if you like ; but the world is hard.
You'll see a river how it dances
From rock to rock, wherever it chances—
In and out, and here and there :
A regular young divil-may-care !
But, caught in the sluice, it's another case,
And it steadies down, and it flushes the race
Very deep and strong, but still
It's not too much to work the mill.
The same with hosses—kick and bite
And winch [1] away—all right, all right !
Wait a bit, and give him his ground,
And he'll win his rider a thousand pound.
Aw dear ! aw dear ! I've had my day,
And it's a merry month is the month of May—
Little Peggies, little Annies,
Little Nellies, little Fannies—
And you with Kitty, and me with Sal,
And coortin like the deuce and all ;
And playin weddin's, and pretendin to go
To the Vicar for a licence, you know—

----

[1] Wince.

And a book, and sayin the very words—
Bless ye! as innocent as the birds!

So what did a lot of us do but join
And persuade this Tommy that Nelly Quine
Was desperate in love with him there—
And, "Spake to her, Tommy! spake to her!
Spake to her, for all!"[1] we said :
"Yes, dyin in love!"   And he hung the head
Like a clout, poor chap!   But we stuck to him still—
And "If you'll not spake, there's others that will,"
Says one of the imps.   And how she'd be blushin
When they'd tell her the bad that Tommy was wushin [2]
To be her sweetheart, but afraid to make free.
"And listen, Tommy! the plased she'll be!"
Says the imp.   Then Tommy looked up, but slow,
And the big blue eyes began to blow
Like——"Bladders" was it I was sayin?
"Rumberellas?"   Try again.
"Bubbles," was it?   What d'ye call—
"Blow'n," I said.   Just aisy all!
"Blow'n," of coorse; and the bigger the lies
The wider Tommy was spreadin the eyes.
"She said you were handsome; she said you were smart;
She said she was almost breakin her heart;"
"She called you a duck;" "She called you a dove;"
"She called you her darlin darlin love ;"
And the tasty dressed, she said she never ;

------

[1] However.   [2] Wishing.

And the splendid trousis he had however ;
And the way they were stitched, and the beautiful gimp.
"She didn !" says I. "She did !" says the imp :
And " Buck up,[1] Tommy, and bring her a present."
These imps is terrible onpleasant.

So one day Tommy took the road
The very earliest he could ;
And into the school as quite[2] as a worm,
And claps his basket under the furm[3]—
His dinner, you'd think—and waited there
Till school began ; but just in the prayer
A fellow gave a shove—worse luck !
At Tommy's basket ; and "Tuck-tuck-tuck !"
And the master stopped, and we all of us stopped ;
And "Tuck-tuck-tuck !" and out she popped—
A beautiful little hen—and she flew
This way and that way—and "*Shish !*" and "*Shoo !*"
And over the desks ; and we all gave chase,
And she flapped her wings in the master's face—
And the dignified he turned to look !
And "*Shoo !*" he says ; and "Tuck-tuck-tuck "—
And away to the window, and scratched and tore ;
And the feathers flyin. "Open that door !"
Says the master then ; and, glad to be shot of us,
So out goes the hen, and out goes the lot of us—
Helter-skelter, boys and gels—
Sticks and stones, or anything else :

[1] Take heart of grace !　　[2] Quiet.　　[3] Form.

"Catch her!"   "Watch her!"

"Stop her!"   "Drop her!"

"Here she is!"   "There she is!"

"Tommy's I'll swear she is!"

"Tommy's! Tommy's! Hop-chu-naa!"[1]

Three cheers for Tommy!—Hip-hip-hooraa!"

And a stone come flyin, and a flip and a flutter—

And down went the poor little hen in the gutter,

And her leg was broken; and "Take her up!"

And "The poor little thing!" and "Stop, then; stop!

Here's Tommy himself!"   And Tommy came,

And he stood like dumb.   "It's a dirty shame!"

Says one of the gels, and begun a-cryin.

Says an imp, " He brought her for Nelly Quine!"

And, " Nelly! for Nelly!" and took and caught her!

And, "Nelly's his sweetheart!   It's for Nelly he brought her!"

So when Tommy heard that, he stooped down low,

Like to take the hen, and the tears to flow

Most pitiful, and shivered all over—

And, " Look at him, Nelly! look at your lover! "

But Nelly sprung like a flash of light,

And her eye was set, and her face was white;

And she put her hand upon his head,

And, "Was it for me then, Tommy?" she said—

"Was it for me?"   And he snuffs and he snivels;

And, " Yes," says Tommy.   " Hooraa!" says the divils.

Then Nelly faced round like a tiger-cat—

[1] Burden of a Manx song.

"You brutes!" she said, "gerr[1] out of that!
Gerr out, you cowards!" and her face all burned
With the fury of her; and she turned,
And she took this hen that Tommy confessed,
And she coaxed it, and put it in her breast,
And kissed and kissed it over again.
"My own little hen! my own little hen!"
Says Nelly; and then she got Tommy to rise,
And took her brat[2] to wipe his eyes.
But away goes Tommy over the street
Like the very wind, and Nelly gave sheet[3]
As far as the bridge; but it wasn no use,
For Tommy could run like the very deuce—
And the hen in her arms and all, you see—
So she stood and laughed; and didn't we?
Laughed and laughed—the little midge!—
And leaned against the wall of the bridge,
And laughed again; but I'll be sworn
There was many a day after that you darn
Say much before Nelly about Tommy—no!
She wouldn't have it! Touch and go,
Was Nelly. Three words, and by jabers you'd gerrit![4]
Aw the gel, ye see, had a splendid sperrit!
Just the least little *chuck!* was enough, and then
You couldn't coax her back again.
"And why did she laugh herself"—did ye say?
"The time poor Tommy was runnin away?"
Well, everythin of coorse in raison!

<hr>

[1] Get. [2] Apron. [3] Ran. [4] Get it.

And the fool he looked, you know, was amazin.
But, even then, when she heard us behind her,
Singin out " Tally-high-ho-the-grinder!"[1]
(The *grinder!* if you know what that is !)
She turned and looked like thunder at us—
And, upon my word, there's a lot of thunder
'll go in a little noddle like yonder.
So she rolled the little hen in her brat,
And its little heart all pit-a-pat—
And as dignified as dignified—
And starts, and away with her home to Kirk Bride.
And no school for her that day nor the next—
Oh, Miss Nelly was desperate vexed !

But Tommy came the very next day—
And if he didn catch it—eh !
By gum ! *He'd make an impression,*
The master said ; and he gave him a threshin
In the good old style, with your thwickumy-thwackumy !
Slishin-slashin ! bick-o'-me-back-o'-me !
And, " Fowls !" he said. " What next ? " he said—
" Ducks and geese !"—and, " Hould up your head !"—
Pigs and geese, as like as not !
Bulls of Bashan ! You couldn tell what !
The whole of the farm ! " But, look ye here ! "
He said—and he caught him a clip on the ear—
" You insolent vagabone !" he says,
" Who's goin to see the end of this ? "

[1] Chorus of an old song.

Was it fowls ! !   Well, well ! had it really come
To fowls ! !   Why, it abslit [1] *struck him dumb,*
He said.   *Of coorse,* he said, *marbles he knew,*
And even, now and then, an apple or two :
And liked his scholars to be cheerful ;
But—fowls ! ! ! he said—*it was simply fearful !*
No, he couldn, he couldn pretend,
He really couldn, to say where would it end.
Abominable, he said, *the habits*
Of childher now-a-days !—the rabbits
And rubbish ! he said ; and " Fowls ! " he said—" Fowls ! ! "
And he lifts his voice, and reglar howls.
And the lot of us poor little blokes
Takin care to laugh at all his jokes.
Oh ! he said, *it wasn no use !*
And down came the cane like the very deuce.
By Jove ! he laid into him like greens,
Till poor Tommy was all in smithereens—
Poor little chap ! the way he was tanned !
But stood it grand ! stood it grand !

So when Nelly come back, the whole of the row
Was over, you know ; but, anyhow,
The master didn say a word
To her at all ; but of coorse she heard—
" Took and pounded him into jammy ! "
We said.   And the way she looked at Tommy !
But Tommy didn look to her.

[1] Absolutely.

Tommy kept his eyes on the floor.
But I never saw anythin beautifuller
Than Nelly's little face, and the colour
Comin and goin in her cheek;
And her eyes, that, if they didn't speak—
Well that was all. And weren't they pretty!
Yes; but now they were wells of pity—
Wells of pity, full to the brim;
And longin to coax and comfort him.
Aw, she couldn take them off him, I'll swear!
But whether this Tommy was aware
I cannot tell; for he wouldn look,
But the head of him down on the slate or the book
Like nailed; but still a way with his back,
Or his body altogether lek,
And a sort of a snugglin with his head
That showed he was a little bit comforted.

So that evening she wouldn let Tommy go home
By himself at all; but collared to 'm,
And wouldn leave him; but, step for step,
The quick or the slow, till they came to the Clip,
Where the roads divide. Then Nelly spoke—
And Tommy fit enough to choke—
And, " I'll give you a kiss," she says, " Tommy, for that "—
And she wiped her little mouth with her brat.
" Here now, Tommy!" and made a lip to 'm;
But Tommy ran; but Nelly gript him;
And Tommy turned this way, and Tommy turned that way;—

And poor little Nelly couldn tell what way—
And first cockin one ear, and then the other,
Till at last says Nelly, " Dear heart ! the bother
There's with you, too !"   And, " Turn, for all !
Turn, ye donkey ! "   But he stood like a wall ;
And whatever she did, and whatever she said,
She was forced to kiss him on the back of his head.
And then if Tommy didn cut !
But Nelly stamped the little foot—
And, " Well, I never !"—and, " Fiddlededee !"—
And, " After all, he's a fool ! " says she.

" *She was right*," you're sayin ?   Poor Tommy though !
" *Right enough ?*"   Well, I don't know——
If a chap won't take a kiss when it's gave him,
You suppose the only way is to lave him ?
Yes, I suppose so.   Aw, Nelly was furious !
But still, for all, it's very curious,
The little foot was slack enough
Before she got home, and all the huff
Washed away in bitter tears—
And as white as a sheet : and so it appears
The mother noticed.   And, *What was the matter ?*
And, " Dear me !" and clitter-clatter.

But if Nelly was sorrowful, then trust me
It was Tommy that was happy.   " She kissed me !
She did ! she did ! she did ! "   And over
The hedge, and into a field of clover,

That was very fine; and he threw himself down
In the thick of it; and never a soun
But the corn-crakes crowin very clear—
You know they're about that time of the year—
Just to be happy, you know, and think—
The little chap! And the last sweet blink
Of the day, and the big cloud sailin across—
And *oh!* he thought, *the happy he was!*
Bless ye! he's tould me many a time.
Why, this Tommy could put it in rhyme!
He was a bit of a poet, was Tommy—aye!
Aw, never say die! never say die!
A poet, I tell ye, reggilar!
And—— *The Star!* that was splendid about the star!
Of coorse, he didn make it then :
It'd ha'[1] puzzled him to do that, my men!
No, the long years after this
(But even at school he wasn amiss
With his little songs). I wouldn trust
But I've got it here—I think I must—
Wrote at Tommy. Aisy all!
That's not it. Rather small
Is Tommy's writin. Wait a bit!
" Star of Hope "—that's it! that's it!
Will you read it, Jemmy? Give him a light?
Jemmy's a scholar. All right! all right!

    Jemmy reads :—

        Star of hope, star of love,
        Did you see it from heaven above?

---

[1] It would have.

Love was sleeping, hope was fled—
Did you see what Nelly did?
I know it was only the back of my head—
But did you, did you, did you, did you,
Did you see what Nelly did?
You're my witness, star of joy!
Was it a girl that kissed a boy?
Was it a boy that kissed a girl?
Oh, happy worl'!
    I don't know!
    Let it go!
I thought I'd have died, and nobody missed me,
But Nelly has kissed me! Nelly has kissed me!

    Come down! come down!
    Put on your brightest crown!
Slip in with me among the clover.
Now tell me all about it—I'm her lover!
Did you see it? Are you sure?
Is she lovely? Is she pure?
Smell these buds! Is that her breath?
Will I love her unto death?
Ah, little star! I see you smiling there
Upon heaven's lowest stair!
    I know, I know
    It's time to go:
But I'm only waitin till you have blessed me,
For Nelly has kissed me! Nelly has kissed me.

First-rate, Jemmy! that'll do!
Capital readin! Aw, it's aisy for you.

Well, however, this Tommy fell asleep,
With the light of the stars on his face, poor sweep,

And when he awoke the night was half over,
And the star was really down in the clover.
So Tommy felt rather shiverin,
And home like the mischief, and creepin in—
Poor craythur ! and never a bite or a sup for him,
But only the father sittin up for him—
And took a stick, and gave it him hot ;
And *for-shamed* him, and sent him to bed like a shot.

But, of coorse, this was rather too much for the lad ;
So Tommy was taken very bad.
It was weeks, I believe, afore he was out,
And even then only creepin about—
And, I really can't azackly[1] explain,
But he never come to school again—
At least to ours—I don't know did they get
To hear the way the lad was beat.
But, however, he was sent to another school—
Somewhere down by the Ballagoole ;
And that would be close to his father's house,
That owned a croft and a couple of cows,
And a pig or two—aw, a dacent ould blade.
The man was a blacksmith to his trade,
And worked at it, too : at least, if he didn,
There was the smithy aback of his midden.
He was a hard man, though—very hard—
And a man that didn much regard
For the people that was over him :

---

[1] Exactly.

Pazons, churchwardens, sumners,[1] and them.
There's no doubt he was rather fond of a fight ;
But any way he'd have his right—
The commons, the quarterlands, the cess,
Intacks, easements, and all the rest.
That's the man that could rattle them off—
And only ownin this bit of a crof'.
I believe the joy of his life was to go
To a vestry meetin, and have a jaw
With the Archdeacon, that was capital
For keepin the temper ; and the louder he'd bawl,
"The bark," he'd say, "is worse than the bite of him ;"
And bore with the chap, but hated the sight of him.
That was Gellin—quarrelsome rather ;
And, anyway, he was Tommy's father.

But "Nelly ! Nelly !"—certainly !
Always after the gels, I see !
Well, I really don't think she cared a toss
About poor Tommy, how he was.
I can't say, of coorse—they're very queer—
But still for all it didn appear
She took up with any of these other chaps—
So that's the way, you know—so p'rhaps—
But dear me ! a fellow that couldn take a kiss
Just in a way of friendliness—
Well, of coorse, a chap that 'd act that funky—
She must have thought him rather a donkey—

---

[1] Officers of the Ecclesiastical Court.

P

Must, you know—a soft sort of craythur—
Aw, there's no mistake—it's only nathur—
And none of us didn say nothin to her,
And she didn stay over a quarter more,
Bein wanted at home for a baby they had,
And fish was scarce, and times was bad.

Well, after a while this Tommy was sent
To work on a farm that was called Renshent—
Jurby way, runnin out on the shore,
Somewhere aback of the Ballamoore;
And a sandy sort of a place; but still
The farm was runnin up to a hill
Slopin south : and, just when you come
On the top, the brews went down like a plumb
To the shilley [1] behind; no rocks at all,
Just clayey stuff, but as steep as a wall,
And the jackdaws workin their holes in it clever,
The divils, bein soft, you'll observe; but, however,
You know the sort of place I mean—
Snug, I can tell ye—Archie Cain
They were callin the farmer—but come with the wife;
But what's the odds! dear bless my life !
Fairish plough-land—couldn be beat,
I've heard, for turmits—a little wet
In the bottom, no doubt, a sort of a gaery,[2]
But splendid for geese; not much of a dairy—
Well, you wouldn expeck—just enough that would do

---

[1] Shingle.   [2] Waste.

For themselves—a nice little meadow or two—
But it paid them well—that gaery piece—
As round as bollans![1] tremenjis geese !

Oh, I knew Renshent—and a beautiful garden—
Bless me! wasn Cain a warden ?
And a round of trees, if it's trees you'd call them,
For, the way the salt of the wind 'll scald them
Over there, they're rather like bushes—
But still, for all, these lumps of [2] thrushes
Of a summer's everin, and the way they'd be shoutin
After the sun, as if they were doubtin
Would he ever come back to them again—
And, "Be sure! be sure!" you'd think they were sayin—
Rum things is birds though—yes, indeed—
Astonishin the places they'll breed—
Very curious that way—
Fanciful I call them—eh ?
Fanciful—Dear me! the dub
That was there for the ducks, and a sort of scrub
Of jenny-nettles [3] and that, where the hens
Was layin on the sly, in the lee of the fence
That ran by the gable ; and a splendid old trammon [4]
For the fairies.[4] But, bless my soul! what gammon !
As if it was any odds to you—
But, ye see, I like them places, I do.

---

[1] A round-shaped sea-fish.   [2] Fine big.   [3] Nettles.
[4] Elder tree, planted at the gable of a Manx house as a protection
against fairies.

However, this Cain had a very nice spot of it—
About a hundred acres 'd be the lot of it.

So Tommy was put to Renshent all right,
And ould Gellin had a desp'rate fight
About the wages, and all the rest of it;
And I don't know which of the two had the best of it—
But of coorse *he'd have a understandin*,
And a row, if it was only to keep his hand in.
But Cain was his match; so, with a deal of bother,
They settled it betwix them some way or another.
And Tommy made a fuss-rate servant—
" Diligent in business, fervent
In spirit "—it's sayin in the Bible—eh?
There's no doubt that Tommy earned his pay—
Aye did he—earned it to the full:
For, ye see, the chap was as strong as a bull,
And handier till men that was twice his size,
And uncommon watchful, and willin, and wise.

Well, now, this Tommy, after a bit,
Got to be a terr'ble favourite
With the misthress there, that was one of the sweetest
Women you ever, about the completest
Every way a woman *should* be—
I don't think a better woman *could* be—
For patience, for gentleness, and that—
She was one of the Shimmins of Ballarat—
They were all of them nice—aw a capital strain !

But the nicest of all was Missis Cain.
And she took to Tommy very much,
For, you know, there wasn the smallest touch
Of divilment in Tommy—no !
But all the other road, and so
The woman was feelin quite at her aise with him,
She said *he had such studdy ways with him.*
For there's some of these country lads is rough,
And cheeky, and impudent enough ;
And carryin on with the gels, and slinkin
Off to the public-house, and drinkin,
And stayin out without any leave,
And not the smallest notion how to behave.

But Missis Cain was a woman that 'd be
Always for order and decency.
She wasn strict, so much to speak,
But pitiful, and lovin, and meek :
And when that woman was in a place
You'd think there couldn be nothin but peace—
It seemed to breathe from her very skin—
The pure and white astonishin !
She wasn a stirrin woman at all,
Nor given to scouldin, and hadn no call ;
For the woman had only just to sit
In any room, and you'd see it lit
With a soft sweet light, that was just the holy
She looked, and the pure ; and all sin and folly
And dirt, and evil talk, was driven

From her; and her smile was like an angel in heaven.
Do you believe, if a picture of Christ was hung
Somewhere, that a fellow could do what was wrong
Before it at all? I don't think he would.
But we're tould these Romans——but what's the good?
God knows the heart; and I don't like to be sayin
Too much, you know; but Missis Cain—
Dear me! it's no use! wasn she a Shimmin
Of Ballarat?—most splendid women!

And Tommy had nice ways with him, too;
Indeed, for his station, there 'd be very few
That would have such sense and manners, both;
The very way he was suppin his broth,
Missis Cain remarked (and she was right, bedad!),
Was showin the proper feelins he had.
No puffin and blowin, no stuffin and chewin,
And scroogin and nudgin, and the elbers goin
Like a shoemaker; but Tommy would dip
His spoon very delicate-like, and the lip
As tight as a puss; and no slushin and sloppin—
And, besides, the fellow knew when to be stoppin.

So that'll do—all right! all right!
Now, Missis Cain she took a delight
In Tommy—reg'lar delight it was,
The decent woman! ye see, because
She was thinkin the nice example he'd be
To all the rest of the family.
And it wasn only eating either,

But just his conduct altogether—
Modest—and when the work was done
Of an everin, and every one
Was gettin sleepy, Tommy would take
His book, and keep them all awake—
Beautiful readin—and a lovely voice,
And the gels would say it was very nice,
And listen, grand ; but the boys would be laughin,
And tryin to carry on with their chaffin :
But the gels would shame them, and then they'd be
    quiet ;
And then some of *them* would take and try it ;
And then the gels would laugh till they were shakin—
The idikkilis[1] mistakes they were makin—
And then they'd give in ; and all the while
The misthress 'd be havin a little smile—
And Tommy as happy, and explainin there—
A good-natured craythur, never fear !
And simple ; and then he'd take the book,
And a gel would look, and a boy would look,
And back into a corner, and start
A little bit of courtin—dear heart !
What harm ?—And you'd hear a kiss go *pop !*
And the misthress would be lookin up,
But no-ways cross, just a sort of surprise ;
But Tommy 'd never lift his eyes.
What was he readin ? All sorts of things—
Lives of pessons—Queens and Kings—

---

[1] Ridiculous.

Travels—history, you know—
Pilgrim's Progress—Robin Crusoe.

And Tommy had a fiddle too,
And I don't know what was there he couldn do
With yandhar [1] fiddle, the way it 'd [2] mock
Everything—it 'd crow like a cock,
It 'd hoot like a donkey, it 'd moo like a cow;
It 'd cry like a baby, it 'd grunt like a sow,
Or a thrush, or a pigeon, or a lark, or a linnet—
You'd really thought they were livin in it.
But the tunes he was playin—that was the thing
Like squeezin honey from the string;
Like milkin a fiddle—no jerks, no squeaks—
And the tears upon the misthress' cheeks.
And sometimes he'd play a dance—and what harm!
But she wouldn have it upon the farm,
The misthress wouldn—dancin, I mean—
It didn matter so much for the play'n:
But she'd often stop him, and ask would he change
To a nice slow tune, and Tommy would range
Up and down the strings, and sliddher [3]
Into the key; and then he'd feather
The bow very fine, and a sort of a hum,
Like a bee round a flower, and out it 'd come—
"Ould Robin Gray," or the "Lover's Ghost"—
That's the two she liked the most:
And the gels, that only a minute afore

---

[1] Yonder, that.   [2] It would.   [3] Slide.

Were ready to jump and clear the floor,
Sat still on the form, but onaisy though,
And terr'ble disappointed, you know.
And sometimes they'd be coaxin Tommy to take
The fiddle out in the orchard, and shake
His funny-bone over a jig or a reel—
Something to tickle a body's heel,
Says one of the gels—and "I'll give you a kiss!
Faith, I will then, Tommy!" she says:
And Tommy that blushed to the roots of his hair;
But still, he said, *no matter where,*
If the misthress wasn willing,
He wouldn—and, "Tommy, we'll give you a shillin!"
And coaxin away: but he didn regard them.
And anyway, you know, she'd have heard them.

But Cain himself? the master, you mean—
Oh, a very nice man was Cain,
Very, very—couldn be beat.
But you'll hear something more about him yet.
Cain was a "Local," you'll understand—
Yes! aw, the very head of the plan.
They said to preach he was only fair,
But you couldn touch him for a prayer—
Soundin out like a trumpet-blast;
And shockin powerful with a class.
I don't know much about their rigs,
These Methodists that has their gigs,
And travels about; but Cain preferred

To stay at home, and preach the Word
To his neighbours there. So he got to be
A sort of Apostle among them, you see,
A prince and a ruler among his people,
A tower of the truth, a reg'lar steeple
Was Cain ; and had his mortgages,
And money out at interest,
With all the *members*—isn that the name ?—
And even the chapel itself the same.
I've heard him there—a tremenjis voice—
" Rejoice ! " he'd say, " my friends, rejoice ! "
And up the high you couldn think,
And up, and up—but afore you could wink,
Down like a gannet, like he wanted to pin
The divil in soundin's ![1] and then he'd begin,
And he'd wrestle and groan, and he'd thump and he'd
　　　thwack—
A black-haired man, and his eyes was black.

So he says one day to Tommy at last—
" You seem to have gifts with that fiddle," he says,
And he flattens his hand like a dab of mortar
On the little chap's shoulder, and a kind of a sorter [2]
Lookin far off—" Now, gifts, my friend,
Is from the Lord, that knows where to send
His gifts," he says ; " and so you see,
They must be used accordantly,"
And a little pat, and the lift of the eye,

---

[1] Shallow water.　　　　　[2] Sort of.

Like talkin to somebody twelve foot high.
I was there myself, and listenin to'm ;
For almost every time I come home
I'd be out, bein allis in a friendly way with them,
And takin joy,[1] and havin my tay with them—
Well, of course, there was gels there too—
But look here ! confound it ! what's that to you ?
" Now," he says, "this fiddle here
Is very pleasant to the carnal ear,
To the ear of sense, that's aisy plaised,
But them that's got their affections raised,
How is it with them ?" and his voice quite holler,
And took a hitch in Tommy's collar,
That was restless rather, and studdied him
Like a little sack—" How is it with them ?"
And a twist with his knuckle, and "the aisy yoke,"
He says, and Tommy fit to choke,
Till at last the misthress said, rather fearful,
She thought the fiddle was very cheerful
And nice, and makin people happy.
Oh, he turned upon her as snappy as snappy—
"Who asked your opinion ?   It's unbecomin,"
He says, " It's clane again [2] Paul for a woman
To talk in the church."   " But at home," she said,
" In the house, I don't see," aw, his face got as red
As the fire, aw, you never seen the complexion.
"Silence !" he said, "Subjection ! subjection !"

[1] *To take joy*, said of persons meeting after a long separation, or
unexpectedly.   [2] Against.

And then he got as peaceful lek,
"And," he says, "I've a propogicion to make,"
And Tommy stoops and Tommy shifts,
"Thomas Gelling," he says, "your gifts
Is only a snare to you, after all,
A snare," he says; "but hear the call—
Take," he says, "and dedicate
These gifts to His service; there's a handy seat
Under the pulpit," he says, "in the middle
Of the aisle," he says. "What! play the fiddle
In the chapel!" says Missis Cain; but he gave
A sweep with the hand, and "By your lave,"
He says, very dignified, "I was comin
To that," he said, "but, of course, a woman!
But never mind (a tongue on a wire!)
This fiddle may go on the back of the fire,
Or the midden, or any other place;
You'll be cultivatin the viol bass,
Of course, the proper instrument,"
He says, "and begin immadient.
We'll get it from Ramsey," he says, "you'll see;
And it'll be the chapel's property,
And paid in instalments out of the fund—
It isn very expensive they run,
These viol basses; and you'll have permission
To use it, but only on condition
You'll lead the singing. So there you have it:
And now your talent 'll be His who gave it,
And you'll be sitting in the front pew,

And God 'll be glorified in you."
And he sniffed, and Tommy said nothin whatever.
" I've no doubt," says Cain, "you'll do your endeavour;
But we're all of us wake," he says, "and you know
Where we're privileged to go,
Thomas," he says, and——on and on,
Till I thought he never would be done.
So at last I left him there in the thick of it,
For, I tell ye what, I was fairly sick of it—
A thund'rin rascal, anyhow;
But, however, you'll hear, you'll hear just now.

So, you see, this bass viol
Was sent for from Ramsey at first on trial,
Apprerbation, or whatever they call it,
And Tommy there to overhaul it,
And see was it right, and couldn take to it
At first at all, *not able to spake to it,*
He said, *like the fiddle ;* aw, longin shockin
For the fiddle, for all,[1] that was used to go cockin
On his shouldher so handy, you know, or sittin
Upon his breast like a little kitten,
Nustlin [2] there agen [3] his cheek,
And coaxin the lovely little squeak
Out of its innards, somewhere or another,
Just like a baby with the mother—
And the misthress loved to hear him like that,
It went to her soul, she couldn tell what

---

[1] However.   [2] Nestling. ·   [3] Against.

She was feelin, no, she couldn, she said,
But, *comforted*, aye, *comforted*—
And she had her troubles with yandhar man,
Poor thing! and it wasn with him they began —
No—and this Tommy delighted to plaze her.
But when he got this roarin baser,
He was put out most pitiful ;
For, however he'd screw, and however he'd pull,
And see-sawin
And Margery-Dawin,
.He'd get nothin, with all his scrapes and his scrowls,
But a sort of booin you'll hear at these owls.

So Tommy was bothered, and you see the
    raison,
For he thought it couldn do nothin but bas'in,
And hadn no notion the awkard brute
Could play as soft as any flute.
And deeper and deeper still he was goin,
And sawin the bass to the very bone,
And no music at all ; till at last the fact is
The misthress axed him to have his practice
Somewhere else.   So away to the barn
Goes Tommy with this big consarn,
Determined, I tell ye, to have it out with it ;
For he hadn the smallest bit of a doubt with it
But the tune was in it somewhere, you know.
So there he was ; and he tried the slow,
And he tried the quick ; till at last, by jing !

He come upon the tannor[1] string,
That he'd come upon many a time afore :
And ript and rapt, and tagged and tore,
And nothin—but now it was different,
Astonishin the way it went,
Whatever the touch, or whatever the turn,
Like butter comin on the churn,
When you're nearly beat—*like butter*, he was sayin,
Like butter, the soft, you'll observe, he was playin—
Like butter—Aw he worked it grand !
Like a livin thing, he said, *under his hand ;*
Like rivers of water in a thirsty land.
So Tommy ran up the string like a paper
Will run up to a kite ; aw he made her caper,
Rejisin, you know, the high he got
After yandhar basser's, aw workin it hot,
And rispin and raspin, and thrimmin and thrummin
Till the very thrashin boord was hummin.
So all the people was wondherin
Outside ; for Tommy had locked himself in.
And the boys to the door, and begun to push,
And shout, and kick : but the gels said—*hush '*
Hush ! they said, and stood like cravin,
For the sweet it was—they said it was *heaven*
Heaven ! they said ; and *to hould their noise :*
Gels is musicaller till boys—
Just so—takin a interest—
Much more easier empressed.

[1] Tenor.

So the next night Tommy began in the kitchen,
And the misthress couldn help droppin her stitchin
And starin at Tommy, the look he had,
Just like a body goin mad—
With his head thrown back, and his eyes like moons,
And his hair all ruxed,[1] and tunes and tunes.
And the lads very quiet, sittin back-o'-behind,
And the women that 'cited they couldn mind
Their wheels, lek afraid if a sound 'd be missin,
And smoothin the brat[2] a purpose to listen ;
And the tannor string as clear as a bell,
And Cain from home, and just as well.

Then Tommy was at the misthress to get her
To think that the viol-bass was better
Till the fiddle itself, *bein full of power*,
Says Tommy, *and the fiddle apt to be sour*,
And thin in the top ; but the viol, he said,
Was studdy, and sure, and keepin its head
On the small edge of nothing ; no baby, not him !
" But a fine big lusty cherubim,
That takes the half of Jacob's ladder
At a leap," he says, or—" maybe, rather,
Like a beautiful man, that loves you," he says,
" And turns your sorrows to happiness."
'Deed the misthress looked to see what he meant ;
But—innocent, bless ye ! innocent—
Hadn a notion, not him, the sowl !
Aw, as innocent as a biddhag[3] bowl !

[1] Disordered.   [2] Apron.   [3] Cream ready for churning.

But, after that, the life they led with him,
I'm tould, was shockin—must have it in bed with him,
This viol, and reachin to his nose,
And the stick of it tanglin in the clothes,
And strugglin, and gettin out on the floor,
And at it still—aw, well to be sure !
At it, I tell ye, from night to mornin ;
And the chaps that was sleepin with him gave them
    warnin ;
And Tommy had to go over the stable ;
But, if he'd been put on the top of the tower of
    Babel,
Tommy wouldn have been offended,
Just the thing for him, got on most splendid—
But terrible partikkilar ;
No ! he said, *he wouldn dar,*
He couldn ; they really must excuse him ;
No ! nothin in the world 'd induce him,
He said, to go in the chapel yet :
And Cain couldn understand him a bit ;
And very impatient ; and no wonder either—
They were runnin away with him altogether,
Them gifts, and *remindin him of Paul,*
That didn think much of them at all,
But rather bothered him, yes indeed !
Aw, there's no mistake, a troublesome breed ;
" And, for all the carryin on [1] there's about them
The church could do very well without them."

    [1] Fuss.

Q

But Tommy was firm : he said he was wantin
To see the Vicar—"what gallivantin !"
Says Cain—"The Vicar ! the Vicar ! eh ? "
"Yes," says Tommy, "he asked me to play
A piece with him, just for a trial
How the piano would work with the viol."
" It's—a very unsatisfactory sperrit ; "
Says Cain, "but, however, lerrit![1] lerrit !
Lerrit !" he said.   So Tommy went
To see the Vicar, that was well acquent
With Tommy, a wonderful aisy man
Was Pazon Croft—he was an Englishman,
But despard[2] shy, for wherever he came,
He was just like walkin in a drame—
Very white in the face.   I've heard it stated
That Pazon Croft was eddikated
In one of them big churches they've got
Over in England—*Cathedrals*—what ?
Cathedrals—aye : and, the lovely he sung,
He was put to the urgans[3] very young—
Not much like this music that's driven in
Hapes of people, but what he was livin in.
For, the finest music that ever was done
He'd hardly be knowin when it begun,
Or when it left off—just so, just so—
Havin it all inside him, you know.
And if the trees, or the stacks in the yard,
Had struck up, he'd been perfectly prepared.

---

[1] Let it (be).   [2] Desperately.   [3] Organs.

Bless me! if yandhar men had met
A quire of angels that was just let
On Snaefell[1] to practise their hosanners,
He'd ha' axed to look over a book with the tannors—
That's all. So, the first he heard
This Tommy and the fiddle, never a word,
Never a wink, as a body might say;
But, still for all, the next day
There he was, and the next, and the next,
Till Cain was gettin rather vexed—
And, *Couldn they bake on their own griddles?*[2]
And, *Well to be lookin higher than fiddles.*
So this was the Vicar. So Tommy come;
And, *If he wouldn be throublesome—*
And this and that; and, "Come in! come in!"
And down to the piano, and at it like sin;
And jingin and jangin, and bahin and bowin,
Till at last they heard the bellows blowin,
For breakfast, you know. So then they left off—
He was a single man was Pazon Croft.

So Tommy come home, and a book at him there
As big as the parish register—
Somewhere about the weight of a sack
Of potatoes, and every bit of it Back[3]—
Back! yes, Back—you don't know what I mean?
Of coorse, of coorse! Well, you see, I'll explain—

---

[1] Highest mountain in the island.
[2] Griddle, or girdle, for baking.   [3] Bach.

Tommy that was tellin me,
And showin the way, and how would it be.
Well, it's a difficult sort of music, look'ee!
Slantindicular, that is, crooky,
Up and down, in and out—
Bless me! what am I talkin about!
Complercated—heads and tails—
Scientific, that is, scales—
I don't know whether you've ever heard—
Fidgets, fuges! that's the word—
Fuges, fuges, that's what I meant—
Excellent, though, excellent!
Fidgets—good! but avast them nudges!
I'm goin to tell you what a fudge is—
Fuge—dear heart!
What a start!
Well, observe! away goes a scrap,
Just a piece of a tune, like a little chap
That runs from his mammy; but mind the row
There'll be about that chap just now!
Off he goes! but whether or not,
The mother is after him like a shot--
Run, you rascal, the fast you're able!
But she nearly nabs him at the gable;
But missin him after all: and then
He'll give her the imperince of sin:
And he'll duck and he'll dive, and he'll dodge and
     he'll dip,
And he'll make a run, and he'll give her the slip,

And back again, and turnin and mockin,
And imitatin her most shockin,
Every way she's movin, you know :
That's just the way this tune 'll go ;
Imitatin, changin, hidin,
Doublin upon itself, dividin :
And other tunes comin wantin to dance with it,
But haven't the very smallest chance with it—
It's that slippy and swivel—up, up, up !
Down, down, down ! the little pup—
Friskin, whiskin ; and then as solemn,
Like marchin in a double column,
Like a funeral : or, rather,
If you'll think of this imp, it's like the father
Comin out to give it him, and his heavy feet
Soundin like thunder on the street.
And he's caught at last, and they all sing out
Like the very mischief, and dance and shout,
And caper away there most surprisin,
And ends in a terrible rejisin.
That's Backs, that's fuges—aw that's fine—
But never mind ! never mind !

Of coorse ! of coorse !   But, however, the day
Come at last for Tommy to play
In the chapel : and they said it was raelly splendid,
But, as soon as the second hymn was ended,
Tommy went on, and it wasn no use,
On he went like the very deuce.

Fuges! aye! just so—for a part
Of the tune they'd been singin was just like a start
For one of these fudgets. So it got in his head.
And he couldn stop—and his face as red,
And his eyes like tar-barrels—only blue,
And—tuttee, tuttee, tuttee, tooh!
I lave it to your imagernation
The feelins of that congregation—
Feelins, is it? Well, I'm blest!
Tremenjers! couldn be expressed!
And first a look at one another,
And then, you know, a kind of a smother
Of a groan; and then—*hush! hush! hush! hush!*
And then a roar, and then a rush;
And Cain on his feet, and—" Hould him! I say;
Hould him! hould him! anyway;
Take the viol from him! fall him!
Lick him! kick him! smash him! maul him!"

Poor Tommy! poor Tommy! aw, Tommy was ragged,
And Tommy was shook, and Tommy was dragged,
And cast into outer darkness; there
Shall be weepin and gnashin of teeth; and I'll swear
If the preacher didn get up, and thumbed
The Bible there; and hemmed and hummed,
And them very words, or very lek them—
And—*this is the way the Lord 'd correck them,*
He said—*this unfortnit young pessin,*
No doubt, he said, *it was very disthressin;*

But here he was!' a figger-head—
Figger, I mean—what's this he said?
A lively figger, he said, *of them*
That's called—but—chosen?   No!   He came,
Like many others, bid to the weddin ;
But hed he the garment?   No, he hedn?
And put to the door, and black in the face,
And very nearly losin his place.
But Cain thought better of it, for all he grumbled ;
And he said he thought *the lad was humbled—*
And that would do.   But, whether or not,
A servant like Tommy couldn be got
Every day, so he stayed ; but he wasn
Suffered to rub a bit of rosin
On that viol again.   And indeed it was bruk [1]
That night in the row, and had to be tuk [2]
Down to Ramsey for repairs,
And if it ever came back who knows and who cares?
Anyway Tommy got over it clever,
And worked the fiddle the same as ever.

   But he'd never go to chapel again,
No, not even for Missis Cain.
Sunday morning, the very first thing,
When his porridge was supped, he'd be off on the wing
For the Curraghs [3] down—and away for hours—
Butterflies, insecks, beetles, flowers—
G'ology, botany, and such,

---

   [1] Broken.   [2] Taken.   [3] Marshy meadows.

And a book to tell him which was which;
And a bit of a glass that wasn as long
As your thumb.   But, goodness me! the strong!——
Microscope.   Hulloah! look out!
Aye, man! aye! and what do *you* know about
Microscopes?   You're took on the sudden.
Well, you know, I wish you wouldn.
But—however.   So he liked the Curraghs well,
Did Tommy; and they've got a beautiful smell,
Upon my word, them Curraghs; yes!
Even in the spring they're not amiss,
When the soft little sally[1] buds is busted,
And all the sthrames about is dusted
With the yellow meal: but—in summer!   I'm blowed!
Just before the grass is mowed—
Kirk Andreas way, St. Jude's, Lezayre—
Just lie down, no matter where,
And you'll think you're in heaven: and the stream and
    the heat
Fit to smother you, the sweet—
Splendid too, when a chap is home
From a voyage; very wholesome to'm,
Clearin the blood—astonishin
The way it exthracks the salt from the skin.

So this is where Tommy allis was hauntin—
Every mortal thing he was wantin
He could find in them meadows—wonderful land

---

[1] Willow.

For harbs! and him that could understand
The sorts, you know, and the virtue they had,
And were they good, or were they bad—
And them that was p'ison—aw, first rate;
Bless ye! the p'isons was just like mate
To Tommy, that liked to feel the strong
They were, and rowlin them on his tongue.
Well, he was curious, I tell ye—
" Look here!" he'd say, " I could take and kill ye
With a drop of this stuff!" For he'd boil it, and strain it,
And still¹ it and steam it, and draw it and drain it,
Till he'd nothin left but the very last squeeze
Of the Divil's own clout—aw, as nice as you please—
What's this he called it—"concockit?" "decockit,"
Aye, stowed away in his waistcoot pocket,
Many a time I've tould the chap
To take care for fear he'd get into a scrape
With this dirt, that nobody never can trust—
Abominable dangerous!

So, flowers springin,
Linnets singin,
Church bells ding-a-ling-a-lingin—
There was Tommy in his glory.
So, one day, I tell ye, afore he
Knew where he was—now, what d'ye think?
Nelly! Nelly! And the start and the blink
Of her bonny blue eye—like some *haythen goddess,*

¹ Distil.

Tommy was tellin; and curtseys as modest :
But dear me ! the mischief and the sauce
There'll be under all that ! and the quick little toss
Of the head ; and then—" I suppose," says she,
" You don't know me, Tommy ? "   " Know you ! " says he,
And his face all burnin like the very fire—
" Know you ! " and daren't look any higher
Than her knees.   " It's lek I've grew," she said—
" Grew ? " says Tommy, and as red as red—
" Grew ? "   " Would ye think," she said, " I'm the same
Little gel that used to answer her name
At Creer's—the same you were such a friend to—
The little gel you brought the hen to ? "
" Think ? " says Tommy, " think ! " and it all
Come over him like the burst of a squall
When the mornin lifts—" Dear me ! " she says,
" Look up ! " and he did, and he saw the dressed,
And the grew and all, and he looked around,
And—*who was he ?* and he made a bound,
And cleared the hedge, and away like a deer—
Did Nelly laugh ?   Well, I didn see her—
But—I rather think not, but—take the hint !
She was goin to church, so of coorse she went.

    But mind ye ! that was the road the gel
Had to go.   So, very well !
Where was Tommy now would ye be thinkin
The very next Sunday ? and sneakin and slinkin
Behind the very same hedge ?   Dear me !

What else ? and hid that a crow couldn see
Where he was hidin ; and as still as a block,
Still,—but felt the whiff of her frock,
And shivered, and waited till she'd pass,
And kissed the print of her foot in the grass,
And kissed, and kissed : so, of coorse, you know,
He loved her again—poor Tommy though !
Again he loved her ! it hadn died
In his heart—this love ; just stupefied
Like a fire that's slacked, like a spark in the tinder ;
Like you'll wake with the light, and jump to the winder—
Jump to the winder—she's comin ! she's comin !
I'll tell ye what ! this love is a rum 'un !

But at last poor Tommy, with all his blushes,
Got pluck, and 'd twiss [1] hisself out o' the bushes
Like a little hedgehog before her there—
A hedgehog makin up to a hare,
Rowlin—his legs were rather crookit—
And maybe flowers for her to look at,
Or tarroodeals,[2] or ladybirds—
That's coleopthars—terrible words !
Aye, but Tommy took heart of grace ;
And, the second Sunday, he looked in her face :
And the third, she didn come alone,
And Tommy gave a sort of a groan,
And cut ; and the fourth, they had a talk ;
. And the fifth, I believe they had a walk—

[1] Would twist.   [2] Devil's bulls (a kind of beetle).

Two fields or so—and left in the lurch with her
At [1] those other gels, but wouldn go to church with her—
Catch him! so she tould him how it was,
And she was come for a sarvint to the Ballaglass,
The principal house in the parish—aye—
Captain Moore—aw, terrible high—
Splendid family them Moores—
Deemsthars,[2] Clerk-of-the-Roulses,[3] brewers—
All sorts of swells, you know, that's goin,
Was belongin to the Moores—no knowin
The ould, that family; blood, man, blood!
Aw, the rael thing—from the time of the flood—
Officials, Staff-of-Government,
And all to that. So this here gent
Was countin among the first of the land,
Not rich, exactly, you'll understand:
But breedin, bless ye! There's plenty 'll cock
Their chin, but still you know the stock.

So this is where Nelly Quine was livin
For a housemaid with them. I don't know were they givin
High wages or not; but it was a sort of a place
That was very grand, for Manx at *laste*—
The people was lookin up to it uncommon—
And the misthress, you know, an Englishwoman—
And a hape of sarvints, and a sort of a style
With them altogether: and the best part of a mile

---

[1] By.   [2] Judges.   [3] Clerk of the Rolls, a Manx official.

Of plantin and that ; and a gardener (Scotch)
And a butler with a gool watch—
And bulls, and hosses, and a little laddy
With buttons runnin all over his body—
Style, you know—his name was Kelly,
So all that summer Tommy and Nelly
Was meetin in the meadows there ;
But still, for all, he didn dare
To ax her would she love him a bit,
Only they'd linger a little, and sit
Till the bell 'd be out.   And once she stayed
So long, you know, that she felt afraid
To go in at all ; and cried and cried ;
Aye, and wouldn be pacified,
And wouldn spake to him.   And Tommy said
He was very sorry—but she turned and fled
Like a pigeon (you know she could run rather fast),
And away with her to the Ballagass.

But when the winter weather come,
Mrs. Moore was keepin the sarvints at home,
And a surt of a praychin, just to shuit
Their hours, and I'm tould it's well she could do't—
For the Captain and the son, ye see,
Were at church as strick [1] as the pazon would be.
So what was Tommy to do?   Every man of ye?
What would *you* have done?   Now, one of ye !
Spake now !—Billy !—all right !   You'd *ha' gone*

----

[1] Strictly, regularly.

After dark, and had some fun
At the Ballaglass?   Well, there's a quid
For your guess!   That's just what Tommy did.
But the *fun?* is it fun? aw no, no, no!
Poor Tommy! Bless ye! if he could only go
To the house at all, it was just as much
As ever he could—aw bless ye! to touch
A thing she'd touched, a can, a besom—
It was wonderful the trifle 'd please him—
Pleasin isn the word!   He'd get it
Away with him somewhere, and coax it, and pet it,
And listen (he tould me, and I wouldn doubt it)
If there was any sound of her about it,
And put it back.   *Did he ever see her?*
Never to spake to her—*aw dear!*
Says you—why, bless ye! you don't know the fellow—
He'd ha' been turnin blue and green and yellow,
And red, and primin, and black and white,
If anybody 'd seen him and brought a light!
Fancy Tommy in the sarvints' hall
At the Ballaglass, and ould Missis Ball
That was housekeeper, and all the rest—
And Tommy lookin east and west!

No, no! but still there'd be gels about,
Bless ye! often slippin out
On the sly, and there they'd wait and they'd watch
For the signs of the boys, and lift the latch
The way no finger on earth will guide it

But a gel's, when her lad is waiting outside it.
So that was Tommy's trouble, the sowl !
The poor little mortal ! out in the cowld,
And no gel in his arms, nor him in hers,
That's better than mittens and comforters,
Out in the cowld—and cowld is bad,
But what was driving this Tommy mad
Was thinkin if Nelly was one of the crew,
And, if she was, then *who, then ? who ?*
Who was the chap ?   And he'd be creepin and creepin
All around, and peepin and peepin,
And seein her shaddher on the blind,
And very nearly out of his mind ;
And hearin a click, and 'd have to jump,
And hidin himself behind the pump ;
And gettin in the way of others that was lookin
After their *own* sweethearts, and hookin
Over into the garden, and stumblin
Against some others, and all of them grumblin—
And often chased, but never caught ;
Till at last they got freckened, for of course they thought
It was ghosts ; and—*the night was very injurious,*
Mrs. Ball was sayin : but the boys was furious,
And had a reg'lar hunt, but no use,
For Tommy would dodge them, and off with his shoes,
And away like the wind.   So the chaps was fo'ced,
As you might say, to give up the ghost.
But a terrible disappointment, it's lek,
For the Captain's gels was the very pick

Of the sarvints about—aw, splendid lasses—
Shuperior, you know, was the Ballaglasses.
So the chaps was comin from far and wide,
Sulby way, Ballaugh, Kirk Bride—
Chaps, you know, that had any consate
Of themselves, and likin to be nate
And dacent—dacent—none of your scum—
Why, light-keepers was used to come—
Light-Keepers ! yes, and eireys [1] too—
Eireys—'deed I could tell ye the who—
But still, for all, it's hardly worth—
Just the tip-top coortin on the North.[2]

    And was Nelly one of them ? No ; *and why ?*
Well, I'll tell ye the raison by and by.
But, of course, you can fancy the disthress
Of this poor little Tommy. I remember a vess[3]
Of a little song he made—let's see—
How's this it is ?—"I think of thee"?
No, that's not it—"So it's home——"—just so—
I've got it now—when he was leaving, you know—

        " So it's home to Renshent
           My weary way I wind ;
        For I must be content
           With her shadow on the blind."

On the blind, ye see. *Renshent,* that's Cain's—
All right ! all right ! I know what you manes,

---

[1] Heirs to farms.   [2] Northern division of the Island.
[3] Verse.

Yes, yes! of course, that's the tune your hummin to—
The misthress and Tommy—that's just what I'm comin to.

Well, I tould ye the way he was punishin
These beetles and things—it was raelly astonishin—
And stores and stores ; and so, if ye plaze,
He took and made a sort of a case—
And every inseck with a little hook through
And a pane in the lid for a body to look through—
For you mustn open—all hatches battened
On Tommy's decks ; and the flowers he flattened
(And still there wasn room for half)
In a big ould Bible he found on the laft.[1]
And often of an everin
The misthress would ax him to bring them in,
And Tommy would sit, and Tommy would 'splain—
And who so happy as Missis Cain ?

Aw, 'deed she was happy though, for all—
" Yes," the misthress would say, " he's small
Is Tommy," she says, " but his heart—his heart
Is big enough." *And he gave her a start
Many a time*, she said, *to see
The perfect happy he could be
With nothin, and the full of it too*—
Yes—and she liked his eyes to be blue,
She said, *it was making them so clear*—
Such room, she said, *he had in them there*—

---

[1] Loft.

Such an arch, such a spread, like the round of the sky—
No cloud, no shadow of a lie.
Some eyes, ye see, is nothin but fog,
And some is just like weak grog;
And some is like leeches, and some is like slugs,
And some is like bullets, and some is like bugs—
Muddy, some is, and some is sharp,
And some like a cod, and some like a carp—
Differin sorts.   But Tommy's was loops
Of light in light, just hoops in hoops
Of soft blue fire, and feathered about
With a kind of gray fluff, and openin out,
And out, and out—the eye of this chap—
Hoops, you know—like ye'll see a map
That's showin all the planets and things,
And the sun in the middle, and rings and rings—
No doubt you've seen the lek in a book.
So the misthress would sit, and look and look,
And give a little nod, I'm tould,
And bless this Tommy in her sowl.

Well, troubles came upon him for all—
Troubles! troubles! where's the wall
That'll keep them out?   As the Scripture saith—
Dig the foundation as deep as death:
Plumb it, and plaster it, every chop of it;
Build it to heaven and put glass on the top of it—
No go, my lads! you'll pay your fine—
And a chap that's in love should spake his mind :—

That's the thing. But this Tommy? What?

Shy? dear bless ye! But, whether or not,

He was over one night at Captain Moore's,

And watchin the windows, and watchin the doors,

And as silent as a little trout,

And a dale o' coortin all about,

And chased at [1] these divils, and couldn see her,

And into the garden, and hid himself there,

Behind the summer-house—Holy Moses!

The smotherin it was with roses,

Yandhar place; but only Spring

The time I'm tellin : but thatched with ling.

So there was Tommy aback of a bush,

When—aisy! aisy! hush, hush, hush!

Two people comin on the walk,

And the nearer they come he could hear them
    talk—

Aw—Tommy, Tommy, Tommy mine!

The young Captain, and Nelly Quine!

Aw 'deed it was! aw 'deed for sure! [2]

Nelly, and young Captain Moore—

The son—and into this arbour place,

And sat, and his arm around her waist,

And—the ould ould music, sweet and low—

Music! music! aye just so—

Whoever was the first to set it—

Music, music, wherever you'll get it.

---

[1] By.   [2] Yes indeed.

And Nelly's tears was just like rain ;
And Tommy could hear what the Captain was sayin—
" Do love me, Nelly ! do then ! do !
Aw Nelly, the same as I love you !
Nelly ! Nelly ! I am in earnest—"
If that wasn a burnin fiery furnace
For Tommy—my gracious ! he said the bite
He took of his tongue to try and keep quite,[1]
And his head goin round and round and round,
Till he thought he'd fall ; but he held his ground
And they looked so lovely ! he said—good Lord !
That's where, he said, *it come very hard*
On the leks of him—and he didn know
Whether to stay, or whether to go,
Or what to do—but, rain or fair,
Of coorse he wasn wanted there—
But—Nelly cryin—and— *Would he take her part ?*
But how ? and the cables of his heart
Goin crackin.   And then he thought, was it right
For him to be sneakin there in the night
Like a spy upon her ? for he wasn apt
To be thinkin evil, wasn this chap—
No, he wasn, and he didn now ;
But he waited till, he couldn tell how,
Nelly's head gave two little slips,
And—aw, poor Tommy ! lips to lips,
Yes, yes ! aw Tommy, my son,
You're beat ! you're beat ! the game is won !

---

[1] Quiet.

Was and wasn—and meant is meant—
But he picked up the bits of his heart, and went—
Bits! aye, bits! and a swish and a swirl
Of all his life, like the wheel of the world
Had gone over him with its lumbering load,
And left him dyin on the road—
Tommy! Tommy! But, afore he got home,
He begun to think what good could come
Of work like that—and—"She's lost! she's lost!"
And he staggered, and his head was frost
And fire in a minute, and he turned to go back,
And—"I'll save her! I'll save her!" and he looked to the
    black
Black sky, and he shouted—"Nelly!" he said,
"Nelly! Nelly!" and fell like dead.

    Aw dear! the little sowl!
And some chaps that was knockin about on the sthrowl [1]
Found him there, and picked him up,
And of coorse they thought he'd had a sup,
And home with him, and laughin and jeerin,
And up to the door, and Cain appearin
With a light, and terrible aggravated,
And—"Here's your Tommy, tossicated!" [2]
And cuts. "Indeed!" says Cain, "indeed!
The pump, I suppose," and wouldn heed
For Tommy, whatever he could say—
"Drunk," says Cain, and drags him away—
"Drunk," says Cain, "indeed!" he says,

---

  [1] Strolling, loafing.   [2] Intoxicated.

And Tommy that wake he couldn resist—
And under the very pump; but then
The misthress came, and—"Cain! aw Cain!
Cain!" she said, "aw listen, listen!
He isn drunk, he isn, he isn!
It's trouble," she says; and—"Lave him to me!"
So Cain dropped him, and—"Come," says she,
"Come in now, Tommy!" Then Tommy to ax
Could he spake to her alone? "The fac's
Is dead agen [1] ye," says Cain; "but still—
Trouble—eh? well—pozzible—
Pozzible"—and shakin the head,
And takes the candle, and off to bed.

So then it was that Tommy tould
All the secrets of his soul—
And Nelly—and how it began at Creer's,
When they were little things, and all the years
He'd loved her since; so she gave a smile,
Did the misthress, you know, and—"Dear me! child,"
She says—"that's not such a terrible case;"
And she took his hand, and she looked in his face.
"But now," says Tommy, and *where he had been*
That very night! and what he had seen!
And the way the Captain was spakin to her,—
"Captain! what Captain?" "Young Captain Moore."
"Captain! Captain!" Aw, she dropped his hand,
And the two of her own was clasped in the one,

---

[1] Against.

And pressed to her heart, like a man when he's shot,
And her face like paper, and just a blot
Of blood on her cheek, and drawin her breath
All tight and shivery through her teeth,
Tommy said—*like shot*, he said—
And, if it hadn been for Cain that was overhead,
There's no doubt, he said, she'd have sent a cry
Right up through the roof, right up through the sky—
Poor thing! to God Himself in Heaven,
But Cain was betwixt—and past eleven.

Now, what had Tommy done? You'll get lave![1]
He'd stumbled into an old grave—
Had Tommy, sent his foot through the lid
Of a coffin—that's what Tommy did—
Of a coffin, where her heart's true core
Was nailed down, stamped down for evermore.
That's what the misthress thought, it's lekly,
But I'll tell you all about it direckly.

Well, whatever it was, it was see-saw,
For a while at[2] the misthress would she hould her jaw
Altogether, or just to spake out
To Tommy at once, like a doubt in a doubt—
For to spake at all wasn aisy to her—
And to spake to Tommy—that was more.
For ould sorrows comes over you sometimes
Like ould tunes, like ould rimes,

[1] All right!   [2] In her mind.

That's runnin in your head, and makin ye
A sort of happy, and sometimes they're takin ye
Like the frost takes the whalers in the fall of the year,
And gunpowder cannot blast you clear.
And still, for all, she had to say something,
For of course this Tommy would think it a rum thing
For her to be carryin on like yandhar :
And besides—she loved him——Alexandher!
I'll throuble you to look sirrious!
Loved him—that's the way it was—
Bless ye! and isn it Natur tells us
To pour our souls into somebody else's?
And that's what she'd longed for, but hard to find ;
So never couldn make up her mind,
Part wondherin if Tommy would shuit,
But stopped at the pint, and didn do 't.
But now—what was it she wouldn dar?[1]
So she tould her saycret, so there you are!
Only just think now!   Pazons and preachers,
Pastors and masters, class-leaders and teachers,
Shuperintendans and conferences,
Archdeacons and bishops, and all their expenses
Paid.   Think of that! the whole machine
That was workin around her, or else should have been—
Priests and Levites, that was used to go
Every day to Jericho,
And back very likely—and never eyein
The craythur that lay by the roadside dyin—

---

[1] Dare.

And this little chap, that just kep in his place,
Like a dog might keep, and look up in her face,
But looks like axin her to tell—
Aye, that's it! aw well, well, well!

Now, listen! this is the way it was—
This Captain Moore, of Ballaglass,
The father, you know, when Misthress Cain
And him was young, lek the people is sayin
Young and foolish—eh? but still—
Fell in love with her terrible,
And her with him.   All right! all right!
True and honest as the light
Was Captain Moore.   But what was the good?
Think of the fam'ly! think of the blood!
First-class—you know! the very first
In the Island—the very! and that's the worst—
What for won't people be content
With their equals?   And—*The heiress of Renshent?*
I know she was, and a Ballarat—
But, bless my soul and body! what's that
When you're spakin of Moores?   It couldn be,
Moores! it couldn! don't ye see?
And they might ha' knowed it.   And of coorse the fuss
His people was makin was scandalous!
Dreadful!   And its only raison too
His love wouldn be that through-and-through
And deep and strong like the misthresses,
So that's, you see, the way it is.

And they had him away to England there—
(He'd ha' married her like a shot, never fear!
And half the parish at the weddin),
But he wasn allowed, and so he didn.
And years afore he was back—behould ye!
He married the English lady I tould ye,
So that's, you see, the way it was done,
And settled down, and had this son,
Their only child, and spoilt him rather,
And went for a Captain like his father.

So Misthress Cain—that's Shimmin, you know,
That was then—was taken uncommon low,
And wouldn ate and wouldn spake,
And gettin very thin and wake.
And it wasn no matter what they were tryin—
Aw 'deed I believe she was out of her mind,
For a while, at least.   And Parson Craine,
A rum ould chap that was vicar then,
Was axed would he come and pay her a visit.
So they tould him the way.   "A dumb divil, is it,
She's got?" and they looked!   "Aw, well, I guess
You'd better lave her alone!" he says—
Like maenin, *It's well to be rid of their talk*,
The *women*, you know.   Aw, a hearty old cock
Was Craine, I've heard, a rael ould Turk.
So then the Methodists went to work,
And the lot of them hummin about her like midges;
And got her to be a sort of religious;

Lek stupid lek, and very meek,

And had her converted in a week—

In a week she got *pace* ;[1] and rather blamin her

The slow she was, like a sort of shamin her,

Pace! Aw, 'deed, I'd aisy belave

She *had* pace ; but was it the pace of the grave?

Well, well, there's many worse places.

Pace! it's a word I'm fond of, pace is.

Pace, pace from all her woes !

Pace, pace ! God only knows—

Perfect pace—the people was say'n ;

Perfect pace——and then—comes Cain !

Yes, he come—he come from the South,[2]

And butter wouldn melt in his mouth—

Yandhar man ! And the holy, you never !

And gettin the name, you know, of the clever !

At[3] the Methodists—bless ye ! brought him over

A purpose to see would he do for a lover—

Renshent's heiress! aw dear ! they knew

Which side their bread was butterin too.

So nither way no *love* was meant ;

She got *religion* (!), and he got Renshent.

She hadn a notion, I expeck,

To have him for a husband lek

Lek husbands is, you know, but just

A guardian lek, that was put in trust

With her sowl, like a guide the Lord had given

---

[1] Peace. [2] Southern division of the Island. [3] Among.

To lead her studdy on to Heaven—
A Christian brother and a Christian sisther,
And if this Cain had ha' took and kissed her,
He'd ha' spoilt it all.   But—cautious! cautious!
Bless ye! that's the stuff that washes!
And her to tell him the whole of her story,
And hand-in-hand with him on to glory—
That's what she thought—*her foot couldn slip*
In such holy communion and fellowship.
The big Tom-cat! the smooth and the sleek
And the soft, and the whisker on his cheek
Just like blackin on a boot,
And his nice white hands, and——ough! the brute!
And—"Oh," he says, "the unselfish love!"
Renshent, you know, he was thinkin of!

Aye, Cain—so the uncle come to die—
Him she was gettin the proppity by—
And rather an awkward way he was givin it—
And so they got married, and come to live in it.
And so you'd think they'd be goin jog-jog—
Aw, bless ye! they turned a new leaf in the log
That day, they did; a leaf that was scored
With blood and misery, every word—
Death sealed it up at last, and tuk[1] it
To owners, that has never bruk[2] it,
And never will till God will sit
Upon His judgment throne—that's it.

---

[1] Took.   [2] Broken.

Well, this Cain was not content—
He'd got the woman, he'd got Renshent;
But there was one thing he hadn got,
The woman's love—he hadn got that—
The bargain! the bargain! she didn pretend—
A pious friend! a pious friend
Here below, and Heaven above—
And she shivered at the name of love.
Obey him? serve him? so she was doin;
But—*love* him? That's another tune.
She couldn, it wasn in her power:
Her love was as dead as a dead flower—
Stick it in the ground! will it grow?
Mould it! water it! just so—
Will it blossom like the rod for Aaron?
Will it bloom and blow like a rose of Sharon?
Its stalk is bruk, its leaves is shed—
Dead! she *tould* him it was dead.

But the pride of the man! the pride of the
        man!
To think he couldn get her love like land—
Rent it, or buy it, so much an acre—
That, if she wouldn love him, he couldn make her.
Make? make? make! No, you won't, my boy!
Let's have that joy! for it is a joy!
You can't! you can't! Oh, isn it glorious?
Love victorious! love victorious!
Victorious—eh! ah dear! the strength of it!

And the height and the depth and the breadth and
    the length of it
Make it—will ye? Make a woman's heart!
Scoop it, and scrape it in every part!
Send blood through its chinks, let it beat, let it
    burn,
Make what you like! make a tub, make a churn!
He was welcome to love her. But was it fair?
That's it! that's it! I have you there—
When she couldn love him, and when he knew,
Was it fair for him—I'll lave it to you—
First to sulk, and then to complain,
Then ragin fury, then sulks again,
Till he settled down in the dead sea
Of bitter hatred and cruelty?
Where was the saint that she thought would direct her
On the road to Heaven, that she thought would pro-
    tect her
Against herself, against the love
That was still in the deep of her heart, and strove
With the love of God? Where was he to lift her
Above everything on earth that could drift her
From the anchor of her sowl
Sure and steadfast, like we're tould
In Hebrews?—do ye remember the hymn?—
Jesus, lover—Say't for them, Sim!
Can he? you're foolish! is it *can he*, ye said?
Now, then, Simon, go ahead!

Simmy repeats :—

> Jesus, lover of my soul,
>   Let me to thy bosom fly,
> While the threatening billows roll,
>   While the tempest still is nigh.

One verse, that's enough, that's all we're wantin,
Just to show the way it's slantin.[1]
He could say every word. Well, you'll easy see,
He wasn the man he was seemin to be
When the misthress married him :—it was just like
     wakin
Out of a dream ; like a cloud 'd be breakin,
Like scales goin peelin off her eyes,
When she saw what he was. There's some of them dies
Directly almost, and some drags on—
But she knew the man ! she knew the man !
So that's the story she had to tell
To Tommy there—aw well, well, well !
Yes, she tould him—he didn try to stop her—
But very nice, you know, and proper—
Like shuitable for him to hear—
Aw, that was the woman ! never fear !
And—"Tommy, Tommy," says Missis Cain,
"The curse is come upon them again—
The curse ! the curse !" And—*she'd send a letter*
The very next day to Nelly, to get her
To come—and most particular.
And Tommy of course, you know, not to be there.

[1] It goes.

And so she did : so Nelly come,
And this Cain, for all, was away from home.
So ups with Nelly, and took and tould her
All about it.   She didn scould her—
No, no ! not her—but just the way
It was ; and the people had got it to say—
" What people ? " says Nelly, and the stiff she stood !
" What people ? if you'll be so good ? "
" A friend of yours," says Mrs. Cain,
" A lovin friend "—" That's the *people* you mean,"
Says Nelly, as sharp !   So she didn deny,
Didn the misthress, but fit to cry ;
For she thought this Nelly was rather hard,
For a young thing like that, and wasn prepared.
And bless ye ! maybe *a bit of a brazen,*
Thinks the misthress : but everything in its saison—
I never wasn for imprince—no !
I don't like it.   But, even so—
Dear me ! there's things—why, bless your noddy !
Musn a body stand up to a body,
When there's one body botherin at him,
And another body at the bottom—
And you don't know, but still you've a guess?
Ah ! I'll tell ye what it is—
That's hard, if you like ! your life, your love,
Your heart of hearts—and they'll take and shove
Their fist in there ! aw I know it well !
And no mistake about this gel,
No mistake ! and the pride and the pluck,

And the *touch-me-not!* look out, my buck!
Will she? won't she? what's the use?
Aye, and see ye at the deuce!
As quite as a lamb, and as bould as a ferret—
Some women's got a terr'ble sperrit.

"He loves you dearly." "Who loves me?" says Nelly,
"Who loves me?" and up with the head like a filly,
Like sniffin the wind—they're splendid craythurs
Is them, lek accordin to their nathurs,
Splendid—like sniffin—"Who loves me? who?"
So the misthress tould her. "Aw, that'll do!"
Says Nelly—and a little laugh—and she says,
"I think I'll go now, ma'am, if you plase;
If you plase, ma'am, I'll be goin, I think"—
And the misthress felt her heart go sink—
But held on, for her sowl was cravin to her,
This Nelly, the very first minute she saw her,
For she saw that she was the rael stuff,
That's it! and no matter for the huff—
Huffed! but wasn it like prent,[1]
The beautiful and the innocent?
The sweet and the true? But—whether or not—
Chut! the misthress loved her like a shot—
And *how to save her?* She seen the sowl
Was trimblin all over, for she couldn hould,
No matter the huffed—aw hard to hide!
Love is a stronger thing than pride.

[1] Print.

S

So the misthress tould her all the same
She done to Tommy, only the name
She didn tell—but *a gentleman*
That was far above her, and how it began,
And how it ended—*no doubt, for the best—*
No doubt—but oh ! the bitterness !
And " Nelly, I wouldn be tellin you this,
If I didn love you—give me a kiss !"
And *Nelly darlin !* and—*Nelly sweet !*
Then Nelly ran to the misthress' feet,
And laid her head in her lap, and flung
Her arms around her, and clung, and clung,
And sobbed and sobbed a good while—
Aw, bless ye ! what was she but a child ?
Then the misthress caught her round the neck,
And spread herself upon her lek—
Aw, Nelly herself has towld me—and she lay,
And the gathered, and sheltered, and hid away,
And nussed, and coaxed, and folded in,
She said it was just astonishin
The complete the world seemed all to go
From her lek—that she didn know
Nothin at all, but just the door
Was shut on all sorrows for evermore.

But when Nelly got a bit peacefuller,
Then the misthress sthrooghed her hair,
And reddied[1] it, and made it nice—

---

[1] Arranged.

Dear me ! the tender and the wise—
Eh ? just so ! till she brought it round
To spake about Tommy, and the way he was down
Altogether, lek low in his mind—
And *the good, and the faithful, and the kind*—
And—*any woman, no matter who,*
Might be proud to marry him ;—and "it's you !
It's you he's lovin more than his life !
Oh Nelly, couldn ye be his wife ?
Aw, try, Nelly ! aw, I think ye could—
Aw, Nelly ! there's no mistake he's good,"
But Nelly shivered in every limb—
And—"Oh ! don't talk to me about him !"
She says, "for if he's as good as gool,
He's a fool," she says, "and a stupid fool."
My word ! she was up again like fire.
But the misthress thought she wouldn try her
That way any more, but just
To pet her, and coax her, the way you must
With the lek, you know, if it's peace you're for—
Or else, you know, look out for war !
Aye—but she got her as quite [1] as quite
And then she went.   But that very night
The misthress made up her mind to spake
To Captain Moore himself, to take
Some order someway with the son—
Hard it was, but it had to be done.
And she saw the captain ; but what occurred,

[1] Quiet.

To tell ye the truth, I never heard—
Only the misthress came home very weakly,
And off with her to bed directly;
And whiter till white; and it was raelly too much—
Ould love is a dangerous thing to touch.

    But listen to me! Just a week after that
I was down at Renshent; and the whole of the lot
Sittin up all night there in the kitchen,
Afraid of the storm, that was nearly hitchin
The roof off the house—Nor-West by Nor—
Dead in, you know, upon the shore—
Great guns—and impossible for me
To get home, so stayed for company.
And Cain was there, with his face in a frown
Like thunder; but the misthress was lyin down,
They said, in the parlour; very sick—
So these boys was up to every trick,
Pretendin they had to hould the gels
For the freckened they were [1]—dear me! what else!
And snugglin up, and whisperin—
And very lovin and comfortin—
And Cain someway didn seem to be heedin,
And he had a book, but he wasn readin—
He seen them well enough, I'll be bail—
But he looked to be thinkin there a dale.
But Tommy wasn with them at all;
And so I says to Harry Phaul [2]—

---

[1] On account of their being so frightened.   [2] Son of Paul.

One of these chaps—" Where's Tommy to-night ? "
And the wink went round upon me straight,[1]
And nudgin and lookin, till one of them said—
" Haven ye heard——? " " Silence ! ye jade ! "
Says Cain, and looks at the gel like murder—
" This talk," he says, " must go no furder—
It isn accordin to your station,
And it isn to the use of edification."
So the gel gave a frump, like *dear me ?*
" Look here ! " he says, " you're talkin too free—
Yes—and very undesi'ble—
And I'll read you four chapters in the Bible
In a minute," he says, " like a shot," he says—
" Four chapters, every vess—"
Four chapters, if a finger stirred o' them !
Four chapters every word o' them !
" Silence ! I say." And he stamps the foot—
" A chatt'rin, aggravatin slut !
But this young Baynes," he says, " may ax
What has happened—I'll state the fax !
I'll state them," he says, " ye jackdaw !
And every one of ye hould your jaw !

This is the fax. Our Thomas Gellin,
For raisons best known to himself, has fell in
Love with a person they're callin Quine—
Ellen ; if I rightly mind.
Now, this gel was a sarvant in Captain Moore's,

[1] Immediately.

That should have turned her out of doors
Long ago—but, however,——this Nancy—
Nelly, I mean, takes the Captain's fancy—
The young Captain's. They'd words—all right—
Him and the father—that's Wednesday night.
Thursday—that's yesterday—Nicky Freel
Brings the captain's yacht from Peel,
And anchors her inside the bay ;
And there she was lyin the whole of the day.
At six o'clock this everin
This young pesson isn in—
Nither's the Captain—can't be found—
And then, wherever she was bound,
This yacht they're callin the *Waterwitch*
Is off to sea with every stitch—
And a woman aboord.—Well, it's nathral rather,
And, puttin two and two together,
It isn cuttin it very fine
To think this woman is Ellen Quine—
No—so the people have got it they're off
To Scotland of course, and I'm tould their craft
Is small, and very bad prepar'd—
And certainly it's blowing hard—
And Gelling—that was allis short—
Don't take his affliction the way that he ought ;
But's gone clane mad, and out on the shore,
And says he'll never come back no more—
See the carnal mind, see !
Where's his faith ? perplexin to me ! "

And when he was speakin there come a strain
That rocked the house—" It's blowin," says Cain :
" Blowin !" says I ; " she'll never live !
That thing 'll go down like an ould sieve,
If she tries her course—I know the boat ;
But she'll never show the canvas to 't ;
Her only chance is to run—d'ye hear ! "
I was gettin rather 'cited theer—
" And where'll she run to ?   I give you warnin
That vessel 'll be ashore afore mornin."

I tell ye the words were hardly gone from me
When the door burst open, and in comes Tommy—
And wet to the skin, and white as a ghost,
And his eyes all ablaze, and his voice all hoast [1]—
And—" Run !" he says, " the lot of ye, run !
She's on the Rue ! she's done ! she's done !"
" The Rue !" I says, " just so ! that's it ! "
(The Rue is a point to the westward a bit)—
The Rue—" Come along !" says I, " let's slope !"
" Get a ladder !" I says, " and plenty of rope !
Light the lanthorn ! bear a hand !"
Says Cain,—" You're quite a perfessional man !"
I raelly thought he was going to bother
About some humbuggin thing or another
Even then—but he wasn so bad as that—
'Deed he was as active as a cat,
Was Cain—and skilful, and houldin out [2]—
Under orders ? no doubt ! no doubt !

---

[1] Hoarse.   [2] Enduring.

Of course! guy heng!¹ and who was he,
To work a wreck, compared with me?
Well, I should think so! only raison!
And everybody in his saison.

The day was broke when we got to the Rue,
And there was the *Waterwitch* full in view.
She wasn on, but very near it,
Just makin her last tack to clear it:
They'd tried to anchor, but the cable went snap;
They'd tried her with the jib and a scrap
Of a mizzen, but it wouldn do—
Closer, closer to the Rue!
And, when we came upon the beach,
They were settin the mainsail reefed to the leech—
And the only chance there was for the ship—
When there came a squall, and the mast gave a rip,
And out of her, and there she was!
Roullin on like a dead hoss²—
Helpless, you know, "Stand by now, men!
She'll strike, and strike, and strike again,
Afore she'll settle"—I says; and she gave
A heel to starboard; and then a wave,
Like an elephant, took her on his back,
And in with a run, and crack—crack—crack!
And then a scrunch, the way I said,
And the *Waterwitch* had made her bed—
Fast—stuck fast in a sort of a jint

---

¹ Bless me!   ² Horse.

Betwix two rocks, that lay off the pint
About a thirty fathom or so,
And covered them ; and the tide would flow
Maybe an hour after that—
Bless ye ! like a mouse with a cat !
And the short seas herryin[1] her,
And the long seas buryin her,
And the tearin and sawin on the rocks—
You could see she was breakin up like a box.
So says I—"The work has got to be done !"
And sthrips—says Cain, "Go on, my son !"
"No !" says Tommy, "I'll go !" says he ;
"I'll go !" he says, "it's me ! it's me !"
"Look here !" says I, "just wait a second !
Look here now, Tommy ! how long do ye reckon
You'll live in that sea ?   The very first flop
Will rowl ye over like a top.
Are you wantin to get drowned ?" says I.
"If I die," he says, "I'd like to die !"
"Indeed !" I says, "aw dear ! aw dear !
Whisper, Tommy !" and I stooped to his ear—
"Whisper—patience just a bit !
Maybe you're goin to have her yet !"
Aw ! I tell ye, he was just like a lamb—
Coaxin ! that's the way I am !

So I says to the chaps—"Is any one wantin
This job ?" I says, "for it's time to be slantin."[2]

---

[1] Harrowing, tearing.   [2] Going.

Not a word—"Are ye sure now?—Right as a
   riddle!"
And I ties the rope around my middle,
And ready coiled, and how—God knows!
But I shut my eyes, and in I goes!
And wasn I divin under the says?
Divin! divin, if ye plase?
Teach your granny to suck eggs!
But it's terrible nasty about your legs
A rope like that—and payin it out
Far too free—bein willin, no doubt,
But no 'sperience, you know—hard work!
And no mistake!   There was a regular turk
Caught me half-way—my eye! what a brute!
I raelly thought I'd never get through't.
And these chaps ashore—it's worse they got—
I'd a mind to go back, and kick the lot—
But—however—what with tuggin and luggin,
And givin and takin, for all their humbuggin,
Just when I thought I had enough,
Somebody gript me by the scruff,
And afore a man could turn on his heel
I had my arms round Nicky Freel.
No time for talk!—"The stump o' the mast!
Bear a hand, Nick! make fast! make fast!"
And gives him the rope—when there come a rowl,
And a bump! and I don't know in my sowl—
But he dropt it—*Nicky?*   Out of his hand!
Dropt it! and these chaps on the land

Haulin, for all[1] they felt the loose[2]—
Haulin away like the very deuce—
Like they'd got a whale—he dropt the rope—
Nicky Freel! like soap! like soap!
And him a sailor!—all very fine!
"Nicky!" I says, "where's Nelly Quine?"
And I looked, and there they had her lashed
To the cabin companion—aw dear! the washed
The craythur looked, the washed and the wore—
Half drowned, you know—"I'll take ye ashore,"
I says, and the Captain standin by—
"I'll take the young woman ashore," says I.
He looked at me very hard, and then
He loosed the lanyarn, and—"Listen, friend!"
Says the Captain, "Suppose I don't live," he says,
"To reach that shore, remember this!
Whatever happens, dyin or livin,
Nelly's as pure as an angel in Heaven."

And so he gave her to me, and so
I says—"It's time for us to go;"
And made her fast across my hips—
"Now, then!" I says, and in I slips—
Easy, you know, very easy, and humours
All I could, and makes these boomers
Ride me as nice as possible,
And treadin the trough, you know; but still
She hung upon my back like death—

---

[1] Although. [2] How loose it was.

Not a word! no, no! not a sound! not a breath!
I thought she was dead—not the smallest tick
In all her body—so I struck out quick
And hard; but a sea come tearin along,
And caught me up, and wrenched me that strong,
And bothered me, that the next that came
Knocked me over like a bame—
Senseless—like a log of timber—
And so, of course, that's all I remember
Till I felt the smell of a body smookin,
And a lot of people round me lookin,
And three of us side by side there lyin—
The Captain, and me, and Nelly Quine—
Her in the middle—but they'd turned her head
Away from the Captain, because he was dead—
Dead, poor chap! But Nelly, the sowl!
Was sleepin just like a two-year-old.
"Hullo!" says I; "hullo!" says Nickey—
Him that was smookin, and likewise Mickey—
Clague, I mean. So then they stated
How the young Captain waited and waited
Till he seen the lot of them landed there,
And then he jumped, and swam very fair,
Strong, they said, but cautiously—
When, all of a sudden! the boom, d'ye see!
That was soulgerin[1] about in the trough,
Gave a heave, and a drop! and hit him, my gough!
Hit him just aback of the skull,

---

[1] Soldiering, knocking about.

And knocked him over like a bull—
Killed him, it's lek, upon the spot :
For when the body come in, they got
No signs of life, nor nothin in it—
Killed him, I expec', that minute.

Aw very bad ! very bad !
And then we took and sent a lad
For a cart for Nelly, and another to go
So quick as he could, and let them know
At the Ballaglass.   So we got the cart,
And Nelly a heisin,[1] and made a start.
But the Captain's body was left in a cove,
And chaps to watch it.   So on we drove,
And the poor gel there hangin all of a dangle,
Sthrooghin [2] just the same as a tangle—
The limp, you know ; and her clothes all twisted
And ruxed about her ; and the way she listed [3]
This way, that way—so we done our endeavour,
And up to the house with her howsomedever—
And *where to put her?* and—bear a hand there !
And—" The hayloft 'll do for the lek o' yandhar—"
Says Cain—" The hayloft !" and I gave a star [4]—
" Is it wantin to feed the rots [5] ye are ?
Haylofts !" I says.   So he grunted though ;
But what was he goin to say I don't know ;
For the misthress come, so soft and swift,

---

[1] Being raised.   [2] Trailing.   [3] Inclined.
    [4] Stare.   [5] Rats.

Like ghoses[1] comes, ye know—just a whiff
Of somethin white—like an owl's wing—
And she ran at Nelly like a greedy thing ;
And Nelly lifted up her head,
And fell in the misthress' arms like dead.

So Cain was lookin rather foolish then,
And of course, you know, no use of men—
So we stood to one side ; and, I'll tell ye what !
Every one of us off with his hat,
Lek round a coffin : and the gels there cryin,
And huddlin and cuddlin, and Nelly lyin
On the whole of their laps, and goin a-carryin
In on the parlour, exac' like a buryin—
And—*to keep away !* and the door shut ;
So Cain stood glasses, and so I cut.

But *Tommy ?*　Tommy, did ye say ?
Aw, he was over the hills and far away
Long afore that.　And, dear me now !
You'd ha' thought ould Cain had ha' kicked up a row
About Tommy breakin articles
Like yandhar—*Noticin,* is it ?　Bills
Of ladin, contracks, charter-parties,
And all the rest of it—go it, my hearties !
Breach of promise ?　Breach of something—
And ould Gelling, too !　But that's a rum thing—
Just when you'd ha' thought the man 'd[2] been furious,
To take it that aisy—wasn it curious ?

---

[1] Ghosts.　　　　　[2] Would have.

Not a bit of it! bless your soul!
But you'll be tould! you'll be tould!

So Tommy was gone; but Nelly got better,
And then the lot of them was at her
To stay for a servant with them there,
And so she did : and the best of a year
No news of Tommy; but the people was sayin
They were hearin a sort of music playin
In the air sometimes—like a sort of disthress—
Like a fiddle cryin about the place—
Like a *cry*, they said, and a surt of a moan to it—
(I've axed Tommy himself, but he wouldn own to it).
So the people said it wasn right
At all : but Cain took a gun one night,
And fired it out at the front door,
And then they never heard it no more.

Aye, aye! but afore the next Mheillea [1]
There was wonderful news of Tommy, I tell ye—
Just so! just so! aw, hould your luff!
Wonderful, wonderful, sure enough!
Well now, this is the way it was—
Nelly's father, ye see, was lost
Off the Shellags one night, with Illiam [2] Crowe,
One-eyed Illiam? exactly so.
And the widda come down most terrible,
And all the mouths she had to fill—

---

[1] Harvest-home.   [2] William.

I don't know the number—and it's hard for such,
And Nelly helpin, but it wasn much—
What could she do? aw a reglar battle,
And *executions*, and I don't know what all,
And the bed goin sellin from under them,
And all to that,[1] till at last it came
She had to give in.   And Nelly took heart
To ax this Cain to take their part,
Just, you know, to spake to the Coroner
For the mother, poor soul! that he wouldn be purrin[2] her
To the road altogether, and no expense,
And did.   But Tommy's tould me since
That Nelly was sayin she'll never forget
The way he looked when she axed him that—
Poor thing! poor thing! but I'll be bail—
Bless ye! looks 'll mean a dale,
A dale will looks: but helped them though;
And then the widda thought she'd go
To Douglas, to live with a sisther theer;
And so the Coroner got them clear,
Or clear of them.   And so Mrs. Quine
Off to the sisther——but—very fine!
Sisthers! will they?   Not a bit o' them!
Showed her the door, and all the kit o' them!
And too proud to go back—you know, the disgrace—
And Douglas is hardly a Christian place:
Bless ye! Douglas, of a rule,
Is just as bad as Liverpool.

---

[1] So forth.   [2] Putting.

So she wandered about on the bare street,
And not a stockin to her feet;
And worer and ragg'der, and thinner and starveder,
Till one of these bobbies took and observed her—
That's their word—and brought her up
Afore the High Bailiff—not a bite or a sup
At the woman for days—and the childher all round her
Cryin; and that's where Tommy found her—
In the Coort? In the Coort. "Is there one of ye knows her?"
Says the High-Bailiff: "I was used *to*, sir,"
Says a little chap in the crowd; and, blow me !
If the little chap they had wasn Tommy—
Tommy, for sure ! And—"I'll take care o' them,"
Says Tommy there—"I think there's a pair o' them,"
Says the High-Bailiff, and he laughed, and he turned
The leaf of his book, and the bobbies girned [1]—
Of coorse ! of coorse ! But still they were plazed,
Aw yes, they were, and the woman amazed ;
But stuck to Tommy, and out on the door—
And—"Mind you'll not come here no more !"
Says the High-Bailiff. But when she got out,
And took a look at the chap, no doubt,
And seen the surt,[2] she lost all heart—
Poor soul ! and actual made a start
To cut and lave him. But Tommy caught her,
And Tommy entreated and Tommy besought her,
And these little midges set up a boo !
And the woman didn know what to do—

---

[1] Grinned.   [2] What sort he was.

"Tommy, ye dunkey! it isn no gud!¹

"Tommy, ye dunkey! it isn no gud!"[1]
Ye cudn!" she says; "I cud! I cud!"[2]
Says Tommy: "try me! try me!" he says;
"I've got a terr'ble shuitable place,"
Says Tommy—"Come, Mrs. Quine, aw come!"
And so she went, but very glum—
Lek shamed, you know, at the undersize
And that, lek thinkin he wasn wise.

So Tommy done the best he was able,
And took a lodgin in Guttery Gable,
Or somewhere—just one room they had;
But he worked like a haythen naygur, he did.
And the woman wasn a bad soul ether,[3]
Only a little cretchy[4] rather—
Cretchy, or somethin of the kind,
And uphouldin[5] the days she lived with Quine.
She shudn!　No, of coorse she shudn;
But—*that's the times she got the puddin,*
Heavin it down the sink, she said—
Plenty of butter to her bread
Them times, she said: you know their way!
Women *muss* have somethin to say—
Muss—and——yes, it was rather hard
On Tommy. But, bless ye! he didn regard.
Tommy had a hope in his bussum,
Had Tommy—and 'd take the childher, and nuss 'em,
Or wash them, or anything at all:

---

[1] Good.　　[2] Could.　　[3] Either.　　[4] Querulous.　　[5] Boasting of.

Till at last the sisther gave a call
One everin : and she saw the nate
And comfible, and—gettin late,
And—*could she sit till mornin there?*
And cuddled her up in a arm-chair,
And had her breakfast, and liked the tay,
And never left them anyway—
Pride, eh? Turn your back, and Pride
'll ate all you'll give him, and more beside.

And all in a little bit of a room
About the length of a lugger's boom—
And dacent lek, ye know, in their habits,
But all in a little room like rabbits.
Bless your sowl! there wasn no harm in,
But the people said Tommy was turned a Mormon—
Two wives, they said, *and it ought to be looked to*,
And—*Pazon Dobson should be spoke to.*

So Dobson come in with a speech to make to them,
But he laughed that hearty he cudn spake to them.
For, the time he come, they were goin to bed,
And the women had rigged a hammock, he said,
And rove it up to the roof with a tackle ;
And the minute they heard him, my gough! the cackle!
And "Tommy, you fool!" and "Tommy, you dirt!"
And Tommy standin in his shirt—
"Here's Pazon Dobson! for all the sakes!
Tommy!!!" and in a brace of shakes

Heaves, and whips him up to a bame,
Like a flitch of bacon, and makes fast the same,
And laves him danglin under the laths,
And turns about, and smooths their brats,
And—"Good evenin, Sir!" and curtseyin—
Aw dear! the Pazon laughed like sin.
And "Tommy, how are ye gettin on upstairs?"
He says, and "Did ye say your prayers,
Tommy?" that's all, bein giv'n to jokin,
And out, and down the sthreet, and chokin.
But still a dale more dacenter
To have the falla slung up there—
Just a block, and a strong hook,
And a promise at Tommy he wouldn look,
And then they could sthrip, and out with the
    light,
And in to the childher with them straight.

So that's the news that come to Renshent,
And Nelly had ha' took [1] and went
Over the mountains like a shot
That very minute, but the misthress said not,
And coaxed and coaxed, and—"Nelly! Nelly!
You relly [2] are too hard now, relly!
Isn it all for you he's doin it?
And it'll be your fault if he's ever ruin it—"
And—*to do unto others* —"arn we bidden?"
And—"Don't, Nelly, don't!" So Nelly didn.

---

[1] Would have taken.   [2] Really.

But still there was other things both'rin the gel—
Cain ?   Aye, Cain—most terrible !
Aw there's no mistake the man was bad,
At laste, ye know, if he wasn mad—
A touch of both—I wouldn thruss [1]—
But Nelly didn see it at fuss—
No she didn—if you'd only ha' ast [2] her,
She'd ha' said he was such a *nice* master—
Nice she'd ha' said, *nice*, d'ye mind !
Pious very, but terrible kind—
Kind she'd ha' said—*such gentleness—*
Such——that's the way the women is—
It's no use o' talkin ! they will ! they will !
That's the way with the women still—
Kind and pious ! folly and blindness !
That's the piety and the kindness !
Vanity and consate—that's it :
Well—howsomdever—just wait a bit !

But the misthress saw it—like a weather-glass
Is these wakely women ; not a speck 'll pass
But they'll have it there—aw, I don't know the wake
Or the what—it's lek the delicake,[3]
And the hung that fine—but let that be—
They'll see what nobody else will see.
Aye, but there's more—there's more though still,
And so I'll confess it, aw, deed I will.
Do you know—ah dear ! it's an ould song—

---

[1] Trust (I rather think).   [2] Asked.   [3] Delicate.

What it is to be right, and yet to be wrong?
Not her fault—no, no!—but look!
Swore upon the Holy Book—
Swore—d'ye see? Aw, it's no use denyin—
Swore—and still, if the woman was dyin,
What could she do? She hadn gorr[1] it—
Love! what love? the only thing for it
Was death, not love : death, death's the cry!
Sell love? sham love? no, die, die, die!

But more than swore, more than swore—
Ten thousand times more! ten thousand times more!
Here was a man that was goin to ruin
Most terrible—and whose doin?
Whose? Aw, don't be hard! aw, don't!
Yes—*she* thought so, but *me!* I won't!
She thought so—yes, just what you'd expeck—
But, oh! be pitiful to the leck!
That's the thought that done the jeel,[2]
Goin like a threddle[3] to a wheel,
Thrib-throbbin night and day,
The wheel that spun her life away.
She hadn loved him! and who could tell
What might have been? aw well, well, well!
I know, I know—if she could have done it,
If she could, if she could? but who begun it?
Who made it unpozzible from the fuss?
No, no, my lads! I'll not cuss—

---

[1] Got.   [2] Did the damage.   [3] Treadle.

But this if—if—if! what's the gud of *if?*
What'll it carry? what'll it lift?
If she cud—just the smallest taste—
Just so—*if, if!* in case, in case!
And all the rest of it, I suppose he'd ha' got
To be a reglar angel—what?
This Cain—an angel, cocked in a bush
Like at Moses theer—ah I only wush
These *ifs* were not so sharp and crook'd,
And catchin, and houldin, and gettin hook'd
In the very flesh, and no aisin to 't
Till Death'll haul you into his boat,
And wrench the hooks, and set you free
From all the throuble and misery.

Too late! too late! I'm glad it was—
The slack'd fire broke out at last,
Lek the Divil had lit a fiery sun
That scorched her face to look upon.
What! Cain? Yes, bless ye! plain as plain—
He didn make no secret, didn Cain—
It seemed as if all care was past,
It seemed as if he was happy at last,
Happy, happy, or goin to be it,
And still this Nelly didn see it.
Wonderful! wonderful, I've heard
About *the state of her sowl!* good Lord!
Yes—aw yes—and 'd give her instruction
Himself, you know—"The introduction,"

He was used to say, "of this young pessin
To the truth is deeply interessin—"
A lamb of the flock, he said ; aw dear !
And wolves, he said, *prowlin everywheer ;*
Wolves, he said ; *but the fold was near.*
The scroundhrel-villyan ! and allis tuk[1] her
To chapel himself, and up and stuck her
In the front pew—and high and low
Could see, but Nelly didn, no !
Such a fatherly man, she thought, *so good*
And holy, you know ; and there she stood
In the chapel, like a primrose in the spring,
And as sweet and as foolish as anything—

But others seen it—what ? *the gels ?*
Seen it of coorse—my gough ! who else !
Likewise the boys—of an evenin theer
At home you know—and the Book, and the cheer[2]—
And—"Aw !" he'd say, "the power of grace !"
And put a finger in the place,
And his other hand on Nelly's head—
"The power of grace ! of grace !" he said ;
And pattin theer, and the big smooth smile,
And—"The Lord is daelin with this child."
"Oh !" he says, "it's grace that's in,"
And the hand goin sliddherin under her chin.
And then he'd be readin all the chapters
That's talkin of love—"Oh !" he'd say, "the rapthurs !

¹ Took.   ² Chair.

The puffick joy! And lizzen to this!
Greet one another with a holy kiss!
See!" he'd say, "my childrin, see
The joy of Christian liberty!
If it hadn been for *the unrighteous leaven*,
See what kisses we'd be hevvin!"
"Dear me!" he'd say, "if you were all God's sons
And daughters, we might begin at once;"
And dhrops the book, and sticks his thumb in
His oxther, and gives a surt of a hummin,
And lookin the way you could aisy tell he
'd like uncommon to begin with Nelly.

Did they wink? did they nudge? enjoyin the spree?
Certainly, most certainly!
And sometimes he'd be lookin very black at them;
And sometimes, d'ye know! he'd be laughin back at them—
Actyall! yes! he wud, he wud!
Dhrunk? No—the pison in his blood;
Or—— I don't know; but in general,
He wasn takin no notice at all;
But just like a body in a dhrame,
As sweet as sugar, and as soft as crame.
I believe in my sowl then—honour bright!—
The man was thinkin he was all right.
Sometimes? Yes; and weeks at a time—
Lek nothin in the world could annoy 'm;
Just azackly as if he was livin
In another world, *saved and forgiven*,

With other loss and other gain,
With another Nelly and another Cain.

Decavin himself?   No, no! d'ye see!
Never not decavin nobody
Such times—like settled long ago,
And no use to be spakin nor nothin, ye know ;
But just to be happy, and have no bother
This way that way, one thing or another—
Happy, happy; allis the same—
Just to go on, and dhrame and dhrame.
Raelly happy.   For this Nelly at Cain's
Made the man's blood go sweet in his veins—
Lifted the falla up from the mire
Of his spite, and his hate, and his hell-fire ;
Grew like a lily or a pink
'll grow by the side of some dirty sink,
Or a midden——   *Hard?*   No, I'm not hard!
A midden in a farmyard !
A midden, by gough !   I'll stick to that.
A midden or a tanyard vat—
My senses ! a midden 's twice too gud for him.
A beauty for pinks and lilies to bud for him !
There now, there now !   Labour in vain !
You've got him, you've got him !   So take your Cain !

It's no use, my men ; keep quiet ! keep quiet !
How could it be right ? how could it be right ?
Heaven above, or earth beneath ;

Right is right in the Devil's teeth.
Lovin Nelly! What did ye say?
That was sugar for any man's tay?
Certainly! and no thanks to be gud,
If you were lovin her; I think you shud!
And her lovin you—aw, at that price,
Ould Nick himself 'd 'a' tuk to be nice—
Yes, there's no doubt; but I can't discover
How he had any right to love her—
Any right, or any sense.
Good grayshurs! he knew he hadn a chance
To get Nelly to love him. What was there in him
But muck and mash and hissin venom?
Could he love? He could hate—he hated his wife!
Put a dhrop of love into that man's life;
Run a river of love—what's the gud of it all?
It'd only turn to the bitter gall.
He had soaked himself in spite—d'ye see?
He had steeped himself in cruelty.
He was pison to the very brim—
All the love on earth couldn sweeten him.
Plant a apple tree in a bog—will it root?
In a hungry bog—will it bring forth fruit?
Plant love in Cain—don't you know what would happen?
It wouldn be love; it wouldn have the sap in,
Nor nathur, nor nothin: it would breed grubs;
It would rot; it would stink. It 'll do in dubs,
Will dirty water; but, so soon as it flows,
Stand to one side, or hould your nose!

Aw, he had to keep quiet—his only look out ;
And as long as he could, there isn no doubt
The man had a surt of happiness,
A surt of peace, a surt of rest—
A surt—but still he knew if he'd spake
One word that Nelly couldn mistake,
One word ! his dhrame would go like a puff—
That's what my lad knew well enough.

So he had to humour his dhrame that way,
To spin it out, to coax it to stay—
Lek all that was ever like to be—
And it made him as peaceful there, and free—
Bless your sowl ! he was gettin quite kind
To the misthress even, lek he'd made up his mind
Lek all to be happy like in a story,
Lek Nelly'd got them up to glory,
Nor where, nor when, nor how, nor who—
And the misthress to be in it too.
But who and how, and where and when,
Must have an answer, must, my men.

And so there was times when the divil awoke,
And seen he was just the fool of a joke,
And sickened at these slops of love,
Or whatever trash he was dreamin of.
And then the seven divils came
And filled his sowl with rage and flame :
And his shouldhers shuck, and his face fell,

And his heart was like a coal of hell.
And he'd take for the shore or anywhere—
Lek chokin, ye know, lek catchin the air—
I've talked to people that heard him there.
It was hard to understand him rather,
They said, bein mostly stormy weather
Such times he was after these games; and mixin
Religion and that; but still they were fixin [1]
Putty [2] middlin; and the despard [3] way
He'd shout to the land, and shout to the sea.

And—"God in Heaven!" he'd say, "O God !
I know Thy rod! I know Thy rod!
She can't be mine! she can't be mine!
O Nelly Quine! O Nelly Quine !
But why? Oh, why? Is'n there a place
In all the world, a little space,
Nowhere? nowhere? a space, a spot—
Oh, is there not? Oh, is there not?
God of mercy, in all these lands,
Where I can flee from Thy commands?
Somewhere! somewhere! there must! there must!
O God, I am but feeble dust,
A worm, a fool, a stupid liar—
O give me but my heart's desire !
God in Heaven! what's the gud o' me?
I cannot do the thing Thou wud o' me—
I was never converted. I only shammed—

---

[1] Describing it.   [2] Pretty.   [3] Desperate.

I'm lost already! O God, I'm damned—
I never loved Thee, nor Thy word—
Lave me to myself, O Lord!
I'm weak, O Lord, I can't stand firm!
What's all this bother about a worm?
Drop me! Lave me! What matter to you?
Give me Nelly, and that 'll do."

That was a praecher—rummish docthrine
For a man that knew the way, and walked therein
With sweet assurance—I've heard him talk—
Rather a curious road to walk!

But Nelly never knew a scrap—
Ye see, the parties that heard the chap
Was terbil deep Methodisses,
That's apt to hide a thing like this is,   .
Hush it up, lek thinkin *it best*,
They're sayin, *for the Chapel intheress*—
Aw, crafty uncommon! a *Christian brother*—
Dear me, but they 'll stick to one another!

But how was it the misthress didn spake
To Nelly? Now, for God's sake!
To Nelly? The misthress? You havn a grain o' sense—
Wasn it just in Nelly's innocence
That the misthress had her only pleasure,
Her only joy, her hidden treasure—
In Nelly's peace, in healin the smart

Of the sore that was still in Nelly's heart?
In seein her bud again and blossom,
That would ha' tuk her to her bosom
Every minute, and rocked her and rocked her
Like a baby there—and Cain for the doctor!
My gough! let's see—
Doctor Cain, M.D.—
And so long as the gel was cheerful
And happier gettin, the misthress was fearful
To move a finger—and she didn know
About his tantrims. She only saw
The smilin the man was got, and the silly,
And evident all by raison of Nelly.

And sometimes she started like a thing that was
    stung,
When she looked at the man, and seen the young
And sthrong he was seemin : and then she thought,
I don't know what! I don't know what!
Death, and darkness, and despair—
But other times, though, sittin there,
Just the three of them, and no winkin nor nudgin
At these boys and gels, it was hard to be judgin
And Cain that tuk up, and contented, and cuddlin-
If it was only a piece of old man's muddlin
After all ; and, if so,
Then he was very happy, ye know—
And was *she* makin him happy? poor woman!
Cud she? and mightn the man be comin

To an anchor lek in still water,
And Nelly to be to him like a daughter !
Besides the religion—aw, deed, I'll bet
The misthress was thinkin a dale of that.
For, ye see, for all the good-hearted,
And the sweet, this Nelly wasn convarted—
No—and still it was rather expected,
After all her trouble, she'd be *directed*
And that—you know—and only proper—
And even talk of Cain to adop' her.
So who was knowin when it'd come—
The great change—very slow with some—
Yes, I suppose so—and to try to forget
The Captain theer—aw, they wouldn be beat—
Poor lad ! Was he in the same thrim ?
I wondher what change there come to him.
" We shall not all sleep," it says,
" But we shall all be changed," same vess—
All, now ? What is he maenin by *all* ?
A terbil hand was yandhar Paul.

But, I tell ye, it got so bad in the Chapel
That these unfornit locals had to *grapple*
With this question—that's what they called it—
And the Shuperintandin overhauled it
One everin with them, havin come
Special o' puppose from Douglas, by gum !
Aye ! but of coorse, you know, they'd contrive it
To be a meetin lek in private—

Private, aw, private—yes, but still
The lek will out, of course it will.

So the meetin was in the everin,
So the next day they summoned Cain
To *appear* before them—*for divers grave
And weighty causes*—aw, you'll get lave ![1]
Like lawyers just—ould Bobby Kirkbride—
And as dignified as dignified.
But the chap that had to sarve this writ
Didn like the job a bit—
No, he didn, aw, deed, no, man !
So he started off the very momen'
It was in Cain's hand, and he over the hill,
And heard him shoutin terrible—
" Young man ! come here !" but he didn mind him,
But ran lek he'd got the Divil behind him.

But Cain to the chapel—and that's the place
They had the row, and every taste.[2]
And who was tellin me ? Tellin ? tellin ?
Why, bless your souls ! ould Harry Gellin,
Tommy's father ; aye, but it was, though,
Just one day there shoein a hoss though—
Aw, whatever there's goin, the blacks and the whites of it,
It's in a smithy you'll get the rights of it—
And him a local : but tuk the huff
About something, and left them long enough

[1] Say what you like.   [2] Bit of it.

After he was tellin me the fun.
So Bobby Kirkbride it was that begun,
Bobby—and " Brother Cain," he says,
" We're in a very great disthress,
Brother—very," he says—" The Church,"
He says, " is troubled. 'Twere gud to search
Your heart, brother, and ascertain
How is it with thee, brother Cain.
It's for our brother's own sake,
And indeed the case is delicake,
Yes, it's delicake uncommon—
I may say it's about a young woman,
Livin under your own roof,
I understand, but kep aloof
From the rest of the sarvants. We've heard this ;
And then, in this sacred edifice,
We're tould of conduck, as one might say,
Conduck, conduck, in a general way.
Furthermore, it's said in the neighbourhood
That this faymale pessin is well-favoured,
Also, we're informed her state
Is hopeful, or *was*, at any rate—
Hopeful—and makin her to be
A pleasin subject—spiritually—
Spiritually—in another respeck,
We've heard of captains and the lek—
We've heard, no doubt, and a trouble that came
On a fam'ly I'm not goin to name—
A trouble, yes. So, if he's inclint

To clear his mind upon this pint,
We think, in a spirit of Christian unity,
Our brother should have a opportunity."

And then he axed the Shuperintandin
To *open the Scripthar for their understandin,*
If so be they might see the light,
And lead the doubtin Church aright.
So then the Shuperintandin prayed,
But *very cautious*, Gellin said—
Cautious, cautious, like an ould drake,
And cautiouser still when he come to spake,
Eyein Cain, ye know, that was theer,
Sittin in the Communion cheer—
Bless ye ! as happy as a bird,
Nid-noddin at every other word :
And when the prayer was over, he set
The Amen as bould as a clarionet ;
And slicked his lips like slickin a label,
And cocked himself on the communion table.

So then the Shuperintandin 'spounded,
And the way it was, and where they found it—
Corinthians—and Paul *enlargin*
How a man is to do with his vargin—
If he thinks he's behavin uncomely toward her,
St. Paul is sayin, he's bound to take order
To get her married some way ; but still,
If the party's got power over his will,

And *hath so devised in his heart*, says Paul,
He needn marry her at all—
"That's Paul," he says; "we've his own word,
It's only hisself, and not the Lord—
But I spare you, says Paul,"—and this and thus,
And whips them back to Leviticus,
And works the texes—*But still, of coorse,*
The law of Moses hadn no force—
And then there was David, when he got ould,
And sufferin greatly from the could,
Tuk yandhar Abishag, that nussed him,
And seemed to be a ancient custom,
But differin from the case in hand,
And not the same for every man—
But no doubt, for the sake of the congregation,
Their brother would gev an explanation.

Says Cain—"It's beautiful, it is!
A splendid exposition," he says—
"Splendid, splendid! Dear me! the way
That Scripthar was opened, just like day,"
He said, "like day. But how? But how?"
Was it larnin? "No, I trow:"
Was it readin, was it study?
Was it pokin in the muddy
Waters of the carnal mind,
Pokin, pokin, till you're nearly blind—
Was it? And he looked around,
And he·smiled like butter a shillin the pound—

"No!" he says, "it's just the habirtual
Comparin spir'tual things with spir'tual "—
And—" Hem !" he said, and ups with the eyes,
And smacks his lips like somethin nice.

  Nice ! by gough ! aw, nice enough !
It was Nelly he was thinkin of.
Aye, aye ! it had got a name,
It was there, *he was spoke to*, it wasn a dhrame—
Spoke to ! spoke to ! Yes, and, beside,
I believe the chap had a surt of a pride
The way he was lifted altogether
Above Shuperintandins, or Locals e'ther,
Lek on wings of the mornin, and these craythurs to run
With their farlin candle to see the sun
Just when it was goin to rise—that's it !
To rise, to rise—that's the thing that lit
His face till it shined like polish just—
Heaven or Hell, love or lust—
Take your chise ! but, as Gellin 'd say,
It must have come from somewhere—eh ?
" The exposition," he says, " is grand ;
But now let's come to the point in hand,
To the point," says Cain ; " I'm not deny'n
A word that was said about Ellen Quine.
I think you'll allow it's only natur,
The way she came to us, we'd trate her
Special lek, bein in a sense
Entrusted to us by Providence—

Trusted," he says, " I think you'll agree,
Trusted to Mrs. Cain and me.
She come to us a poor lost sinner,
But we seen the seeds of grace that was in her,
And—the beauty, yes, the carnal beauty—
No doubt, no doubt; but what was our duty?
That's the thing.   Our duty was plain
Before us—me and Mrs. Cain.
Seeds—now ought we to leave them there,
To be picked and pecked by the birds of the air?
To be choked with the thorns, to be burnt with the heat—
Is that our duty?   I beg to state
It's not.   No matter the time or the place,
Seeds of grace is seeds of grace.
To raise the fallen, to seek the lost,
That's our duty, whatever the cost.
But the gel is good-lookin? that's admitted—
Is she any the less fitted
For a vessel of grace?   Good-looks is fac's—
What *is* there in good-looks, I ax?
Must she be ugly?   Is there anything carnal
In good-looks?   Is the life etarnal
For ugly women and ugly men
Only?   No, no! my brethren.
That's carryin Election out of all raison :
The works of Nature, in their saison,
Might teach ye that.   The very flowers
Of the field, God's work, you know, not ours—
Has the blossoms of Spring a lovely breath,

Or are they a savour of death unto death?
They're beautiful—aye! There ye gorrit![1]
Beautiful, and ye like them for it.
And then in the Bible everywhere
The beautiful the women are!
Not one neither, but every one of them,
Aye, bless ye! every mother's son of them.
They're all beautiful! Look at the way
They're in the picthars—as you might say—
Puffeck beauty, not a stain nor a spot,
Not an ugly one in all the lot.
Yes, and holy women, too.
Of coorse! of coorse! we've nothin to do
With Jezebel and Herodias,
And hapes of the like, as bould as brass:
But Queen Bersheba that wouldn be done
But she'd hear the wisdom of Solomon;
And the Shunamite, that we're taught to consider
A type of the Church; and—altogether—
What do ye say to the likes of them?
And "the daughter of Jerusalem."—
See the Prophets, see the Psalms;
See that Hagar of Abraham's,
And Ruth, and Rahab, that hid the spies,
And Leah—only the blinky eyes—
And dozens more, if they were wanted—
See the way they're represented!
Beautiful? Of coorse they were—

[1] You have got it.

Beautiful—and I'll tell ye the for.
It's a gift is beauty, a gift it is,
And used for improper pupposes
At[1] the Divil—no doubt a snare to catch
Unwary souls : but God's his match.
This gift is *His* gift after all,
Not the Divil's, in spite of his gall ;
And God is usin it to bend
Our hearts, that so we may befriend
Poor things that has been led astray,
That so His banished may find a way
To return to Him ; the effeck of whuch,
My beloved brethren, is such
That this beauty, this snare of the ould Dragon's,
Is the banner of love : ' stay me with flagons
In the banqueting house ; yea, comfort me
With apples from the apple tree—
I am sick of love,' the bride is say'n ;
And so with me and Mrs. Cain.
We love this young pesson ; the Lord has guv[2] her
Unto us that we might love her,
That we might lead her unto Him ;
And if she was like a cherubim
For beauty, or just the *vice versies*,
We umbly thank him for his mercies."

And he stopped.   To hear ould Gellin arrit[3]
Was good ! he had every word, like a parrot—

   [1] By.   [2] Given.   [3] At it.

Stopped a minute, did Cain ; and the fashion
Of his face was changed, Gellin said ; no passion,
No love nor hatred to be seen ;
But just the cunning of a fiend—
Cunning.   And then he says—" The occasion
Was seemin to want an explanation :
And now ye have it," he says.   " But still,
If you're only convinced against your will,
If this meetin isn satisfied,
Then," he says, " I wouldn divide
A Christian body," he says ; " no, no !
I can go," he says, " and I'm willin to go.
But," he says, " I'll always be jealous
Over you with love : no malice
Has place in my heart, but only a yearnin
In the bowels of the Gospel for them that's returnin
Evil for good.   But—no more of that.
One thing," he says, " I musn forget—
It's a matter of business," he says, " I fear,
But better perhaps to have everythin clear.
I'd be very sorry, certainly,
To give any trouble to the Cōmmĭttee,
Or the congregation in general,
Very sorry : but—still for all—
There's certain moneys ; and it's handy, rather,
For the man and the money to go together—
So no doubt you'll be makin arrangements for payin
The mortgages on the chapel," says Cain,
" With all the interest that's owin,

For I think there 'll be foreclosin goin.
But I'd better give you a day or two
To think about it—that 'll do,"
Says Cain, "Good evenin!"   And takes
His hat, and a smooth of the elber, and makes
For the door.

    "Stop!" says Gellin, "Stop!"
He says, and he gave a skip and a hop,
And got hoult of the door.   "Stop!" like commandin;
"Aisy!" says the Shuperintandin;
"*Aisy*, Mr Gellin!" he says;
"*Aisy?*   What sort of talk is this?"
Says Gellin.   "*Aisy!* I'd have you to know,"
And set to work, and gave them the jaw,
Most terrible—the way he was tellin;
Aw, by gogh! he could do it, could Gellin—
Could and would—*They'd heard a lecthur,*
He said, *about women that's drew in a pecthur.*
Concubines, and ould men's misses;
Was this the talk for Methodisses?
Were they Protestans?   See, then, see!
Was'n this flat Popery?
What else in the world?   "Pecthurs!" he says,
"Pecthurs, graven images!
It's as clear as daylight," says Gellin; *but then—*
The mortgages!   And at it again.
Mortgages, he said, *indeed,*
He'd like to see the trust deed;

He called for it to be produced—
Yes, and he'd hev it. They couldn be loosed
From the obligation under the Trust—
Was it gud in law? Was it right? Was it just?
Mortgages! There couldn be—
And how about the mortgagee?
He could tell Mr. Cain, if he'd lent that money,
The position he was in was more till funny;
It was danger's it was, a reg'lar fix,
And he'd better be makin quick sticks
To get out of it, or he'd see what the Coort
Of Chancery would say. And he roort
And he shouted: *and he'd hev it tried,*
He said, *if it beggared him, if he died;*
He'd take it to every Coort in creation—
It was just "a corrup' consideration."

And Cain looked thunder, and well he might;
But the Shuperintandin got a light
From all this talk; so he stroked down Gellin
The best he could, that was puffin and swellin
Most awful—and then he turned to Cain,
And—"I think we'll let the matter remain
As it is," he says, "I believe I express
The general feelin—as it is, as it is;"
And looks round at the others, that gave a sort
Of a grunt or a groan, or a sniff or a snort,
Maenin yes—and "Let us pray;"
And down on their knees and pegged away:

But Gellin only said—*Chit!* and *Chut!*
And tuk and slammed the door, and cut.

    So one Sunday though ould Cain was as clever,
Fiddlin there with Nelly as ever,
And wrappin the shawl—and it wasn rainy—
But just like the gel was made of chayney.
And Nelly as rosy as an apple
With the blushes, and linkin down the chapel,
As happy, bless ye! and content—
Innocent! just innocent!
For the capers this Cain was carryin on
She didn hardly understan';
Only she thought it was maybe a way
With pious pessins—but as good as a play;
And the praecher lookin rather glum—
But the hour had come, the hour had come!
Come, I tell ye! make or break—
For on the road he begun to spake
About the young Captain, and worked it round,
Till she *must* understand; and she gave a bound,
And off like a deer, and the night was black,
And this rascal couldn follow the track,
And lost her there; but Nelly went
Across everythin, everythin, straight for Renshent.
Ah, think! what *would* the poor craythur be?
Just mad with fear and misery!

    The misthress! the misthress! That was her thought:

She wasn freckened to be caught—
Poor thing ! not that—but *there ! oh there !*
To be with her ! to be with her !
Safe, safe with her !   And just the strength,
And in on the parlour, and fell full length
At the misthress' feet.   And—*what was there at her ?*
And—" Nelly, Nelly ! what's the matter ? "
And never a word, and never a moan—
Poor Nelly lay as dead as a stone.
But coaxed her, and petted her, and raised her—
And—" Nelly, Nelly ! " and 'mazeder and 'mazeder.
" What is it, Nelly ? " (you understan'—
A pious man ! a holy man !
Where was *he ?*   Ah dear !   What odds ?
The heart of an innocent gel is God's—
Let scoundrels skulk, let divils chafe !
Nelly was safe ! Nelly was safe !
Safe with the misthress).   But when she woke,
And when she looked, and when she spoke,
And when she tould—the misthress heard,
But she didn say a single word,
But turned like a sheet.   It had come at last,
And the bitterness of death was passed.

" Misthress ! " says Nelly, " Misthress ! mother !
My own ! my own ! for I haven no other,
Or if I have—O kindest friend !
O sweet ! O good ! O . . . *mother* then !
Mother, my heart is like to break ! "

But the misthress, you know, she couldn spake—
"O Misthress, is your heart turned hard to me?
O Misthress, won't you spake a word to me?
Just a word! a word!   Oh spake
Any word—for Jesus' sake!
Am I a naughty gel, Mrs. Cain?
Am I? am I?   I didn mane—
Misthress! Misthress! I didn know—
Am I! am I!   Must I go?"

But the misthress sat in her chair quite stiff—
So Nelly got in a sort of a tiff,
Lek, you know, the way with such,
Half-cock, hair-trigger, and off with a touch—
That was the wuss o' Nelly, aw yes!
'Deed it was, and 'deed it is.
But—dear me! clean your own winder—
Flint is flint, and tinder is tinder—
And knew no more till the man-in-the-moon
All the mischief she was doin—
Nelly! Nelly!   And "Misthress," she said,
And she stood on her feet, and she back with the head,
And her bonnet fell off and draggled there—
"You won't hear, you won't hear!
I'm not worth, I suppose; I see't! I see't!
I'm only the dirt beneath his feet!
I'm no matter.   I haven a friend,
And you think I'm a liar, and——there's an end!
I believe ye knew! I believe ye knew!

Yes, I do! yes, I do!
I believe ye made it up between ye,
And I'm sorry the day that ever I seen ye."
Quick work—you'll say; aw, quick is the road;[1]
But oh, if Nelly had only knowed
What the misthress was feelin then!
But—however—what's the use, my men?
So Nelly gave an awful cry,
Like the yowl of a dog, but no reply
From the misthress, no reply at all.
So she took her bonnet and her shawl,
And away, and locked herself in her room,
And left the misthress to her doom.

And the sarvints was freckened, and didn go near,
But they heard the misthress on the stair
Lek staggerin lek—and then—no more,
Not even a foot upon the floor—
And sat up for Cain: but he didn come in
Till daylight, and *blew about with the wind*,
They were sayin, *rather*, and up to bed—
And there was the misthress lyin dead!
She was lyin dead. *Pison?* yes!
A mug of it upon the chiss[2]—
Pison, though—poor thing! she was gone
To the happy place, where it's all one—
Prepared? aw dear! what *is* prepared?
And the ould murderer stood and stared!

[1] Way.   [2] Chest.

And he shouted?   Yes, enough for three !
Shouted—but not immadiently.
No, no; but aisy ! wait, then, wait !
Don't get 'cited, at any rate !

Well, now, you may think the work
There was in that house ; and Christy Quirk,
The Coroner, comin and the inquest arrim,[1]
And everybody on the farrim [2]
Callin [3] there : and couldn agree
For *temporal insanity ;*
But just it was pison, pison—what's
The name of that pison they're given to rots ?
But by whose hand administered—
Minis, minis—that's the word—
I think so.   Well, they couldn say ;
So to bury the body anyway,
And service over it all right—
And so they did, but late at night.

And poor Nelly, they said, was just like a ghose,
Creepin about, and packed her clothes
To be off; but the women coaxed her for all
To stay with them over the funeral.
But Cain knew well that she'd settled to lave
When the misthress went out : so before the grave
Was filled—aw bless ye ! hardly a spatter
On the coffin-lid, he was home and at her—
Aye he was, and had some tay

[1] At him, held by him.   [2] Farm.   [3] Being called.

In the kitchen, and tould the rest to stay
Outside till he'd want them in to prayer;
But *he'd something very particular*
To say to Ellen Quine, he said—
Yes, indeed! and so he had.

And—*would she forgive him?* That was the game,
Would she forgive him? He felt the shame
Of his conduck the other night—aw dear!
The shame, he said, *but still it was clear*
He was left to himself, he said, *that time—*
And would she forgive him? and would she try him?
What was man? he said—*the best*,
He said, *the very holiest?*
No doubt, no doubt, he said, *it was sudden:*
But what was he to do? He couldn
Allow her to go, and his heart to break:
And if he didn spake now, when was he to spake?
It was his one chance, he said, *and he took it:*
And the dear departed would overlook it.

And Nelly tried to stop the man—
But, bless me! she said, the tongue of him ran
Like a wheel, she said. *And would she be this?*
And would she be that? and all the list
Of the things he'd do, and the things he'd give her- -
And—"I will! I will!" and on like a river—
And promisin *the kind* (!) *he'd be*—
And—"Oh, I'll make you happy!" says he,

And—"Will ye, will ye be my wife?"
And he stopped to get wind. "I'll send this knife,"
Says Nelly, "through your black heart,
If you'll spake another word." The start
He gave! and the cup fallin out of his hand!
"Through your black heart, you bad man!"
Says Nelly, and she took a step
Towards him, and the fella kep
His eye on her still; but he backed and backed,
And out on the door; and—aw it's a fact,
Nobody said another word
About *prayers* that night that ever I heard—
No: and next mornin the gel was sayin
Good-bye to them there, when in comes Cain.
"Clear out of this!" says Cain to the gels:
"I must spake to this pessin, and nobody else
Is wanted here." So of course they went.
"Now, Nelly," he says, "you're leavin Renshent;
And you'll return," he says, "for Lammas,
And marry me. Promise now! promise! promise!"
But Nelly made a dart at the dresser,
And had a knife in a minute, bless her!—
The gel was quick. But Cain gave a sign,
And two policemen, that was eyein
The whole, unknownced, gript Nelly, by George,
Like a shot,—and "I give this pessin in charge
For the murder of Mrs. Cain," he says;
And he stands like a rock, and his hand in his breast.
Poor Nelly! poor Nelly! and haulin and pushin,

And a car there to take her to Castle Rushen.[1]
But just when they started he tried once more,
And stooped, and whispered somethin to her.
But the people didn hear what he said,
And Nelly only shook her head—
And, "All right!" and nothin more to say with them,
And up goes the driver, and off and away with them.
The divil! I think I see his hoofs!
But he'd got his proofs, he'd got his proofs.
His proofs—aw yes: for who was it bought
This pison but Nelly, that little thought
What was goin to happen: and then the fight
She had with the misthress that very night—
The servants would swear to as soon as wink,
And lookin middlin ugly, I think.

Now, when Tommy heard this news,
He was clane crazy. "Don't be a goose!
Don't be a goose!" says Mrs. Quine;
"Of course the case will be goin a try'n;[2]
And Nelly was allis a bit of a fury,
Aw, 'deed she was: but no doubt the jury
Will consider the young the craythur's yet—
And it's only transportation she'll get."
"*Transportation!*" says Tommy, "and *me!*"
"Well, well," says Mrs. Quine, "we'll see."
"See!" says Tommy, "I'll go to Duddon
This very minute." "Well, I wouldn,"

---

[1] The jail of the Island.   [2] Will be tried.

Says the mother, " I wouldn be so selly.[1]
She was allis very short-tempered, was Nelly.
And Duddon the very first lawyer goin.
Duddon !   Bless ye ! it's only throwin
Your money away—it is, indeed !
And, goodness knows, there's not much need.
Look at the childher !" and so she went on.
And, "Stop now, Tommy !" but Tommy was gone.
Ye see the chap was doin fair :
He'd got in with some masons and builders there—
And contraks and that, and good at the measurin,
And plannin, and cipherin, and takin a pleasure in
All sorts of inventions, and layin the gas—
Aw, bless ye ! makin money fast.

But Duddon that was the chap for the law—
Terr'ble, but terr'bler for the jaw—
Aw, a mortal hand !   He's laid on the shelf
Since then.   But he'd bully ould Harry himself
Them times.   Aw bless ye !—fire and slaughter !
Put Duddon on them, and they'd cry for quarter.
So it's Duddon Tommy wanted to see,
And tould him all ; and, "Lave it to me !"
Says Duddon, and bitin his pen, and lookin
As deep as deep : so Tommy was hookin.
Poor Tommy, though—the shaky and shivery
He was.   And "The General Jail Delivery"—
That was the time.   And them words seemed cut

---

[1] Silly.

In every stone the craythur put
In a wall. They seemed to be wrote in the air,
On the sands, in the harbour—everywhere.

And Tommy got lave for the mother and aunt
To see this Nelly. And so they went,
And Tommy with them, in a car,
And into the Castle ; but didn dar'
To go in the place where Nelly was,
But pretended to be lookin after the hoss.
And Mrs. Quine was weepin a dale,
And the sisther, of course she wouldn fail—
Aw, dacent women ! But when they were done,
And just sittin together, the mother begun
To ask a hape of questions, you know ;
And this and that, and terrible though—
Till at last she said, "And, Nelly, then,
What did ye give her the pison in ? "
Aw, Nelly jumped to her feet, and she turned
Away from them, and the cheeks of her burned
With fire and shame ; and she wouldn spake,
And didn—and so they had to make
Tracks of coorse ; and—"She's very queer ! "
Says the mother to the jailer theer.

But just it was goin about a week
To the trial, Duddon sent to speak
With Tommy. And—*everythin was in train ;*
But he'd like to have a talk with this Cain.

And would Tommy go with him at once? and statin

The for.[1]   And the two of them off in the phaeton.

So when they got there, it was—"How do ye do, sir?"

"You know me," says Duddon. "Who wouldn know you, sir?"

Says Cain, very smilin.   But when he seen

Tommy there, his face got as keen

As keen ; and—"Thomas Gelling, is it?"

He says, and "What's the cause of this visit,

May I ax?"—quite stiff, ye know.   But Duddon

Wasn the chap to wait for the puddin,

But in it at once : and—"A pessin is lyin

In the Castle, by the name of Quine—

A servant of yours—in custody,

Upon your information, it seems to be,

For murderin your wife by pison.

Now, Mr. Cain, it's very surprisin

You don't perceive how much better

It would have been for ye all to have dropped this
      matter.

If your respected pardner had died

By her own hand, by suicide,"

There you were : but there was people enough

That didn know when they were well off.

And the jury hadn seen their way

To " temporal sanity," and he dare say

He could guess the raison.   "But I don't care a toss,

It was suicide, and *you know* it was !

That's my conviction, and you can't remove it ;

[1] Reason.

You know it, my friend, and you can prove it—
Yes, you can. And look here, Mr. Cain—"
And he eyed him sharp—"Look here, I'll be plain.
There's no doubt at all the law will considher
The two of you to be in it together,
Her the insthrument, and *you*—
Well, Mr. Cain! But here's my view—
Mr. Cain, Mr. Cain, the law 'll go furdher,
And bring you in yourself for the murdher—
Yourself alone!" (Ould Cain gave a jerk)—
"So just you set your wits to work,
And give me that proof—you know what I mane—
Or I'll have you arrested, Mr. Cain.
By this time to-morrow—the proof! d'ye hear?
So now you know the way to steer.
Good-day, Mr. Cain—" and turns on his heel.

That everin Cain was off to Peel,
And a Tommy Artlar[1] in the bay,
And her anchor tripped, and goin to sea
Directly. And Cain just settled his passage,
And sent a passil[2] and a message
By a chap on the pier—aye! it's a fac'!
And away to Ireland aboord of this smack,
And got the steamer at Queenstown, bedad!
And off to America—Catch my lad!
Apt to come back? Indeed he isn—
If he'd show his nose, he'd be clapt in prison

[1] An Arklow fishing-boat.   [2] Parcel.

Like a shot—not him! else what did he run for,
Eh? and so that villyan is done for!

But what was this paper? The paper! wup![1]
This was the paper. When Cain went up
And found the misthress lyin dead,
He found this paper on the bed,
And took it, and read it, and kept it by 'm—
The dirty rascal! all the time.
This paper was written by his wife,
And statin *the tired she was of her life—*
And the wishful to die—that's the way it was tould—
And the Lord to have mercy upon her sowl!
And somethin about her weddin-ring—
Disthracted lek; poor thing! poor thing!

So the trial was held, and the jury sat,
And—"Appear to coort!" and all to that—
And Duddon got up, and the speech he made
Was grand—aw bless ye! he knew his trade—
And the foreman at them was Corlett the Draper—
And Duddon handed up the paper.
And the Deemster read it, and "Do ye agree?"
And "Not guilty! not guilty!" what else could it be?
"Three cheers! three cheers!" aw I'll engage—
And the Deemster black in the face with rage!
And Tommy outside of the Castle wall
With a car; but he hadn the mother at all

---

[1] Woa!

That time : and Nelly, and the people expectin
Lek she'd go to Tommy, lek a sort o' directin,
And in with her straight, and stooped the head,
And—"You've beat me, Tommy! you've beat me!" she said.
But, half-way to Douglas, this Nelly got bouldher,
And the head was slipt on Tommy's shouldher,
And the whisperin in Tommy's ears,
And his arm round her waist, and tears—tears—
Tears—I'll lave it to any man livin,
Sweeter to Tommy than the rain from heaven.

And so of coorse they got married at once ?
Bless ye ! where would be the sense ?
But it's married they got ; and this little wutch
Worked with Tommy, and Tommy got ruch.
And the farm on the North—Renshent, ye know,
Was comin to the heir-at-law,
That lived in England, and willin to let it,
And Tommy terrible wantin to get it,
And got it—the very primmisis,[1]
And there he is now—aw 'deed he is !

It was only last year I had a spell there,
And Tommy and Nelly and me and the childher
Went out for a walk on the Mooragh[2] there,
Just to enjoy the lovely air :
And we took for the beach, and we come to the Rue,

---

[1] Premises.   [2] Waste land on the shore.

And Tommy looked, and I looked too—
And we thought, you know ; but it wasn grief—
And the water floppin upon the reef—
And the little things busy with their play—
And Nelly as happy as the day.

THE END

Printed by R. & R. CLARK, *Edinburgh*

MACMILLAN AND CO.'S PUBLICATIONS.

The Poetical Works of John Keats. Reprinted from the Original Editions with Notes. By Professor FRANCIS TURNER PALGRAVE. 18mo. 4s. 6d. [*Golden Treasury Series.*

The Poetical Works of Robert Burns. Edited from the best printed and MS. authorities, with Glossarial Index and a Biographical Memoir by ALEXANDER SMITH. In 2 Vols. Fcap. 8vo. 10s. *Globe Edition.* 1 Vol. Globe 8vo. 3s. 6d.

Poetical Works of John Milton. Edited, with Introductions, Notes, and Memoir, by Professor MASSON. With three Portraits engraved by JEENS. 3 Vols. Fcap. 8vo. 15s. *Globe Edition.* 1 Vol. Globe 8vo. 3s. 6d.

Matthew Arnold's Complete Poetical Works. New Edition, with Additional Poems. Three Vols. Crown 8vo. 7s. 6d. each. Vol. I. Early Poems, Narrative Poems, and Sonnets. Vol. II. Lyric and Elegiac Poems. Vol. III. Dramatic and Later Poems.

Charles Kingsley's Complete Poetical Works. New Edition, with Additional Poems.
>EVERSLEY EDITION. Two Vols. Globe 8vo. 10s.
>UNIFORM EDITION. One Vol. Crown 8vo. 6s.
>POPULAR EDITION. One Vol. Crown 8vo. 3s. 6d. [*Just ready.*

Charles Lamb's Plays, Poems, and Miscellaneous Essays. Edited, with Introduction and Notes, by the Rev. ALFRED AINGER, Canon of Bristol. Globe 8vo. 5s.

Ralph Waldo Emerson's Poems. Globe 8vo. 5s.

The Poems of Arthur Hugh Clough. New Edition. Crown 8vo. 7s. 6d.

Poems. By STOPFORD A. BROOKE, M.A. Globe 8vo. 6s.

Riquet of the Tuft: a Love Drama. By the same Author. Extra crown 8vo. 6s.

BY GEORGE MEREDITH.

Poems and Lyrics of the Joy of Earth. Extra fcap. 8vo. 6s.

Ballads and Poems of Tragic Life. Extra fcap. 8vo. 6s.

A Reading of Earth. Extra fcap. 8vo. 5s.

BY F. W. H. MYERS, M.A.

The Renewal of Youth, and other Poems. Crown 8vo. 7s. 6d.

St. Paul. A Poem. New Edition. Extra fcap. 8vo. 2s. 6d.

BY ERNEST MYERS.

The Puritans. A Poem. Extra fcap. 8vo. 2s. 6d.

Poems. Extra fcap. 8vo. 4s. 6d.

The Defence of Rome, and other Poems. Extra fcap. 8vo. 5s.

The Judgment of Prometheus, and other Poems. Extra fcap. 8vo. 3s. 6d.

BY CHRISTINA ROSSETTI.

Poems. Complete Edition. With Four Illustrations. Extra fcap. 8vo. 6s.

A Pageant, and other Poems. Extra fcap. 8vo. 6s.

MACMILLAN AND CO., LONDON.